Quarterback
DRAW

JACI BURTON

B
BERKLEY BOOKS, NEW YORK

THE BERKLEY PUBLISHING GROUP
Published by the Penguin Group
Penguin Group (USA) LLC
375 Hudson Street, New York, New York 10014

USA • Canada • UK • Ireland • Australia • New Zealand • India • South Africa • China

penguin.com

A Penguin Random House Company

This book is an original publication of The Berkley Publishing Group.

Library of Congress Cataloging-in-Publication Data

Burton, Jaci.
Quarterback draw / Jaci Burton. — Berkley trade paperback edition.
pages ; cm. — (A play-by-play novel ; 9)
ISBN 978-0-425-26300-6 (softcover)
1. Models (Persons)—Fiction. 2. Quarterbacks (Football)—Fiction. 3. Man-woman
relationships—Fiction. I. Title.
PS3602.U776Q37 2014
813'.6—dc23
2014037298

PUBLISHING HISTORY
Berkley trade paperback edition / February 2015

PRINTED IN THE UNITED STATES OF AMERICA

10 9 8 7 6 5 4 3 2

Cover photo by Claudio Marinesco.
Cover art direction and design by Rita Frangie.
Interior text design by Kristin del Rosario.

Siblings play an important role in this book and, for those of us who are lucky to have them, an important role in our lives. Despite the teasing and torture we sometimes endure at the hands of our siblings, we'd be lost without them. This book is dedicated to my sister and brother. To Angie and Gary—love you both.

Quarterback
DRAW

ONE

IF THERE WAS ONE THING GRANT CASSIDY HATED more than anything, it was PR. Doing commercial shoots was a necessary evil, and some he disliked more than others.

But right now he was in board shorts and bare feet, standing on a beach in Barbados, about to do a shoot for the annual swimsuit edition of a pretty damned famous sports magazine. There were about two dozen barely clad, tanned, and gorgeous models who were going to take part in the shoot along with several athletes.

All in all? Not a bad gig.

"This I could get used to."

Grant grinned as one of his best friends, Trevor Shay, stood next to him.

"Don't get too used to it. Your girlfriend will kick your ass if you get too close to any of these models."

Trevor crossed his arms. "Yeah. I really wish Haven could be here in Barbados with me. But she's in school right now and couldn't make it. She did tell me to behave myself. Like that was even necessary. Trust me, none of these women are as beautiful as mine."

Grant laughed. "You're blinded by love, my man."

"It's true. I am. And perfectly happy to go back to my bungalow at night all by myself. How about you? You like dating models. Got one scoped out yet?"

He had dated models in the past. They were beautiful and fun. "I wasn't exactly looking."

"It's still early in the day. I have high hopes for you." Trevor slapped him on the back as the assistant director motioned for him. "Hey, I'm up. I'll catch you at the bar later."

"Okay."

Grant stayed close and watched as Trevor was put into a shot on a hammock with a beautiful, dark-skinned model. The model straddled Trevor, who Grant had to admit handled the whole thing professionally. As soon as it was over, Trevor shook the woman's hand and wandered off in the direction the pool.

"You'll be up next, Grant," the assistant said. "We're pairing you up with Katrina Korsova."

"Sure." He knew who she was. Korsova was a big deal in the modeling world, one of those supermodels whose face and body were plastered all over billboards, in magazines, and on television. She was a beauty. He was lucky to be doing the shoot with her. It would advance his profile, and he was all about exposure.

If he had to be here doing this shoot for the sports magazine, at least he was being paired up with one of the best in the business.

Once they readied the shot on the beach, he was called over and set up on his marks. He stood in the water up to his ankles. They'd already primped his hair, his face, and his skin. It all felt weird to him, but he'd done photo shoots before. They told him it was to combat shine and to make sure his hair would be gelled appropriately enough so it would behave.

Whatever. He was paid to do what he was told, just like in football. So he stood where they told him to stand.

"We're ready for you, Katrina," he heard the assistant say.

The models were clustered in shaded cabanas before the shoot, so he'd only caught glimpses of them on and off.

Katrina stepped out, a gorgeous woman with long hair the color of midnight, wearing a swimsuit bottom that barely clung to her hips. It was more like two tiny pieces of cloth tied together with scraps. There wasn't much to the top, either. Just a couple of triangles that hardly covered her generous breasts.

She was curved in all the right places, and after she bent over so they could spray her hair wet, she straightened, flipped her hair back, then gave him a look.

Wow. Those eyes. They were so deep blue they were almost violet. Maybe they were violet. He had no idea, because he'd been struck dumb as she approached him.

He'd been around plenty of beautiful women before, but Katrina was . . . wow. Photos of her didn't do justice to what a knockout she really was.

"Grant Cassidy, this is Katrina Korsova."

She gave him a quick nod, then turned to the director, obviously all business and not as thunderstruck by him as he had been by her.

He was going to try not to be offended by that. Then again, she likely worked around good-looking male models all the time. He was no big deal, at least not in the modeling world.

"I want your arm around his, Katrina," the director said. "Katrina, your right breast against his chest, with you facing him. Let's see some heat here."

It was as if they were on a movie set and the director had said, "Action." Where she had previously ignored him as if he didn't exist, now Katrina moved into him, her body warm and pliant as she slid her hand into his hair and tilted her head back. Their hips touched, their thighs made contact, and then she made eye contact with him.

He'd never felt that pow of instant connection before, but he sure as hell felt it now. It was as if lightning had struck the center of his universe, and every part of him felt it.

Katrina blinked a few times, then frowned.

"Something wrong?"

"The angle. Give me a second," she said. He'd expected some type of Russian accent, but there was none, just the smoky hot darkness of her voice spilling from her lips. It was like drinking whiskey on a cold night. The sound of her voice heated him from the inside out. He'd never been slammed so hard like this before.

Katrina adjusted, her fingers tangling in his hair, giving him a bit of a tug.

His lips curved. "So, you like that?" he asked.

"Just a job," she responded, then gave him a smoldering look, tilted her head toward him, and jutted her hips out enough to hit him right in the crotch.

Goddammit. She'd done that on purpose.

He could do it as well. He raised his hand and laid it above her hip, knowing he couldn't obscure the swimwear. After all, that's what they were advertising. His fingers bit into her skin, enough that he caught the flash of awareness in her eyes.

"Yes, that's perfect," the director said. "Hold it there."

Grant heard the click of the camera several times.

"Now move. Get into each other. Lean in, touch. Be mindful of your angles, Katrina. And Grant, follow her lead."

"Yes, Grant," Katrina said, shifting a little, then picking up his hand and placing it on her butt. "Follow my lead."

It wasn't like he hadn't had to pose for a photo session before. He wasn't a rookie here. He knew what he was doing, how to move and react to the camera, and when to be still.

Katrina might be the pro here, but he could play the game, too. He cupped her butt, making sure he didn't squeeze. He slid his fingers lightly over her skin, tucking his fingertips slightly inside the edge of her suit.

He heard each breath she took, saw the smoldering look in her eyes, and his body reacted.

So did hers, as her nipples pebbled, brushing against his chest.

His lips curved.

Just a job his ass.

He moved with every few clicks of the camera, turned his head, shifted his body against hers, making sure their clothes remained the focus while keeping his gaze intently on hers. When he drew a strand of her hair between his fingers, letting his knuckles brush the swell of her breasts, he heard her sharp intake of breath.

"Just a job, right?" he asked, turning her around so her back was to him. That way he could skim his hand down her arm, letting his fingers rest at her hip.

"This is perfect," the director said. "Keep doing what you're doing."

He listened to the sound of Katrina's breaths, got comfortable with her ass nestled into his crotch.

They fit damned perfect together. She was tall—taller than the average woman. He didn't have to crouch down to fit her to him. She had long legs. Really nice legs, too. He'd noticed . . . everything about her.

"Okay, let's break for a few," the director said. "You both need an outfit change. Then we'll resume."

Before he had a chance to say anything, Katrina pushed off and walked away, heading into the cabana. Her assistant, or whoever, handed her a bottle of water, and she disappeared without a word to him.

Friendly, wasn't she?

He wandered off at the direction of the staff to change his board shorts and to have his hair and makeup adjusted. When he came back out, Katrina was in a short robe.

He was called out toward a tree facing the sun.

"Ready for you, Katrina," the director said.

She dropped the robe, and Grant blinked. Katrina wore only a thong bottom. She stood still while they arranged her hair to partially cover her breasts.

And what fantastic breasts they were, too. He decided to look elsewhere, like out on the water, until she showed up in front of him. In this game they were playing, it was best for him not to show a physical reaction.

"Katrina, you against the tree. Grant, you plant one hand above her head to start, lean into her body."

Some of the assistants positioned them while Grant and Katrina made eye contact.

She met his gaze with a cool one of her own, a challenge to him, as if she'd done this a million times, as if rubbing her breasts against his chest wasn't a big deal. To her, it probably wasn't. She wanted to know if he'd react.

To him, he had a gorgeous, half-naked woman pressed up against him, and his dick was trying very hard to respond to that, while he was trying equally as hard to convince his dick nothing was going to happen out here on the beach with twenty other people watching.

"Ready?" the director asked.

Katrina tilted her head back toward the sun. "Yes."

Grant gave a quick nod, hoping like hell this wouldn't take long, especially since every time Katrina moved, she rubbed her breasts against his chest. And because she was topless, they had to take special care that no nipple was visible. They took every shot carefully, stopping to rearrange her hair or strategically place his arm or hand.

It was interminable. Katrina was patient through every shot, but to Grant, it was like a goddamned eternity.

"Is it always like this?" Grant asked Katrina during one of the many breaks.

Clearly comfortable standing around having her hair and makeup retouched, Katrina cocked her head to the side. "Like what?"

"Hours of this. Click and change positions. Click and redo the hair. Click and clothing changes."

"Oh. Yes. Always like this. Why? Are you bored?"

His lips curved and he took a glance downward where her hair barely covered her generous breasts. "Hardly."

She rolled her eyes. "I doubt these are the first set of breasts you've seen. Not from what I've read about you."

"And here I thought you had no idea who I was."

"Oh, I know who you are, Grant. You've dated a few of my friends."

He wondered which ones. None of them were on location with him, and he'd always remained friends with the women he dated, so he doubted they had anything bad to say about him. "Is that right. And did you get a full report?"

"Yes."

"So that means you'll have dinner with me tonight."

She laughed, and he liked the sound of it.

"I don't think so."

He wasn't insulted, and he liked her confidence. They finished the shoot for the day since, according to the director, the light was leaving them. Katrina grabbed her robe and wandered off, and Grant went back to his bungalow to shower off the makeup and hair gunk. He checked his phone and answered a few e-mails and text messages.

Trevor had sent him a text stating he was going to set up a face-to-face call with Haven, so he was staying in his room.

That meant Grant was on his own tonight, which was fine with him. He returned a few calls, one to his agent, Liz Riley. She talked to him about finalizing his contract since the season would be starting soon. He told her he'd come in and see her as soon as he got back to town.

Football season was gearing up, and he was due to the practice facility in St. Louis in two weeks.

He was ready. He'd been in training and was in shape, and was more than ready for the season to start. This was a nice mini vacation prior to getting back to work, though. Soon enough he'd have his head in the game, and it would be all he thought about.

After getting dressed in a pair of shorts and a sleeveless shirt, he made his way to the main bar at the hotel and ordered a beer. He grabbed a seat at one of the tables outside, content to sip his beer and people watch, one of his favorite pastimes.

He saw a few of the models come outside. They sat at a table not too far from where he was, all of them talking and laughing.

They were all beautiful women. Tall and slender, with great hair, pretty smiles, and amazing bodies. But he found himself searching for only one woman.

He had no idea why, when she'd clearly blown him off. She was probably out on a date tonight with some hot male model. He'd seen a few of those guys today as well.

But then he caught sight of Katrina coming through the bar. She was by herself, carrying a tote bag. She stopped to talk to the bartender, who nodded. Then she walked past Grant without saying a word, and pulled up a chair at a table by herself.

Not with the other models, who seemingly ignored her as much as she was ignoring them.

She pulled out a book and a pair of glasses, and one of the waitresses brought her a tall glass of what looked like iced tea with lemon. She opened the book and started to read, oblivious to everything—and everyone—around her.

Huh. Not at all what he'd expected.

He watched her for a while, waiting to see if she was meeting someone. After about thirty minutes, he realized no one was going to show up. He stood, grabbed his beer, and went over to her table and pulled out a chair to take a seat.

She lifted her gaze from her book and settled it on him. She didn't offer a smile.

"Did you get lost on your way to some other table?" she asked.

"No. But you were alone."

"Precisely. On purpose."

She waited, as if she expected him to leave. He didn't take a brush-off all that easily. "I thought you might want some company."

"You thought wrong."

"Does that icy-cold stare work on all men?"

"Usually."

"Why aren't you with your friends over there?"

She took a quick glance at the other table, then back to him. "Do you think models travel in herds?"

She had a sharp wit. He liked that about her. "Sorry. I guess not. What are you drinking?"

"Iced tea."

He signaled for the waitress, then held up two fingers and motioned to their drinks. She nodded and wandered back inside.

"Really, Grant. I'm fine. And I'd like to be alone."

"No one wants to be alone."

"That's bullshit."

"Okay, fine. I don't want to be alone. I figured we'd have dinner together."

With a sigh, she set down her book and took off her glasses. "Just because we worked together today doesn't mean we have anything in common, or that we shared a moment or anything."

"Didn't we?"

She paused for a few seconds, and he held her gaze. Damn, there was something about her eyes. He liked women just fine, and always had a good time with them. He'd had a few relationships that had lasted awhile and had ended amicably. But not one woman had ever shocked him with the same spark he'd felt with Katrina today.

He wanted to explore that, see if he could push through her frosty exterior.

"I'm reading a book."

"So you said. It's a good one. I've read it before."

She frowned. "You didn't even look at it."

"I saw it when I sat down."

She crossed her arms. "Okay, fine. What's it about?"

"There's this guy, and he works for the CIA. But he's a double agent, working both sides. You don't know throughout the book if he's a good guy or bad guy, or if the other CIA agent he hooks up with in Seoul is on his side, or out to kill him. So when they both show up on the train—"

She held up her hand. "Stop. I haven't gotten to that part yet. Fine, I get it. You've read it."

"You thought I was bullshitting you."

"You wouldn't be the first."

The waitress brought their drinks. "Thanks," Grant said. "Can we see some menus?"

"I don't want to see a menu," she said to the waitress, who

walked away anyway. She turned her attention back on Grant. "I don't want you to sit here with me. Honestly, are you always this rude?"

"Not always. You bring out the best in me."

She rolled her eyes.

"So tell me why that book."

"I like suspense and crime fiction."

"You don't strike me as the type."

Her brows lifted. "Type? Why? Did you expect I'd be thumbing through a fashion magazine? Or perhaps you thought I didn't know how to read, so I would just look at the pictures. Do you expect all models to be dumb?"

Man, was she ever sensitive. "That would be stereotyping, and I'd be the last person to do that. And no. You looked like the type to read books on . . . I don't know. Psychology or something."

She laughed. "Why?"

He picked up her dark glasses. "You look so smart wearing these."

"I am smart. With or without the glasses."

He could tell he was digging the hole even deeper with every word he said. "Sorry. I'm not getting this out right. I've dated a few models."

"So I've heard."

He sighed. "A lot of them have different interests. One was a certified scuba diver, so I learned to dive when I was dating her. One was a hiker and a climber. I did some heinous climbs with her."

"You dated Elesia?" she asked.

"Yeah."

She wrinkled her nose. "She's a pit viper."

He laughed. "I'm not even going to comment."

"You have interesting taste in women."

"I like women who intrigue me and challenge me. Not just a pretty face."

"Good to know the modeling world isn't growing old and moldy with no men to date as long as you're around. After all, where would we be without our sports stars to take care of us?"

"Now who's stereotyping? I've also dated a schoolteacher, an accountant, a microbiologist, and a landscape architect."

She took a sip of her tea. "It's nice you're spreading it around."

He couldn't help but laugh. "So tell me what interests you, Katrina?"

KATRINA DIDN'T WANT TO LIKE GRANT CASSIDY. SHE didn't want him sitting at her table, yet there he was, drinking his beer and looking absolutely gorgeous.

She'd wanted to be alone, and she thought about spending the evening in her room, so she could read. But it was too beautiful here, and the beach and sea air beckoned, so she'd put on a pair of shorts and a tank top to come sit beachside for dinner.

Obviously a huge mistake, because no matter how hard she tried to insult the man, he simply wouldn't leave.

And no matter how hard she tried to deny the chemistry she felt during their photo shoot today, she couldn't.

She posed with male models all the time. Sometimes fully naked. She'd never felt anything. It was her job. She knew it, and so did the guys. But making eye contact with Grant Cassidy today, there'd been some kind of . . . she didn't even know how to describe it. A zing somewhere in the vicinity of her lower belly. A low warming that had spread when he'd laid his hands on her.

Even now, hours later, she could still feel his touch, the way he'd looked at her. She'd wanted . . . more. And if there was one thing Katrina never wanted from a man, it was more of anything. She was too focused on her career to spend any time at all thinking of men. Work was everything to her, and men were a distraction.

Like now. He sat across the table from her, all big and tan and smiling at her like he had exactly what she wanted.

Only she didn't want it. She wanted no part of anything he might have to offer.

She couldn't want it. Still, she couldn't help herself.

"I'm surprised you read that book," she said.

"Now who's stereotyping? You think I'm a dumb jock, that all I read is sports magazines."

"I didn't say that."

"I actually have a degree in accounting. And yes, I did graduate before I went out for the draft."

She studied him. "Accounting. I don't see it."

"I was going to go for a law degree, but I like numbers better. I minored in finance. I wanted to make sure I could oversee my earnings with knowledge. I've seen too many football players blow it all or not know where their money is going, and a few years after they retire, the money is gone."

He was smart, too. She liked that.

She leaned back and looked at him. "Do you have an investment portfolio?"

"As a matter of fact, I do. With the high income a successful model commands, I imagine you do as well."

"I do. And I know exactly where my money is going."

"See? I knew you were a smart woman, Katrina. Smart and beautiful—a lethal combination."

She couldn't help but appreciate that he mentioned the smart part before the beautiful part. Too many men never paid attention to the fact she had a brain. All they saw was her face and body and never even wanted to have a conversation with her. Which was why she didn't date. She didn't have time for men who were that superficial.

Grant seemed . . . different. Yes, there'd been that spark of chemistry at the photo shoot today, but so far all he'd done was talk to her. He hadn't sat down to ogle her or hit on her. It was kind of refreshing.

Not that she had any interest in dating him, but when was the last time she'd spent time talking with a man she wasn't connected to in the industry? She wasn't going to bed with him, but there was no harm in sharing conversation and having a meal with him, was there?

"Okay, fine. Let's see what's on the menu for dinner."

TWO

FOR SOME REASON, KATRINA AGREEING TO DINNER felt like he'd won some kind of battle, that she didn't do this type of thing all that often. Grant would take that as a victory, even a small one.

"How long have you been a model?" he asked her.

"I was signed by an agency when I was seventeen. Close to my eighteenth birthday. So almost ten years now."

"That's a lot of your life. Ever want to do anything else?"

She shrugged, and took a sip of water. "I make good money, and modeling isn't something most of us do all our lives. I'll do something else later. Since I started modeling early, I didn't get a chance to go to college, so that's one of my long-term goals for after the modeling career is over."

"College is a good goal, especially since you didn't get to it after you graduated high school."

"Unfortunately, no, I didn't. It wouldn't have been an option for me anyway."

"Why not?"

She stared at him for a few seconds, then waved her hand back and forth. "Not an interesting story. Forget I said that."

"Why don't you let me be the judge about what's interesting or not? Why wasn't it an option for you?"

Their waitress brought dinner, so she didn't answer him. But he got the idea she'd said something she wished she hadn't. Now he was curious and wanted to know more about her.

"Are you going to make me guess in a twenty questions kind of way, are you going to tell me, or will you just tell me it's none of my business?"

She lifted her gaze from her plate. "What?"

"The reason you couldn't go to college."

"Oh. That." She hesitated. "It was nothing."

He wasn't buying it, because if it was nothing, she would have just told him. Like something inane to talk about over dinner. "So you did jail time and had to put your college career on hold?"

She laughed. "No."

He waved his fork at her. "You're an international spy?"

That made her laugh harder. "Nothing that exciting, I'm afraid." She went back to eating. Her way of dropping the subject.

"You're really not going to tell me. This makes me think you're harboring a deep, dark secret. Maybe I wasn't so off the mark about the spy thing. Or maybe you were held prisoner in a foreign country during your formative years."

She laid her fork down and gave him a direct look. "My mom died and I had a younger brother and sister I had to take care of. Around the same time, I got the offer from the agency and started booking modeling jobs, so it all worked out great. That was the reason I didn't go to college. Sorry, nothing nefarious or exciting."

She made it sound so matter-of-fact, when it must have been a nightmare for her. "Katrina. I'm sorry about your mom. You were seventeen, right?"

"Yes."

"That must have been so hard for you. Your dad—"

"Was not in the picture. It's just me, Leo, and Anya."

"Leo and Anya are your brother and sister?"

"Yes."

"Tell me about them. How old are they?"

"Leo is fifteen. Anya is seventeen."

Having finished his fish, he pushed his plate to the side. "They're young. So they must have been really young when your mom died."

"Yes."

"Who took care of them after? Did you have aunts and uncles?"

She laid her fork on her plate. "No. It was just me. We had no other family."

This story kept getting worse. "Jesus, Katrina. You raised those kids? And worked full-time as a model?"

"You make it sound like it's a big deal."

"It is a big deal. You were just a kid yourself."

She shrugged. "They're my family. We're a family. We had no one else but each other. What was I supposed to do? Child services wanted to take them away and put them in foster care. Can you believe that? I wouldn't allow it—couldn't allow it to happen. I booked jobs right away and fortunately I turned eighteen not too long after my mother passed away, so I filed for custody of the kids. Since I had immense earning potential, the courts let me have guardianship over them."

Grant's chest tightened at the thought of what Katrina must have gone through. Losing her mother, being all alone, and having the burden of raising her two younger siblings thrust upon her all at the age of seventeen. The pressure of her situation must have been overwhelming.

"You had no one to help you?"

"I hired a really good au pair, because I had to travel for work. I put the kids in good schools and I bought a really nice apartment in New York. I was home as much as I could. We've managed just fine."

"I'll bet you did." He looked at her. "I have to admit, I'm damned impressed. You could have bailed."

She lifted her chin. "I would have never done that. I love my sister and brother."

"A lot of girls that age would have, faced with that responsibility. I admire you for taking it on, for having the balls—or the courage, I guess I should say. You're an amazing woman."

"I did what anyone else would have done, given the same circumstances."

"I don't think so. You don't give yourself enough credit. I'm not sure I would have done the same thing. At seventeen all I wanted to do was play sports and party. The thought of that much responsibility—of having to raise my siblings?" He dragged his fingers through his hair. "No way in hell would I have been able to take that on."

She smiled at him, and it was like the sky had lit up. "Oh, I don't know, Grant. You don't know what you're capable of until you're backed into a corner. I'm sure you would have done the same thing."

He thought about his brothers. Hellions, all of them. A lot like him. He wasn't the oldest, Flynn was. But still, with three brothers? Plus a little sister? Could he have done it? He didn't know.

Hell, he did know. No way.

"Maybe. I'll never know because I have two parents who raised me, and I lived a very comfortable life."

"Then you're very lucky."

"Goddamn right I am. And you just made me realize how very lucky I am. And how very special you are for what you've done."

"I didn't tell you that story to make you admire me, Grant. I shouldn't have told you at all."

She was uncomfortable. Embarrassed, even. He had no idea why. "I'm glad you told me. It's nice getting to know you."

She shook her head. "I never tell anyone about that."

The waitress came and took their plates. "Can I get you something else?"

"No, I'm fine, thank you," she said, and started to gather her things, sliding them into her bag. "I should go."

"Wait. What?" He signed the ticket, charging the meal to his room. "Why are you leaving?"

"I've told you enough." She stood. "Too much."

She hurried away. Grant followed, though she was hard to keep up with because she was practically running.

"Katrina, wait."

She ignored him, so he hustled to catch up with her, grasping her arm as she made it down the walkway in between the restaurant and the cabanas.

"Stop. Talk to me."

She wouldn't make eye contact. She had her arms wrapped around her bag.

"Hey. I'm sorry if I made you uncomfortable, if I made you say something you didn't want to say."

She lifted her gaze to him. "I never tell anyone about my past—about the kids. That's . . . private. I don't know why I told you."

He took her elbow and led her down toward the beach, where it was quiet. Fortunately, she came willingly. Whatever was bothering her was clearly upsetting. "I'm glad you did, but don't worry. I'm not planning to broadcast it to anyone."

"I don't like those models with those sad backstories, you know? They use it to get media attention and that's just not me." She slung her bag over her shoulder, seeming a little more relaxed now. "I want my work to speak for itself. And I need to protect the kids. They have enough to deal with without having the media hounding them."

He grinned as they walked along the beach. She glared at him.

"What?"

"You go all protective mama bear when you talk about Anya and Leo."

"Shut up. I do not." But her lips tilted upward. "Okay, maybe I do. You don't even know what it's like—" She stopped herself. "Right. Of course you know what it's like."

"Is that why you don't date anyone famous? To keep the cameras away?"

"I have enough cameras on me in my work. I need to keep them out of my personal life. And it's not like I'm going to meet a guy at the corner coffee shop."

He nodded. "You are a little intimidating. You probably scare the shit out of men."

She stilled, then turned to face him. "I do not. I'm very nice."

He pinned her with a look. "Yeah, you were all warm and welcoming when I took a seat at your table tonight."

"That was different. You barged in on my time with my favorite book."

"Duly noted. Don't get between you and your books. Otherwise you're totally approachable."

"Okay, maybe not so much. It's not that I don't date anyone famous. I don't date . . . anyone."

He pulled her to a sitting spot on the sand. "Okay, now I find that hard to believe. You're young, you're beautiful, and well traveled. This is the time of your life you should be dating your ass off. And you're telling me you don't go out. Why not?"

She shrugged and stared out over the ocean. "I don't have time."

"Okay. I get that you're busy, and you're in high demand. But you get time off."

"I spend my time off with the kids."

"They're teenagers and likely want to spend their time off with their friends."

She didn't answer.

"I'm right, aren't I?"

She still didn't answer, but that gave him time to study her profile. A lot of women didn't like to be viewed at certain angles. Especially the models he'd dated. There were all these angles they'd preferred. Something about head-on being their most attractive feature, or they liked gazing into his eyes, or some such bullshit. Katrina didn't have a problem giving him her profile. And why not? She was stunning from any angle. Or maybe she just didn't want to make eye contact with him, because he was hitting too close to the truth.

"Katrina. You took on a lot of responsibility at such a young age. You're entitled to go out and have some fun, ya know."

"I have plenty of fun when I travel."

He cocked a brow. "Do you? Are you having fun now?"

She gave him a half smile. "Loads."

"I'll bet." He stood, brushing the sand off his butt and legs. He held his hand out for her, then tugged her up. "Come on."

"Wait," she said as he held tight to her hand and pulled her back toward the hotel. "Where are we going?"

He shot her a grin. "To have some fun."

THREE

KATRINA FELT LIKE SHE WAS ON SOME ROLLER coaster, being dragged to the top, only to plunge down the abyss at around a hundred miles an hour.

In the dark.

While blindfolded.

In the short span of an hour, she'd been sent to her room to change. Grant had told her "comfortable," and since she had no idea what he had in mind, she changed into a sundress, plus sandals. She'd thought about objecting. Hadn't he been listening when she'd told him she didn't date?

Why did she even agree to this? She could have told him to kiss her ass, which was her typical response to pushy, aggressive men, especially the ones who asked her out. Though he hadn't asked her out, had he? He hadn't even given her time to ask what the hell was going on. He'd told her to change, that it was high time she have some fun.

Whatever. Fine. She'd have "fun," because it was obvious he wasn't going to go away until she did. Then she was going to bed, because they were shooting again in the morning.

When she'd come out of her bungalow, Grant had been waiting for her. He'd changed, too, into cargo shorts plus a short-sleeved shirt. She had to admit, he was some rather nice eye candy, and not in the typical pretty-boy-model way, either. He was real. Rugged, tall and lean and good to look at.

"Ready to go?" he asked.

"Where exactly are we going?"

"You'll see." He held out his arm, which she took, letting him lead her to the front of the hotel, where there was a private car waiting for them.

"Seriously," she asked. "Where are we going?"

"You said you don't get out much. So we're going out."

"I already had dinner."

He held the car door for her. "Never said we were gonna eat."

She knew she should have hidden out in her room tonight. This was ridiculous. Still, it might not hurt to get out a little, and she was curious now.

She slid into the seat and he climbed in after her. The car took them for a ride around the island, to the bay, where they got out at the docks.

"You're not going to throw me in the water, are you?"

He laughed, then took her hand as they walked down the dock. "No."

At the end of the dock was a catamaran.

"I thought we'd take a cruise tonight—see the sunset."

Normally she worked, then she went to her room to read, or hung out near the water. She very rarely went in it—or on it. She loved the water, and getting out on it wasn't the worst idea ever. "Sounds okay."

He held her hand as she climbed aboard, then kept hold of it, forcing her to meet his gaze. "Don't get too enthused."

"I'll try my best."

They were met by the captain and two crew members, one named Jay, who told them all about the catamaran and the cruise, including where they'd be sailing.

"We'll take a tour around the coast of the island, and make sure you're able to catch an awesome view of the sunset tonight. If you'll come forward, we have some champagne."

Grant looked over at her. "I suppose you don't object to champagne."

"I do not."

He held her hand as they moved toward the front of the catamaran when they took off. She took in the sensation of the breeze blowing through her hair. They leaned against the front of the catamaran, and Katrina watched the view of the shore as they pulled out farther into the water.

The sea was like turquoise glass, the waves calm as they turned and began to make a slow, leisurely trek parallel to the shore.

When Jay brought champagne, Grant picked two glasses and handed one to her. Katrina looked around.

"Where are the other people?"

"Just us."

She blinked. "You rented the entire boat?"

"They offered private sunset cruises. I thought that sounded fun. Maybe a little romantic."

She shook her head. "Seems a waste of money. You could fit a lot of people on this thing. And don't go looking for romance with me, Grant, because it isn't going to happen."

"You're welcome, Katrina. I thought it sounded nice, too."

She cocked her head to the side. "Fine. Thank you. But I'm still not interested—"

He held up his hand. "How about you stop worrying about all the things that *aren't* going to happen, and just enjoy the view—and the champagne?"

She still couldn't believe they were alone on the huge catamaran. What was he thinking? Even worse, what was the boat owner thinking? She mentally counted the number of people that could fit on there, and how much money he could have made fitting all those people on here.

Then again, maybe he'd charged Grant the same amount.

Whatever. Not her problem, since she wasn't paying. She sipped her champagne and decided that was Grant's problem, not hers. If he wanted to waste his money taking a private cruise, he could. She wouldn't have done it, but since he had, she walked along the side of the catamaran, taking in every view since they had the run of the boat. Grant followed behind, commenting about things he saw on the land like fishing boats or shopping areas or hotels and places where people lived.

"Must be nice to wake up to a view like this every morning," he said, noting some of the beachfront property.

"It would be, wouldn't it?"

"I sometimes think about retiring to a place like this someday," he said, his gaze searching out over the shore. "But then I figure after a month or so, I'd be bored as hell and I'd miss civilization."

"I don't know. I could get used to the island life. It's pretty decadent. You wake up in the morning and throw on your swimsuit. If you have to run an errand, you put on a sundress and your flip-flops and head into town or wherever the nearest market is. You get to know all the locals, so you feel safe and protected, and everyone takes care of everyone else. Since I live in such a big city, that idea sounds idyllic to me."

He nodded. "I can see your point. Still, I'd miss going to football games. I'd miss my family."

She looked at him. "They have airplanes for that. You could visit."

"True. But then there are the kids. Wouldn't they be missing out on city life?"

She shrugged. "Who'd miss city life when they could grow up with something like this?"

"You raise valid points, Katrina."

"Or, wait until your kids are grown, then retire to your island paradise."

"Then I'd miss my grandkids, and someone's got to teach them about football."

She laughed. He was a pretty good companion, but she wasn't going to say that because she didn't want him to think she was interested in him. She was just along for the ride because he'd more or less bullied her into coming with him. And okay, the champagne was pretty good.

The boat had slowed. The sun had started to set, a beautiful orange glow sifting through the clouds and melting into the water. The glow sizzled as it sank lower by the second.

With no buildings or trees to obstruct her view, she had to admit this was a stunning way to see the sun set.

Grant held out his hand for her. "Come on, let's move to the front and watch."

She slid her hand in his, mainly because the boat was rocky and she didn't want to fall overboard. They headed to the front of the catamaran, where nothing stood between them and the sunset but the water.

It was a little cooler here, and she shivered.

"Cold?" he asked.

"A little."

He wrapped his arm around her and tugged her against him.

"Kind of makes you feel like you're hovering at the edge of the world, doesn't it?"

She watched the sun dip into the water, imagining she could hear it sizzle. "When I was little, I was always an early riser and I'd dash up to our building's roof whenever I could and watch the sun come up. My mom hated for me to be up there all alone. She was always afraid a strong gust of wind would blow me off the roof. But I loved it there. I felt so free. It was just me up there, all alone, waiting for the sun to greet me."

It took her a few minutes to realize Grant hadn't said anything. She pulled her gaze away from the setting sun to find him looking at her. "Shouldn't you be watching the sunset?"

"You're a lot better to look at than the sunset. And I liked your story about the roof."

She laughed. "It wasn't a big deal."

"Still, you shared it with me and I appreciate it."

She didn't know why she had. Another part of her past she'd divulged to someone who was practically a stranger. Maybe it was the champagne loosening her tongue. Then again, she'd been drinking iced tea over lunch when she'd told him about her parents and siblings, so she had no excuse.

What the hell was wrong with her tonight? She normally kept her past locked up tight. No one knew about it, yet in the space of a couple of hours Grant now knew more than she'd ever told anyone.

Not that it mattered, since after this shoot she wasn't going to see him ever again.

After the sun set, the boat turned around and made a leisurely sail back to the dock. Katrina couldn't recall having a nicer, more relaxing evening, other than being alone and reading one of her favorite books.

Grant didn't talk incessantly, and when he did, it wasn't all about himself like a lot of men she knew. The man was good company. She liked her own company just fine, and mostly preferred it that way, since men were a complication she didn't need in her already too-complicated life.

They both thanked the crew for a nice sail, and he held her hand as she stepped off the catamaran.

There was a car waiting for them at the end of the dock.

"It's like you planned it that way," she said as the driver got out and held the door for them.

"Kind of," Grant said, and slid in beside her.

The ride back to the hotel didn't take long. Grant took care of the tab for the driver, and then held her hand as she got out of the car. There was still a lot of activity at the resort, since it wasn't all that late.

"Care for a drink at the bar?" he asked.

She shook her head. "I need to get a full night's sleep since we're shooting again tomorrow."

He nodded. "I'll walk you back to your room."

"It's not necessary. I know the way."

"I'll walk you anyway."

She shrugged, and he stayed close to her as they made their way to her bungalow. She fished her key out of her bag, then turned to him.

"I had a nice time. Thanks."

"That was probably painful for you to say."

She nudged him with her elbow. "It was not. I can be charming and polite. Even fun."

"I'm sure you can. But I can tell you don't go out much. And you obviously aren't comfortable around men."

She pinned him with a look. "I'm extremely comfortable around men, since I shoot with them all the time."

"That's work. I'm talking about fun. Dating. Romance. You

know, romance? That thing you said we weren't going to have together? Or is it just me you don't like?"

Now he was putting words in her mouth, and irritating her. "I never said I didn't like you."

"So you do like me."

She rolled her eyes. "I didn't say that, either."

He laughed, then took the key card from her hand and opened the door to her bungalow. "Get some sleep, Katrina. I'll see you in the morning."

She was kind of shocked he didn't push to come in for a drink, or even try to kiss her. "Okay. Good night, Grant."

He nodded, and waited there while she closed the door and locked it. She put her purse down and kicked off her sandals. When she went to the window to check, he was gone.

Interesting man.

And one she couldn't figure out at all, which was odd, because she thought she knew men very well. But this man she intended to avoid, like she had made avoiding men a practiced art her entire life.

She had made independence her priority, knew better than to trust any man.

I'll never leave you, my printsessa.

She could still hear her father's voice in her head, promising he'd always be there for her.

Right up until he'd disappeared from her life forever, abandoning her and her mother without a word, shattering her world and her trust.

And then her mother had died, and she'd been on her own, spending years carving out the independence she'd worked so hard to attain for herself, and for her siblings.

She'd never let a man—any man—screw that up.

Even if her libido thought otherwise.

Grant Cassidy might be hot and sexy, and her sex drive might be revved up, but her sex drive could be tamped down.

She'd worked for ten years to make a life for herself, to make sure she'd never end up broke and alone. She'd made a careful plan, never once deviating from it.

And no man would ever interfere with her plan.

She just had to keep her body and thoughts under control. She'd done it for twenty-seven years; she could do it for another couple of days.

Easy enough, right?

FOUR

IT WAS DAMNED HOT TODAY, AND THEY DIDN'T HAVE
to do much oiling of Grant's skin, because he was sweating like
he'd just taken the ball himself and run it forty yards for a touchdown.

Good thing they decided on a shady shot, and in the water by
some caves, which suited him just fine.

It also suited him that they decided to pair him up with Katrina
again. The director told him he liked the chemistry between him
and Katrina.

Yeah, Grant was into that chemistry, too. All over it, in fact.
He'd like to find out if yesterday was just a fluke, or if it continued
today.

They were at the mouth of the rocks in the shallow water.
Katrina was in a turquoise swimsuit, some skimpy thing again
that barely covered her. And again, she was oblivious to it all, just
following directions as they set up the shot.

Grant had to lean against the rocks, with Katrina draped over him. The director was hot about this, saying it would be sexy as hell. Right now it was uncomfortable as hell and the rock was digging into his back. Good thing he had a gorgeous distraction, and as Katrina eased over his body, her breasts mashing against his chest, his back forgot all about the pain.

"Stretch out, Katrina," the director said. "Now slide your fingers into his hair and extend your legs. That's it. Grant, I want your left hand on her lower back, your fingertips just above her swimsuit bottom. Hold it—that's perfect."

With her close like this, he easily got lost in the blue violet depth of her eyes. And she could really work the camera. Or maybe she was working him, because once again he was struck by her, by the way she looked at him, at the connection he felt when their gazes met.

Nope. Not just a fluke. That pow of attraction was still there.

She shifted, her center colliding with his hip. They were both wet from the water that had been sprayed on them, her hair falling over her shoulders, tickling his chest. At that moment, she started sliding off him.

He grasped her hips. "Are you okay? Uncomfortable?"

"No, I'm fine. Just realigning."

"It's really damn hot today," he said.

"I know."

"I hope I'm not sweating all over you."

"Don't worry about it. A little sweat isn't going to bother me."

"When we're done today, I'm going to take a dive in the ocean to cool off."

Her lips curved. "It's not the worst idea ever."

The makeup and hair team dashed over to fix Katrina's hair and dab some powder on her. The shoot seemed to go on for hours, with adjustment in positions. They draped Katrina over the rock, with Grant leaning over her. He felt bad for her, because he knew how damned uncomfortable that rock was, though she never even winced or complained, just did what she was told.

Though he noticed she arched her back. Now he knew whenever he saw those sexy shots of models thrusting their breasts up, it was probably because they were uncomfortable on whatever surface they were on. He had a new respect for what they had to go through.

Finally though, they finished off on their knees facing each other in the water. They'd taken off Katrina's top, and strategically placed her hair over her breasts. She and Grant were body to body.

"I want your lips practically touching, breathing each other's air. Make this sexy, you two. This is the last shot before we lose the best light."

Her head was angled, her lips full and as he moved in, he could feel her breath sail across his mouth. It was much cooler here in the water, which meant he was focusing a lot less on it being so goddamned blistering hot, and focusing a lot more on the sizzling woman in his arms. He tuned out the cameras and assistants and crew, and concentrated only on Katrina, on the feel of her body against his, the way she breathed, the way her eyes darkened as her lips touched his.

It wasn't a kiss. It was an almost kiss, and it was damned frustrating. Her lips were right on his, but he couldn't move in. He wanted to jerk her fully against him and take what she teasingly offered. Their gazes were locked, their bodies entwined, and it was a good thing cold water rushed over him, because he'd never been hotter.

"Goddamn awesome," he heard the director say, but Grant could only suffer through the tease, sliding his hands down her bare back, feeling the silken softness of her skin, her breasts against his chest, and bide his time.

But this time, he knew she felt it, knew it from the way her heart pounded against his chest, from the fast way she breathed, from the passion he saw in her eyes. This was no work-related, I'm-bored-and-let's-get-this-over-with kind of look. She was engaged and in this with him.

"Okay, we're done," the director said.

And this time, instead of pulling away immediately, her gaze drifted. Reluctantly, as if she wanted to stay locked with him like this, as if she wanted everyone to go away so they could finish what they'd started.

Yeah, he wanted that, too.

He stood and took her hands, pulling her to a standing position.

"Are you through with me for the day?" Katrina asked the director.

"Yeah, we're done. Good job. Both of you. I think these shots are going to be amazing."

"Thanks," Grant said.

Katrina accepted her top from the assistant, and looped the string around her neck. Still staring at him, she put it back on.

"Want me to tie that for you?" he asked.

"Sure." She pivoted and lifted her hair while he fastened the back of the bikini top for her.

When she turned around, she smiled.

"Now, how about that dip in the water you mentioned."

Before he could answer, she was off, walking past the rocks, and disappeared into the waves. He followed right behind her, diving into the water.

When he surfaced, she was right next to him.

"You're right. I needed that. It was hot out there," she said, then started to swim back to shore.

He caught her ankle and spun her around. She kicked at him, laughing, but he brought her leg up and pulled her around him.

"You're like a mermaid. Elusive."

He thought she'd push away, but she held on to his shoulders. "I'm exhausted. I did a solo shoot at sunrise this morning. And I need to pack."

"When do you fly out?"

"Tomorrow morning."

"Plenty of time. And you're probably hungry. I know I am."

"I am a little hungry."

"Then let's get something to eat. We'll hang out by the water. Enjoy this view before we both have to leave it."

She hesitated, then nodded. "Okay. I need to take a shower and scrub all this makeup and oil off."

"Me, too. Meet you at the pool in a half hour?"

"Sure."

He was reluctant to let go of her. She felt good against him, and he wanted to kiss her, but she was still resistant and he knew better than to push it, so he let go and they made the dash to shore.

After taking a shower and checking messages, he ran into Trevor in the lobby. He was packed and on his way out.

"Done?" Grant asked.

"Yeah. I had an early shoot this morning, so fortunately I have time to catch a flight this afternoon and get home to my woman. How about you?"

"Just finished a shoot, so I'm going to hang out and enjoy the beach. I'll fly home tomorrow."

They shook hands. "See you at one of the games," Grant said, "or we'll have dinner next time you're in St. Louis."

"I think we're playing you this season, so we'll definitely get together."

"Okay. Have a safe flight."

Grant picked a table close to the water, and ordered an ice water with lemon. It wasn't too long until Katrina showed up, her hair still wet from her shower, and no makeup this time. It didn't detract from her beauty at all. In fact, without makeup, she looked so young, and yet so incredibly pretty.

He stood when she came to the table.

"Thanks. Were you waiting long?"

"I just got here and ordered a water."

The waitress came over, and Katrina ordered the same. The waitress left menus for them while she went to get Katrina's drink.

"I'm sorry. I wanted to check on the kids."

"And how are they?"

"They're fine."

"What are they doing over the summer?"

"They have camp."

He grimaced. "Camp? What kind of camp?"

"Anya has music camp. She plays the flute. Leo has theater camp."

"Do they enjoy those things?"

"Of course they do."

"So your brother doesn't play sports?"

She gave him a half smile. "Not every boy plays sports, you know."

"Has he ever expressed an interest in it? Or your sister?"

"They get plenty of physical exercise."

"Now you sound like a mother."

"I'm going to take that as a compliment and not the insult you intended."

Their waitress came and they ordered food. After she left, Grant looked at her. "I'm not saying every kid has to play sports. But music and theater? I mean yeah, those are great additions, but summer is a time to take off and do something fun."

She sighed. "Those are fun activities for them, and keep them engaged. Would you prefer I let them hang out in front of the local drugstore in the summer and join a gang?"

"Okay, now you're being dramatic. And overprotective. Not every kid who isn't involved with a scheduled activity every single day is doomed to gang life."

He could see the defensiveness in the way she raised her chin and the straight line of her lips. "I'm doing the best I can."

"I'm sure you are. And I can't imagine it's easy raising kids in New York. Have you ever thought about moving?"

"Often. But I work there. It's easier to me to stay there since I'm on call a lot for shoots."

"Which means you shoot in New York?"

She took a sip of water. "Not exactly. But my agency is there and I meet with them a lot. And it's a good location for flights. It's convenient."

He shrugged. "Something to consider for the kids. A big house in a great city. Lots of friends. Less supervision."

"Oh, come on, Grant. Teenagers can get in trouble in any city."

He laughed. "This is true. I got in plenty of trouble growing up in Green Bay, and Texas."

She leaned back in her chair. "Now this I want to hear. I've told you about me and my family. Tell me about yourself and this trouble you got into."

"I don't think we have enough time for all that. I might miss my flight tomorrow."

She laughed. "Surely you weren't that bad."

"According to my mom, I was. Then again, she'd likely say the same thing about all my brothers. Maybe not my sister."

She arched a brow. "You have brothers?"

"Three of them."

"Wow. Your poor mother."

"You obviously haven't met my mom. She rules with an iron fist. We're all a little afraid of her."

She laughed. "I'd like to meet her."

"You'd like her. She'd like you, too, with your music and drama lessons."

"And here we go again with that."

The waitress brought their dinner, so they settled in and ate.

"What's up next for you?" he asked.

"I have a shoot next week, then a bit of a break, fortunately, so I can spend some time with the kids."

"Taking any trips with them or doing anything fun?"

"Not really."

"Do they like to travel?"

"I don't know. I've never asked them."

He leaned back. "You should take them on a summer vacation before school starts up. Maybe to the beach, or go horseback riding or something other than that camp stuff."

She finished her salad and took a long swallow of water. "I'll definitely give those ideas some thought."

"Yeah, I'm sure you will." Grant figured she'd give it no thought whatsoever. "Hey, I'm going to be playing against New York in a few weeks for a preseason game. I'd love to see you and meet the kids."

She gave him a flat look. "That wouldn't be a very good idea."

"Why not?"

"For the very obvious reason that you and I aren't involved in any way."

He shrugged, set his fork on his plate and wiped his mouth with the napkin. "So? What does that have to do with anything? I like you. I'd probably like your brother and sister. And frankly, I'm a fun guy. I know they'd like me."

"Yes, I'm sure they would. But I don't want to confuse them."

"In what way would meeting me confuse them? Because I'm a

guy that you know? It's not like you'd introduce me as your boyfriend or some dude you're dating. We met on a photo shoot. I'd be in town, and we could go do some fun stuff. You could show me the city."

She wrinkled her nose. "Tourist things?"

He laughed. "Yeah, even tourist things. Something wrong with that?"

"I guess not."

"Great."

They finished their meal, the waitress cleared their plates and brought the check, which Grant signed. Katrina stood. "Well, thank you. I had a nice time."

"Do you want to hang out by the pool for a while?"

"No. I think I should start packing."

She acted like she couldn't get away from him fast enough, and he knew it wasn't because she didn't like him. He hadn't been pushy—okay, maybe a little pushy. So maybe it was time to back off a little. But not too much. He liked this woman and he wanted to get to know her better.

He walked with her back to her bungalow, and waited while she dug her key out of her bag. When she turned around to tell him good-bye, he figured he'd push just a little bit more.

"So about New York . . ."

Her head was down, but she lifted her gaze to his. "I still don't think that's a good idea. I mean, it's been great meeting you and all, but I don't see us continuing our relationship beyond today."

She was a tough one. So skittish. "I'm not asking you to marry me, Katrina. But we have chemistry. We can be friends, right?"

Katrina didn't have friends. Especially not guy friends. She worked, then she went home and hung out with Leo and Anya. That was all she had time for. She didn't socialize, and she absolutely did not date. She had no idea what Grant's motive was, but she was not on board for this.

And it wasn't because she didn't like him. She liked him a little too much, and that was the problem. Just doing the photo shoots with him for the past couple of days sparked feelings and interest she hadn't felt in . . .

Well, never.

She had no business feeling those feelings. Not with all she had on her plate. She couldn't afford to avert her concentration when she had people depending on her.

"No. We can't be friends."

His brows rose. "We can't. Why not?"

"Because . . . well, because."

She inwardly cringed at her lame excuse. She was usually so adept at shutting men down, so cool at expertly pushing them away. Now she fumbled for a valid excuse, and she had no idea why.

Because you don't want to, that's why.

He stepped in, and picked up a strand of her hair. She looked down at where his fingers had hold of her hair, and recalled the way his fingers had felt in her scalp during the photo shoot.

She'd liked his hands on her. She wanted more of that. Her body wanted a lot, lot more of him touching her.

"You can do better than that. It's because you think I'm an arrogant asshole."

Her head shot up. "What? No. I never said that."

His lips curved. "I know. Which is why I'll be calling you when I come to New York." He pulled out his phone. "Give me your number."

Her number fell out of her mouth as if she were possessed. What was wrong with her, anyway?

"Great. Just a friendly call. We'll have dinner. Go do some fun touristy things. You, me, and your brother and sister. No strings attached. Promise."

She frantically searched for one of her expert shutdown comebacks, but all thoughts fled as he wrapped his arm around her and tugged her against his hard, muscular body.

"Until I see you in a few weeks, Katrina, I'm going to do what I've wanted to do since your director put our lips so close together today."

He slid his hand into her hair—and, dear God, she really liked that. And then he kissed her, and she had no thoughts at all except how soft and full his lips were, how much passion he poured into the kiss, and how he backed her against the door of her bungalow so he could press his body against hers.

Oh, that body. She felt every inch of it aligned with hers, and she wanted so much more.

She dropped her bag and held on to his shirt, felt the mad wild beat of his heart against her hand as he pressed the kiss deeper, his tongue sliding against hers. She wanted to straddle him, to rock her center against his, to massage the thrumming ache he'd brought to life. That ache roared with demand and it wouldn't be denied. She wanted to beg him to push open her door and get her naked, then lick her all over until she came about a hundred times.

But he finished the kiss, brushed his lips against hers, then leaned his forehead to hers.

She heard him swallow while she fought to catch her breath.

He took a step back and she saw fiery passion in his eyes. "I'm going to be honest with you here, Katrina. After that kiss? I'm not so sure about the just friends thing."

He turned and walked away, and she fumbled behind her for the door handle, turning it and backing inside.

Just friends? Who was he kidding?

The man was dangerous.

She was going to have to figure out a way to never, ever see Grant Cassidy again.

FIVE

"TWENTY-FOUR AND OUT, SIX, HUT HUT!"

Grant backed away from center, ball in hand, and searched the field, scouting receivers while his front line did their job, keeping the defenders away.

He spied Cole Riley on an open route and threw the ball into Jamarcus Davis's waiting hands.

It was a good play.

The whistle blew and he regrouped with his offense.

Both the running and passing game were going well. The team looked good this preseason. All their key players were healthy, and the rookies were coming along. If they were lucky and everyone stayed injury-free, they had a shot at a damn good season.

Practice today was long, but productive. Coach Tallarino was happy with their progress, and Grant liked what he saw on offense. He had a lot of targets to hit with his receivers, and that's all he wanted.

"Looking good out there, Grant," the coach said after practice. "How's the arm?"

He'd had some stiffness in his shoulder during the off-season, but he'd worked it out with therapy and weights. "Doing good. No pain, no stiffness."

"Let the trainers check you out. I don't want to take any chances. And be sure to check in with the team docs before we take off for New York."

"You got it, Coach."

He met with the trainers, who went through his range of motion. He felt no pain, which was a relief to him. A quarterback was only as good as his throwing arm. When the doc came in, they went through even more.

"No stiffness? And don't lie to me, because I'll know if you do."

He liked Martin Ashwell, the team doctor. "A little in the morning when I first get up. But I do the range of motion exercises the PT staff gave me, and after a hot shower, I'm fine."

Marty nodded. "That's to be expected. But no sharp pains?"

"No."

"Good." The doc tested his range of motion, and pressed on some of the spots he'd complained were tender during the off-season. He'd had a cortisone shot, and some physical therapy.

"I really feel great, Marty."

"Your MRI looked clear. I don't see any scar tissue. PT staff said you worked it during off-season like you were supposed to and you didn't miss any appointments. You're a better patient than most of the guys. And you lifted weights and built some muscle mass in your upper body. That'll help."

He laughed. "I kind of need my arm. It's my moneymaker."

Marty slapped his back. "You're a smart guy, Grant. And a good player. You can put your shirt back on."

The doc made some notes on his computer, then turned around.

"You're good to go. Monitor your movements and pain level. I'd say as long as you don't do anything stupid, and stay in tune with the signals of your body, you'll be fine. If you feel any sharp pains, let me know."

"Will do."

"I'll let the coach know you're fully cleared."

"Thanks, Marty."

He didn't fully exhale until after he left the team facility and was in his car. Then he took a minute and let out a deep breath.

Yeah. He was clear. His shoulder was fine, and his career wasn't over. He'd never said it out loud to anyone, never told his family about it, just kept it to himself. But the issue with his shoulder had scared the shit out of him. Things like that could end a quarterback's career.

He wasn't ready for it to be over yet.

He closed his eyes, gripped the steering wheel, and . . . breathed.

His phone rang, so he fished it out of the cup holder and checked the display.

It was his agent.

"Hey, Liz."

"Hey, yourself. How did the shoot go in Barbados?"

"It went good."

"So detailed as always, Cassidy. Who were you paired up with?"

"Katrina Korsova."

"Outstanding. She's one of the best. I can't wait to see the pictures. Anyway, there's a thing when you're in New York next week."

He loved Elizabeth Riley. She was one of the best agents in the business, a shark when it came to contract negotiations. She was also great with exposure, working with his PR team to make sure he was as noticeable off the field as he was on. He didn't necessarily mind that.

"A thing? What kind of thing?"

"A charity function for the Merritt Foundation. They do all kinds of great things for disadvantaged youth."

"Sounds right up my alley."

"Good. You just need to make an appearance, take some pictures and sign some autographs. Can you make time for it?"

"I can, as long as it doesn't interfere with practices or the game."

"It won't. I'll send you the details."

"Okay. How's the little one?"

"She's great, thank you for asking. Getting bigger all the time. Starting to crawl, which means I need two more sets of eyes and about four more hands."

He laughed. "Good thing you're multitalented like that. And you have Gavin to help you."

"When he isn't playing baseball, which is nearly all the time. But I have his family to help out, so it's all good."

"You were lucky to marry into the Rileys, weren't you?"

"Thanking my lucky stars every day, Grant. Now play good, and I'll be in touch."

"See ya, Liz."

He hung up, and thought about New York, which reminded him of Katrina. He was going to have to do something about connecting with her when he was in town. He'd thought about her a lot since the shoot. Practice and games had kept him busy, but he hadn't forgotten he'd promised her he'd see her, even though he figured she hadn't believed he'd pursue it.

He wanted to pursue it, and her. He wanted to meet her brother and sister.

He intended to follow up.

SIX

"HEY, KIDS, I'M HOME."

Katrina laid her bag down in the entryway and headed down the hallway into . . .

Dead. Silence.

Never a good sign.

She picked up her phone to check the time. It was four p.m., which meant both Anya and Leo should be home by now.

She checked the living room, but saw no sign of them. They weren't in the kitchen, either, so she rounded the corner and went down the hall toward the bedrooms. The doors were open to both their rooms.

Both empty.

Goddammit.

She went to her room, though they wouldn't go in there, but still, she checked anyway.

Not there.

Their bathroom was empty as well.

There were no messages on her phone, either.

Shit.

Just as panic was about to set in, she heard the front door open, and the sounds of their voices, both of them laughing. She hurried to the front room.

"Oh, hey," Anya said. "You're home."

Both of them had Styrofoam cups, Leo sucking from a straw.

"Sup," he said.

"Where were you?"

"We went down the street to get a drink."

"There are drinks in the refrigerator, and you know you're not supposed to leave the apartment."

"Chill, Kat," Anya said, sliding onto one of the couches. "We went to the market. It's just a block down the street."

"Without texting me to let me know where you were. Without permission."

"Uh, okay, Mom. We're fine," Leo said, heading to his room.

"Stop." Her voice came out sharper than she intended. "We need to talk about this."

Leo kept going, and then closed his door.

Sonofabitch. She hated raising teenagers. She had never been like that when she was their age. She'd been cooperative and respectful. Where did all this attitude come from?

With a sigh, she took a seat on the sofa, feeling tired and defeated. It had been like this for about a year now—the constant battles, the defiance. She had no one to turn to for advice. No relatives, no friends to talk to. She was a novice at this. She hadn't even gone through her own period of rebellion, because at barely eighteen she'd been in charge of two young children. She'd had to grow up in a hurry.

"You need to relax about this, Kat," Anya said, leaning back against the sofa cushions, her feet up on the table as she scrolled through her phone. "It's no big deal."

She was too tired to deal with them. She'd been on the road for three weeks straight, and then after barely unpacking had spent an entire day in meetings.

At least she'd be home for a while now. Maybe they just needed some attention. And some reminders about the rules.

"I'm going to take a bath." She pushed off on her knees and stood, heading down the hall.

"Oh. Hey, Kat?"

She stopped, turning toward her sister. "Yes?"

"I have a new recipe in mind for this homemade pizza I'd like to make. Can we do that tonight?"

She tried for a half smile. Anything that would engage her with her siblings was a good thing. "Sure."

GRANT GOT SETTLED IN HIS HOTEL ROOM AFTER DO-ing the signing and photo shoot for the Merritt Foundation that Liz had set up for him. He debated whether he wanted to go out for something to eat or wander around the area. He grabbed his phone and decided to call Katrina first. He dialed her number. It rang several times before someone who definitely wasn't Katrina answered.

"Yo, hello?"

"Hi. Is Katrina there?"

"Who's this?"

"This is Grant Cassidy. And who's this?"

"Anya."

"You'd be Katrina's sister."

"And how would you know that?"

"I did a photo shoot with her a couple weeks ago."

"You did, huh? Are you two dating?"

He grinned. You had to love the nosiness of teenagers—and siblings. "Jury's still out on that one."

"She's resistant. Thinks all her free time should be babysitting us, but I can assure you we don't need babysitters."

"I'm sure you don't. So is she around?"

"She's in the tub. So why are you calling?"

"I'm in town and thought we could all get together and do something."

"So, by 'all,' I'm assuming you mean me and Leo, too?"

"I do mean you and Leo, too. Are you all free tomorrow during the day?"

"Hang on. Let me check with her."

She laid the phone down, Grant assumed to check with Katrina. He could only imagine the response. But she came back about a minute later.

"She said that sounds fine to her."

Grant was shocked to hear that. "Are you sure?"

"Absolutely. I think she's bored hanging around us. You're probably a nice distraction."

He laughed. "Okay, then. How about I pick you all up about ten tomorrow morning?"

"Sounds like a plan. Do you need our address?"

"I do."

She gave him the address.

"What should we wear, Grant?"

"Tourist clothes."

Now Anya laughed. "Awesome. See you tomorrow, Grant."

"Okay. If Katrina has any questions, she can call me."

"Noted. See ya."

She hung up, and Grant shook his head.

Tomorrow should be interesting.

He couldn't wait.

KATRINA FELT A LOT BETTER AFTER A LONG SOAK IN the tub. She helped Anya make the pizza, plus salad.

At least she and the kids were eating together. It always took her a while to get balanced again when she got back from a long bout of travel. She felt out of sorts, and they would hit her with a wave of rebellion, so this wasn't unusual. She'd just have to set some firm ground rules and stick to them and the universe would right itself again.

She took a drink of the merlot she'd poured herself and felt a calm settle over her.

She'd tried to engage Leo and Anya with questions about camp activities. So far, she'd gotten nothing but grunts and monosyllabic responses, so she'd given up, figuring she'd try again after dinner.

Leo needed a haircut. His hair was long and hanging well past his brows, which made it easier for him to hide his emotions, which she could always see in his blue eyes, so much like hers. She made a mental note to make a haircut appointment for him this week.

Anya, on the other hand, had no problem at all expressing her emotions. And did it on a regular basis. Her sister sat on the cusp of adulthood, with one foot still firmly planted in the land of bitchy teenager. Katrina never knew which sister she was going to get on any given day. The laughing, smiling, let's-talk-smart-topics one, or the sullen, angry-with-Katrina-about-everything one.

Such a joy.

"By the way, Grant Cassidy will be picking us up at ten tomorrow morning," Anya said.

Katrina nearly choked on her sip of wine. She laid the glass down on the table. "What?"

"Grant. Cassidy. Hot football player. You didn't tell us you were dating him."

She shot Anya a glare. "I am *not* dating him."

"You know Grant Cassidy?" Leo leaned forward, lifting his head and shaking his hair back. "Since when?"

"I did a photo shoot with him in Barbados." She looked over at Anya. "And what do you mean he's picking us up tomorrow?"

Anya gave her a saucy grin. "He called while you were in the tub. Said he's in town and wants to take us all out tomorrow. I said yes on our behalf."

And there went her stress level again. "Anya. You shouldn't have done that."

Anya shrugged. "Why not? He told me that he told you he was going to call you and set things up when he was in town. He's in town. I didn't want to bug you while you were in the tub. You seemed wigged out when you got home today, so I figured you wanted some downtime."

"Grant Cassidy's coming here tomorrow? Cool." Leo took a sip of his soda.

"I can't believe you did that," Katrina said. "I'm going to have to call him and cancel."

Leo frowned. "Why? Is he a dick?"

"No, he's not. And don't say dick."

"So if he's not a dick—"

"Anya. Come on," Katrina said, pleading for either an end to this conversation or for some return to civility. It wasn't looking like she was going to get either.

"Okay. So if you don't dislike him, then you like him," Anya said.

"I didn't say that, either."

"He had your phone number. And he seemed like a pretty cool guy."

"Based on what? A five-minute phone conversation?"

"More like three minutes, actually. But he's taking us out tomorrow. And we're going. You don't want to be rude and call him back now and cancel. Then you'd be the dick."

"Oh. My God. I don't know what to do with the two of you."

"There's nothing wrong with us," Anya said. "You, on the other hand, are way too tense. You probably need to get laid. Maybe Grant Cassidy can help you with that."

Leo snickered, then raised his hand up high. Anya high-fived him.

"I am not having this conversation with you two. Finish your pizza, then clear the table and do the dishes." She took her glass of wine and went into the living room to turn on the television.

"That means we're going out with Grant Cassidy tomorrow," Leo said.

This was a nightmare. Her entire life had somehow spiraled completely out of control and she no longer had the capacity to deal with it.

So tonight, she was going to drink wine.

Tomorrow, she'd figure out how to handle her unruly teenage siblings who obviously had no sense of boundaries.

And then she'd deal with Grant Cassidy.

SEVEN

GRANT HAD GOTTEN PERMISSION FROM THE TEAM TO fly in a day early, claiming he had some promotional things to attend to. Which he had, and he'd handled in about two hours. Hey, what they didn't know—they didn't have to know. He wanted this day to see Katrina.

After checking in early at his hotel, he took a cab to Katrina's condo on the Upper West Side of Manhattan.

This place had a doorman. Fancy. Grant gave his name, and the doorman buzzed, looked at Grant, then motioned for him.

"You can go on up, Mr. Cassidy."

"Thanks."

He went to the sixth floor, and once he found Katrina's door, rang the bell.

The door was opened by a very tall teenage boy with long hair and eyes the same color as Katrina's. The kid leaned against the doorway, not exactly blocking it, but not letting him in just yet, either.

Protective. Assessing. Grant liked that Katrina's younger brother wasn't going to let just any guy through the front door.

"You must be Leo. I'm Grant Cassidy."

"I am."

Grant held out his hand, and Leo shook it. The kid had a firm handshake, so he had that going for him.

"Hi. Come on in."

He stepped inside and Leo shut the door. Before he could completely walk into the apartment, a very pretty, dark-haired girl hurried to Leo's side. Tall and slender, also with blue eyes like Katrina's.

"I'm Anya, Katrina's sister. She's still deciding what to wear. Apparently you freak her out because I've never seen her take so long to get ready."

He tried not to smile at that thought. "Nice to meet you, Anya. I'm Grant."

"Oh, I know who you are. I watch a lot of football, though I'm a big fan of our New York teams. Still, you're very good. Hey, can you get us tickets to your game this weekend? Leo likes football, too."

She talked a lot and reminded him of his sister at that age. "I'm sure I can." He turned to Leo. "Do you play?"

"Football? Nah." Leo shrugged, then moved aside so Grant could come in.

"So you don't like football?" Grant asked as they moved down the hall.

"No. I like football. A lot, actually."

"But you don't play."

Leo shrugged. "I might want to, but I haven't yet. You should, like, sit on the couch or something."

"Okay." He followed them into the very spacious apartment, giving it a thorough once-over. It was modern and classy, but not fussy. A lot like the woman who owned it. There were windows that let light in, plus plenty of space. She didn't clutter the place up with antiques or expensive furniture. Only necessary items like a dining room table, a couch, and a couple of chairs.

Nice.

He took a seat on a cream leather sofa. "Does Katrina like football?"

"She watches the games with us when she's home," Leo said. "I'm not sure if she pays attention. She likes to read a lot."

"I noticed that about her when we were in Barbados."

Anya took a seat next to him on the sofa. "She's always got her head stuck in a book. Me, I'd rather be out doing something instead of stuck inside. Unless I'm cooking. But speaking of getting out, what are we doing today?"

"I thought you all might like to show me New York. I'm kind of a tourist."

Anya laughed. "Yeah? We never get to play tourist. This could be fun." She took out her phone and started tapping away.

With Anya focused elsewhere, Grant turned his attention to Leo, who seemed a little nervous. Remembering what it was like to be that age and faced with a strange adult, Grant figured it was up to him to ease the tension. "Okay, so you don't play football, Leo. Do you play any other sports?"

"Lacrosse. Tennis."

"I never played lacrosse. And I sucked at tennis."

That made Leo smile.

"Do you like playing those sports?"

He shrugged. "They're okay. I only do them because Katrina makes me."

Interesting. "So you don't like sports."

"I do. But not those. I'd rather play football, but I'm a little light, weight-wise. And Katrina would bust a brain cell or something if I told her I wanted to play football."

"Why is that?"

"She thinks it's dangerous."

Oh, now he was starting to get the picture. "Have you tried talking to her about it?"

Leo shrugged. "No point in it. She's like the law around here, and freaking her out doesn't do any good."

"This is true," Anya said, her focus still on her phone. "Though it's fun to mess with her a little."

It didn't take Grant long to grasp the dynamics here. Katrina was obviously in over her head trying to wrangle two teenagers. Who wouldn't be? He remembered the shit he and his brothers used to cause, and they had two very firm parents to shut them down. Katrina was barely past her mid-twenties and these kids were smart. They didn't seem like they'd step back easily when confronted. Katrina probably fought a lot of battles and didn't win them all.

If any.

Teenagers could be a giant pain in the ass. But these two didn't look dangerous.

Grant heard a door open behind him, so he stood and saw Katrina making her way down the hall dressed in black capris, a black-and-white-striped T-shirt, and a pair of slip-on canvas shoes. Simple, yet on her, elegant. Her hair was pulled in a high ponytail, making him think about wrapping all that hair in his hand and giving it a hard tug. He wondered how she would react and figured he shouldn't be thinking thoughts like that with her young siblings in the same room.

"Sorry. It took me a little longer to get ready because *someone* keeps borrowing my clothes and makeup."

"Yeah, I can't help myself. Your turquoise eye shadow looks so good on me," Leo said, giving Katrina a crooked smile.

Anya snorted and shoved into her brother. "And don't forget how her pink miniskirt highlights the dark hairs on your legs."

Leo looked at Anya and gave her a short nod. "This is true."

Katrina, on the other hand, rolled her eyes. "Comedians. See what I have to deal with?"

Grant laughed. "I don't know, Leo. Somehow I don't think pink and turquoise are in your color wheel."

Katrina blinked. "I can't believe you said color wheel."

He turned to face her. "I have a little sister. She might or might not have painted my nails once or twice."

"Recently?" Anya asked, arching a brow.

"Yeah. Last week, as a matter of fact. To match my team uniform."

"Now who's the comedian?" Anya asked, looking at Katrina.

Leo laughed. "Anya did that to me when I was five."

"Hey," Anya said. "Katrina was out of town and the au pair wouldn't let me paint hers. Besides, they turned out pretty, didn't they?"

Leo sent Grant a look that communicated what brothers had to go through when they had sisters. Grant nodded, because he totally understood.

"You two, your bathroom looks like a hurricane swept through it. Go clean up. The cleaning lady is coming today and she shouldn't have to pick up underwear, socks, and wet towels from the floor."

Leo sighed. "Really? Now?"

"Yes, now."

"Come on, Leo. It'll only take a few minutes." Anya slipped her arm through her brother's and they disappeared down the hall.

After watching them, Katrina turned to him. "I'm sorry about them. They're a handful."

"They're awesome kids. Funny, too."

"They can be. They can also be terrors. Watch your back."

"Did I mention I have three brothers—and a sister? I think I can handle this."

"You say that now. You haven't spent a day with them."

He put his hands on her upper arms. "You need to relax. Maybe we should stop at a bar for alcohol first."

"For me or for them?"

"For them, of course. It's important to get them loaded early in the day. Makes them easier to control."

This time she laughed. "The thought is tempting."

"Actually, we could stop and get you a mimosa or something."

"Even more tempting. It's been an intense few weeks, and I wasn't prepared for you to actually show up."

"Why not? I told you I'd call when I got to New York."

"I know. I just didn't expect you to really do it."

He moved closer, the urge to touch her more tempting than he wanted to admit. "Why? Do men typically flake on you?"

She stepped back. "No. I told you, I don't . . . make dates."

"You mentioned that before. And you should make dates. Obviously you need to get out more."

"I get out plenty. I travel all the time. When I'm home I like to relax and spend time with the kids."

"The kids spend a lot of time at home," Anya said, reappearing. "And we're ready to get the hell out of here."

"Anya. Watch your language," Katrina said.

"Like we're babies. Please." Anya grabbed her purse and turned to face them. "So are we going?"

Grant looked to Katrina.

"Hey, you're in charge today. I'm just along for the ride."

"Great. I'm going to let Anya and Leo tell me what I should see today as a tourist."

"You've been to New York before, though, right?" Leo asked as they headed out the door.

"Yeah, but I'm in and out and I never spend much time here. It's always for games or meetings. I've hit some hot spots, but I've never played tourist or seen the things I think I should."

"Honestly? We haven't, either. Most native New Yorkers don't," Anya said as they rode down the elevator.

Grant stopped them on the sidewalk. "So you're saying you don't want to go? Because we don't have to."

"Are you kidding?" Anya asked. "We're dying to see this stuff. It's not like we've ever been to the Statue of Liberty or the Empire State Building. We've been to all the art museums because that's educational, of course, and Kat insisted on it. God forbid we be denied culture."

Katrina shot him a look. "It's like I'm the devil." She pinned her sister with a glare. "And for your information, we all went to the Statue of Liberty when we were kids. Mom took us. You and Leo were just too young to remember."

"So it's like I was never there, right?" Anya shot back before turning to Grant. "We're going there today, right?"

He laughed. "Sure. I've never been. We have to go."

Anya shot a smug look over at Leo. "And again, we win."

They piled into the car Grant had hired for the day. "Where to first?"

"Statue of Liberty, I guess," Katrina said. "If we can even get in. Those tours book up early in the day. We'll be lucky to even get one."

"Oh, I can get us a tour," Grant said pulling tickets from his shirt pocket. "I took a guess that maybe everyone would want to go there today."

Leo cracked a smile. "Score."

"Like always." Grant grinned.

Katrina shook her head.

"What?" he asked.

"Nothing."

He could tell she was irritated, but had no idea why. He aimed to change her mood.

Today was going to be a fun time for all of them.

EIGHT

KATRINA HAD GONE INTO THIS WHOLE DAY RELUC-
tantly, and mainly because Leo and Anya were excited about doing
the tourist thing. But after spending hours touring the Statue of
Liberty and Ellis Island, then moving on to the Empire State
Building, and seeing the sparkle of excitement on their faces, she
finally admitted defeat.

There was a magic quality about Grant Cassidy that she obviously did not possess, because while Leo and Anya were mesmerized by him, they pretty much wanted nothing to do with her. He
brought out the fun in her siblings, got them to laugh and relax,
and she was clearly unable to do that. With her, they were sullen
and bitchy and rebellious. With him, they said yes to everything
he suggested, no matter what it was.

She chalked it up to the "new" factor, and also because they
liked being contrary. If she disliked something, they were bound
and determined to love it.

Whatever.

"I've always wanted to get a hot dog from one of these corner vendors. What do you think?" Grant asked as they strolled near Central Park.

This was where her finicky brother and sister would draw the line. This was where they'd dig in their heels and say no, especially Anya, who prided herself on her culinary skill and wouldn't be caught dead eating food from one of those vendors.

"Sounds great," Anya said, and got in line behind Grant and Leo.

Katrina blinked. That was it. Her brother and sister had been kidnapped by aliens, and these two currently slathering mustard on their hot dogs were clones. Or robots. Or something.

"You do realize you're eating a hot dog," she said to Anya.

Anya took a bite, then spoke with her mouth full. "Yeah. So?"

"You don't even like hot dogs."

"Today I do."

Her sister gave her a mouth-filled grin.

"Whatever." Katrina wasn't going to even try to figure out these kids today. They were obviously in worship mode or something.

"Hot dog?" Grant asked.

She grimaced.

"Oh, come on, Kat, one won't kill you." Leo pushed into her.

"Fine. I'll have a hot dog. With mustard, please."

Grant took his loaded with relish and onions. She made another face. "Are you sure about that?"

"Hell yeah." He bit into it and groaned like he was having some kind of mouthwatering steak.

She didn't get the appeal since it was a basic horrible hot dog, but she took hers and ate it.

It was fine. Mediocre, but at least it was edible.

They sat on park benches and ate. Katrina tried not to think about what was in the hot dog. Anything but actual meat, she suspected. She washed it down with a bottle of water and listened to Grant talk to Leo about sports while pretending not to listen as she checked her e-mail.

"Tell me about lacrosse."

He shrugged. "It's okay. I don't really like it." He leaned forward to take a peek at her. Now she tried really hard to pretend she wasn't listening. She scrolled through her e-mails, but she wasn't focusing on them.

"Why don't you like it?"

"I mean it's competitive and all, but it's just not a sport I enjoy."

"What sports do you enjoy?"

"I like football, but like I told you earlier, I need to add some muscle."

Grant nodded. "Do you lift weights?"

"I've been spending some time in the weight room at school and at the condo. I could use a trainer, though, because I'm not sure if I'm doing it right."

"I could help you with that. And you could get a personal trainer to help you add muscle in the right areas. You're fifteen, right?"

"Yeah. I'll be sixteen in a few months."

"What position are you interested in?"

"Wide receiver."

"Okay, so you need some muscle in your legs for sure. Are you fast?"

"Very."

He laughed. "You know I'm going to want to test you on that. Do you have a running track at the condo?"

"We do."

"When we get back we'll test how fast you are."

Leo turned his back to her so he could face Grant. "You'd do that?"

"Sure. I could find out from the New York team who the good trainers are in the area, maybe make some recommendations. Providing it's okay with your sister."

"She might not like that idea. She doesn't want me playing football."

Katrina had no idea Leo was so passionate about playing football. He'd mentioned it when he was younger, but she'd pushed the idea aside, because he was so small at the time. And, okay, she'd been fearful about him getting hurt.

Now, though, she'd be fine with it since he was older and much more capable of taking care of himself on the field. She wished he'd brought it up again sooner.

She stood and walked over to him. "Leo, I'd be more than happy for you to play football if that's what you want to do."

He pushed his hair away from his face. "You would?"

"Sure. Why didn't you say something before?"

"You hated the idea before."

"You were seven. I was . . . worried."

He blew out a breath. "I'm not a baby, Kat. I wasn't when I was seven, either."

She folded her arms over her middle. "You were a lot smaller when you were seven."

"And I would have played with kids the same size as me. No difference then."

He had her there. She was terrible at this parenting thing. "I guess not. But if you're interested now, we'll see what we can do about it."

He looked at the ground. "It's probably too late, anyway."

"Hey," Grant said. "It's never too late if you want it badly enough.

A lot of really good pro football players don't start until high school. Don't give up before you've even given it a shot."

Leo lifted his gaze to Grant. "You think so?"

Grant gave him a grin. "Well, we'll see how fast you run. Then we'll decide where to go from there."

"Can we go now?"

"I think you should digest those two hot dogs you ate first, buddy. How about we take a walk around the park?"

"Okay."

LEO AND ANYA WALKED OFF AHEAD OF THEM, GIVING her a moment alone with Grant.

"Thanks for that."

"For what?" he asked.

"For what you did for Leo just now. He doesn't have a ton of confidence, and you gave him a boost."

"He's a good kid, and I'll bet he is as fast as he thinks he is. A large percentage of what an athlete needs is in his head. The other is doing what you love. He hates lacrosse, by the way."

"So I heard. I didn't know because he never told me. Or maybe he did and I just didn't hear him. When he wanted to play football as a kid, the whole idea of it terrified me because it was so damn physical. I thought he could get hurt."

Grant laughed. "Of course he can get hurt. Little boys get hurt doing all sorts of things. It's in our nature. You have to loosen up the reins a little and let him do what he wants. As long as that isn't standing on top of the roof of a car while it's speeding down the highway at a hundred miles an hour."

She arched a brow. "Tell me that's not something you did."

"I was dared to do it as a teenager. By one of my brothers who obviously was trying to get rid of me. I'm not that stupid, though."

"Good to know."

She still didn't know if it was a good idea for Leo to play, but Grant might be right that she had to let go a little.

They made it back to the condo, and she wasn't sure she'd ever seen Leo move that fast—at least not recently. He dashed into his room and was back out in record time, having changed into his workout clothes.

"Ready to go?" he asked Grant.

"Sure." Grant looked over at Katrina and Anya. "Are you two coming along?"

"Why would I be interested in watching Leo run?" Anya asked.

"Because he's your brother, and you want to give him a hard time in case he sucks."

"Oh." She laid her phone on the table. "Good point."

They piled into the elevator and Leo was the first out, Anya on his heels.

"I can't believe you encouraged Anya to give her brother a hard time," Katrina said. "Believe me, she needs no encouragement."

"Hey. Siblings can be great motivators. Trust me. He needs her here."

"I disagree. I think *you* being here is making him nervous enough."

Grant laughed. "He's going to do just fine, and you worry too much."

Grant marked off a hundred yards, and set a starting point for Leo while her brother finished his warm-ups.

"You ready?" Grant asked.

Leo nodded.

"Don't strain anything," Anya said, pulling up a spot on the ground at the makeshift finish line. "You might need your groin for something important someday."

"Bite me," Leo said.

Katrina shook her head, more anxious than she should be.

"Okay," Grant said, stopwatch in hand. "Let's see what you've got. You ready?"

Leo nodded.

"Okay, on the count of three. Three, two, one, go."

Leo shot off the mark. He looked so fast to her, but she knew nothing about this other than races she'd seen on television. When he finished, Grant clicked the stopwatch and looked at the time. Leo made the trek back.

"Not bad, kid."

Leo came around and looked at the stopwatch. "Really? That's my time?"

"It is. Faster than you thought you'd be, isn't it?"

"It is."

Leo grinned.

"You put some muscle on, it'll propel you even more. And you need a haircut. You look more like a beat boy than a football player." Grant ruffled his hair.

Leo actually blushed, then smiled. "Yeah, okay."

Katrina was stunned. "You've agreed to a haircut? I've been after you for months about this."

"But you're not the great Grant Cassidy," Anya said, pulling herself to her feet. "So you have no stock."

"Apparently not."

"Come on, Leo," Anya said. "Let's go fix some iced tea."

Leo seemed reluctant, until Anya grabbed his shirtsleeve and pulled him along.

"We'll meet you upstairs."

Katrina had no idea what kind of scheme Anya was cooking up, but before she knew it, her siblings had disappeared, leaving her and Grant alone in the gym.

She turned to face him. "Again, thanks for doing this for Leo.

I really had no idea he hated lacrosse, or that he still wanted to play football."

"Kids don't tell their parents—or in this case, you—what's on their minds half the time. They think you won't care. And if you shot him down on the football thing years ago, he likely figured you wouldn't give it a thumbs-up now, either."

She sat on one of the weight benches. "This is hard."

He took a seat next to her. "Of course it's hard. Plus, they don't make it any easier on you. They're teenagers, and they're sullen and moody and given an opening, they'll take advantage. Or they'll make everything seem like it's your fault."

She turned her head to look at him. "You sound like you know what you're talking about."

He laughed. "I have no idea. But I've been a teenager, and we all ganged up on our parents. I just know all the moves."

"You do, huh? Care to take on a couple of difficult ones? I'll gladly turn them over to you since you seem to be their hero today. You can give them back when they're adults."

"No, thanks. And they just like me because I don't have to tell them to do their homework or give them curfews or tell them no. Trust me, if I had to do that, they'd give me shit, too."

"Probably."

He laid his hand on her leg. "Cut yourself some slack, Katrina. They're really great kids. They're smart and funny and they ask excellent questions. But they're also very respectful. You've done a good job raising them."

Their teachers and other parents had always been complimentary of Leo and Anya, for which she was grateful. But it was nice to hear Grant give her positive feedback. So often she felt like she was flying blind.

"Thanks. I've done my best, and I freely admit I've had to leave them in the care of nannies and au pairs while I traveled. I tried to hire exceptional ones. And I've tried to be here for them as much as I could."

"You're only one person. You've worked your ass off to be both mother and father and breadwinner. You can't do it all, ya know."

"I had to. Who else was going to do it? Someone has to be here to make sure they're taken care of."

He brushed her hair away from her face. "Yeah? And who's been here to take care of you?"

The way he looked at her made all those responsibilities, that tight knot of tension she always felt in the pit of her stomach, fall away. And when he brushed his lips against hers, she leaned against him, letting herself draw some of his strength.

Only a minute. Just a few seconds of his touch, the way he squeezed her leg, the way his tongue slid so intimately against hers, and then she'd pull away so they could head back upstairs.

But then he'd pulled her onto his lap and the kiss grew more intense. She knew she should engage some common sense. They were in the gym where anyone could walk in at any moment, but for the life of her she couldn't summon any of that common sense right now, because his hands were on her hips, digging in, and she felt wanted. When was the last time that happened? When was the last time she allowed herself to fall into a kiss and feel a man's hands on her?

She couldn't remember. All she knew right now was that she was on Grant's lap, nestled against some very strong thighs, rocking against one very promising erection, and all she could think about was herself.

Just this once, she wanted something for herself.

She wanted Grant.

But then she heard the ping of the elevator door. She broke the kiss and slid off his lap in a hurry, taking several steps backward. Grant picked up the workout bag Leo had brought with him and placed it on his lap, giving her a crooked smile while she lifted a shaky hand to her mouth.

Her lips felt swollen from his kiss and as the guy who'd come in passed them and gave them a short nod, Grant nodded back.

"Ready to head upstairs?" Grant asked.

"Yes."

He stood and she walked in step with him to the elevator. They stepped inside and she pushed the button for her floor. Her cheeks were still red and she put her cool hands on them, hoping to douse the flames.

It didn't help when Grant moved into her, his hand sliding around her waist.

"We're not finished here," he said, his warm breath caressing her cheek.

It was stupid to even start. She had responsibilities. The kids. Her job. She had no business making out with Grant.

But oh, she wanted so much more.

NINE

GRANT HAD TO RIDE UP THE ELEVATOR WITH THE BAG in front of him to hide his erection. But it had been worth it to feel Katrina on his lap, to touch her and kiss her.

Too bad they'd been interrupted by the guy coming into the gym, but he knew he'd been taking a risk by kissing her there. They needed some privacy, which they weren't going to get at her condo. Leo and Anya were already waiting for them and hungry. He was going to take them out to a restaurant for dinner, but Katrina insisted on cooking.

"I eat out all the time when I'm traveling. I like to cook when I'm home," she said. "Besides, I already have food here."

He shrugged. "Up to you, but I didn't intend for you to cook." He was leaning against the island drinking a beer and watching her pull out pots and pans.

"Like I said, I enjoy cooking. Anya and I cook together all the time."

"Okay. What can I do to help?"

She gave him a suspicious frown. "A man in my kitchen? I don't think so."

"Now you're being sexist." He moved around the island and washed his hands, grabbed a towel and dried them. "My mother taught us all to cook so we could fend for ourselves."

"Good for her. You can cut up these vegetables, and then the meat."

"Now you're talkin'." He grabbed the chef's knife from the butcher block on the counter, and went through the vegetables, then sliced the meat and handed it to Katrina. She'd already set the rice in the cooker and had the wok warmed, so he picked up his beer and watched her work. She added seasonings to the meat and let that simmer, while Anya had taken the rice out and started making fried rice.

"My stomach is grumbling just watching you two—and smelling whatever it is you're seasoning the food with."

"It's my own recipe," Anya said, cracking two eggs to fry before adding those to the rice. "And Katrina has a special marinade for the meat."

Katrina looked up at him. "See? We work as a team here. Though, honestly, Anya does a lot of the cooking. It's kind of a treat when she lets me in the kitchen."

Anya smiled. He liked seeing the kid so happy. And maybe there wasn't as much animosity between the two sisters as Katrina thought.

Katrina seemed relaxed, easily moving around the kitchen, as if this was something she did all the time. Maybe he had preconceived notions about supermodels—like they had personal chefs to cook for them and butler service. He'd dated plenty of high-profile and high-maintenance women, the kind who liked to go out to fancy restaurants—the type that liked to be "seen." And here was this woman who was happy to stay at home and cook with her sister.

Katrina definitely surprised him.

"Leo, time to set the table," Katrina said as she poured out the vegetables onto a serving platter and set the meat into the wok.

"Anything else I can do?" Grant asked.

She motioned with her head. "There's a wine fridge over there. Pick something out and open it up?"

"Sure."

He selected a bottle and opened it, setting it on the dining room table to breathe. Then he helped Leo finish setting the table, bringing some of the food over as well.

"It smells good, doesn't it?" he asked Leo as Anya and Katrina brought the meat, vegetables, and rice to the table.

"Anya and Kat can definitely cook," Leo said, taking his seat. "We don't complain about that."

"Kat taught me a lot about cooking," Anya said. "She brought me in the kitchen with her when I was little and let me start helping her. And I learned more on my own."

"No," Katrina said. "You don't complain about the cooking thing. You just complain about everything else."

Anya shrugged. "It's in the teenager handbook. Chapter three is titled whining, moaning, and complaining. Didn't you read it?"

Katrina placed her napkin in her lap and graced her sister with a benevolent smile. "Read it, highlighted it, and made notes in the margins."

Grant smiled. "This conversation is making me miss my brothers and my sister."

"You have brothers?" Anya asked.

"Three of them. One is older and two are younger."

"How old is your sister?" Katrina asked as everyone began to scoop food onto their plates.

"Mia is twenty-one."

"And your brothers all play sports like you," Leo said.

Katrina shifted her gaze to Leo. "You know a lot."

He shrugged. "You just assume I only play video games in my room. I know sports and players. Like Grant. His family is famous. They're a dynasty. His dad is a Hall of Fame football player, too."

Katrina looked at Grant. "Is that right?"

Grant swallowed, then nodded. "Yeah. He played football for Green Bay for his entire career—fifteen seasons—until he retired."

"Wow," Anya said. "And your brothers play football, too?"

"Barrett and Flynn do. Tucker plays baseball."

Katrina leaned back in her chair. "Fascinating. Does your sister play sports?"

"She plays for the soccer team at her college. As far as I know she isn't planning on a professional sports career. She says the rest of us have that covered."

Katrina laughed. "It certainly sounds like you all do. Your poor mother. I can only imagine what that must have been like."

"What?"

"Wrangling all you boys to all those practices? I assume you all played when you were little?"

"Yeah. We all played baseball, soccer, and football."

She laid her fork down and stared at him. "While your father was off playing pro ball? How did she manage?"

"A lot of helping hands. We have a big extended family, so that helped. My dad has three brothers, so they and their wives would help out taking us to practices and games since Mom couldn't be everywhere at once, especially if Dad was on the road."

"Oh, that's nice. I'm sure they were a huge help to her."

"We didn't have a large family," Anya said. "So when our mom died, and Dad was gone, it was just Kat around to take care of us."

Grant looked over at Anya. "That must have been tough for all of you."

"We managed. We give Kat a hard time, but we could have ended up in foster care if it wasn't for her. She dug in and made them give her custody of us. It was hard for her."

Big statement for a teenager to make. Anya understood a lot. Grant wondered if Katrina realized she wasn't the only one who understood the responsibility she'd carried.

"It wasn't hard at all," Katrina said. "We're a family and it stays that way."

"That's been her line for the past ten years," Leo said with a wry grin.

He liked this family, the way they gave each other a hard time, yet he could still see how much she loved these kids—and how much they loved her back. It reminded him so much of his own, and made him realize it had been a while since he'd seen his family. He was going to have to make time for a visit.

They finished dinner and Leo immediately set about clearing the table, loading the dishwasher and washing the pots and pans without complaint.

"Good setup for you," he said as he sat back and finished his wine. "You and Anya cook and Leo cleans up."

"Anya actually does most of the cooking now. I don't have to do much at all."

"Free labor, is what she means," Anya said from the kitchen.

Grant laughed. "Yeah, we all had chores when we lived at home, too. Someone was on yard duty. Someone had dishes and trash duty. Somebody had to clean the bathrooms—which, by the way, was the worst."

"That's because you had all those boys," Anya said. "Thank God we have housekeeping service to deal with that. Ick."

"Yeah. Doing dishes is bad enough. And speaking of those,

we're done." Leo hung up the dish towel and came into the living room. "Bobby asked if I could come over tonight. Do you mind?"

"And Leah wanted me to spend the night," Anya said. "Is that okay?"

Katrina looked at both of them. "You guys. No. We have company."

"Really. It's okay with me," Grant said. "I had a great time with both of you today, but it's not necessary for you to hang out with me the rest of the night. Providing it's all right with Katrina."

She looked at Grant. "Are you sure?"

"Positive."

"Awesome," Anya said. "I'm going to go pack a bag then call Leah. She said her mom will come meet us."

"I'll go grab my stuff." Leo started to turn away, then stopped and pivoted to look at Grant. "Hey, thanks for today. It was fun. And for the football stuff."

"You're welcome."

"Yeah, what Leo said," Anya said. "Except for the football stuff, though it was interesting."

And in seconds, they had both disappeared into their rooms, only to reappear about five minutes later, both of them hustling out the door.

"That was fast," Grant said.

"It always is when they have things to do with their friends. Leo's best friend lives in the building, which is convenient, and Leah only lives two buildings away, so Leah and her mom will walk down to meet Anya."

"It's great they have friends so close."

"Yes. At least one thing I don't have to worry about."

He tucked a strand of her hair behind her ear. "You should worry a lot less. They're great kids. Awesome, really. You've done a fantastic job raising them, Katrina."

She stood, stretched. "Well, thanks."

He could tell she was uncertain, maybe a little uncomfortable now that they were alone.

"Kat. I like that name. It suits you."

Her lips curved. "They've called me that since they were little. It just kind of stuck."

"Does everyone call you that?"

"No. In professional circles I'm Katrina. Only people close to me call me Kat. Just the kids, really. I should check on them, make sure they got where they were supposed to."

"Sure. I'll open another bottle of wine while you do that."

He had no intention of drinking any. He had practice tomorrow. But she was wound up tight and needed to relax. He had no idea if he was the one making her tense, or if it was something else. He intended to get her to drink another glass and see if he could wind her down some, get her to talk to him.

He grabbed a glass of water for himself after pouring wine for her, returning to the living room just as she hung up the phone and laid it on the coffee table.

"Kids okay?"

"Yes."

He handed her the glass. She took it, then looked at him. "What are you drinking?"

"Water."

She sipped her wine. "So you're trying to get me drunk?"

"Nope. Trying to relax you. You seem tense."

She took a deep breath, then sat on the sofa. "You're probably right. I am tense."

He laid his water on the coaster on the table, then sat next to her. "Why?"

"I don't know. You, probably."

"Me?"

"Yes." She took another swallow of wine.

"I make you tense? Why do you think that is?"

"Because you make me think about things I don't have time to think about."

Now it was getting interesting. "What kinds of things?"

She shrugged. "Maybe we should talk about something else."

Before she'd been direct, even doing her best to get rid of him with blatant honesty when they were in Barbados. So why was she avoiding him now? "Oh, no. You don't get to throw that out there, then deflect." He took her glass and laid it on the table, then grasped her chin in his hand, forcing her to look at him. "What are you thinking about when you're with me?"

She drew in a breath. "Kissing. You touching me. I liked your hands on me when we were in the gym earlier."

There it was, and oh, man did he like hearing her say it. "I can do something about that, you know."

She shook her head and stood, wrapping her arms around herself. "Not here. Leo's just a few floors down. He could pop back in anytime."

He went over to her and wrapped his arms around her, inhaling the sweetness of her scent. "So why don't you find out if Leo can spend the night with his friend?"

She pivoted to face him. "They could still come back. I wouldn't be comfortable or relaxed enough to . . . enjoy being with you."

He got the idea there was more to it than that, but he'd have to respect her decision. "Okay. How about another night?"

"Don't you have to leave town after your game?"

"Eventually. Make arrangements for the kids and come stay with me at the hotel the night after the game."

"I couldn't. The kids would know I was with you."

He rubbed her arms. "And that's a bad thing?"

"I . . . I don't know."

"You're an adult, Katrina. You're entitled to have a relationship. Leo and Anya seem like smart kids. I don't think they'd mind if you spent some time with me."

She walked away and went over to the door leading out to the terrace. "I know that. It's just me, really. I'm a lot more concerned about things like this than I should be."

She turned to him. "Maybe it's better that we're just friends."

He had no idea what was going on with her, but he wasn't going to walk out and let it end like this.

He stalked over to her and drew her into his arms. "I don't fucking think so. And I don't think you want that, either."

He held her just a breath away, his gaze meeting hers, a storm of emotions in her eyes. He felt the draw, and this tension wasn't the kind that made her want to pull away.

He put his mouth on hers, felt her surrender even before his tongue slid between her lips. He wrapped an arm around her waist as he explored the softness of her mouth, tasting her, claiming her, letting her know that friendship wasn't at all what he wanted from her. And when she sagged against him, when one of her hands wound around his neck, her fingers sliding into his hair, the other hand clutching his shirt, he tasted victory.

Her moan was as sweet as her taste, and he let his hands slide down over her back, relaxing a little now that he knew she wasn't going to bolt. He wanted to touch her everywhere, to take his time kissing her neck, that sweet spot on her collarbone, and her back. He wanted to get her naked and explore her skin with his hands, his mouth, and his tongue. He'd seen so much of her body in Barbados, but they hadn't been alone and it had been for work—his hands on her then had been professional.

Now he wanted to get really goddamned personal with her body, but he understood she wasn't relaxed enough for that. He needed to get her alone, behind a locked door where neither one of her siblings was likely to burst in at any second. He needed her calm, tranquil, and stress-free, not thinking about anything but what the two of them were doing together.

But right now he enjoyed having her mouth under his, tasting and teasing her lips and having her body snake against him in a way that felt urgent and needy and made him hard. Which he had to agree was probably not a good idea since they didn't have a guarantee to be alone.

So he was the one to lighten the kiss, to slide his hands from her back to her arms, even though what he wanted to do was grab a nice handful of her sweet ass. He was the one to eventually break away, take a deep breath and rest his forehead against hers, fighting for control when all he wanted to do was gather her in his arms and take what she seemed so willing to give.

She tilted her head back and her eyes were a storm of emotion. Confusion, desire, and regret, all packaged up in a blue purple haze. It took every ounce of strength he had not to kiss her again.

"Grant," she finally said, her voice a strangled whisper.

"Yeah, I know. I need to go, because otherwise I'm going to take you to your bedroom and I'm not going to give a damn who comes through the door."

She swallowed. "Yes. You need to go."

He blew out a breath. "Mind if I finish my water first? I have an issue here that needs dealing with before I go out in public."

Her gaze drifted to his erection and lingered there before moving back up to meet his eyes. Yeah, that did nothing to help.

"Oh. Sure."

He needed to get away from her, away from the looks she was giving him. Otherwise he was never going to leave.

He downed the contents of the glass in three gulps, mentally thinking of football plays and strategies for the game as he did. Getting his mind off Katrina and onto the game helped. By the time he turned back to her, she had moved into the kitchen, putting some space between them.

"I'll get tickets to you for Sunday's game."

She nodded. "Great. The kids will like that."

"I'll talk to you."

He walked out the door, feeling like he'd left unfinished business in there.

He had.

Katrina.

TEN

KATRINA HAD NEVER BEEN TO A PROFESSIONAL FOOT-
ball game before. She'd watched games on TV with Leo and Anya,
and she liked football, but she didn't know as much about the game
as they did.

When the tickets had been messengered over, Leo had been so
excited he'd had to text all his friends about going to the game, and
that Grant Cassidy himself had gotten them tickets.

He'd even gotten a haircut, which had shocked her.

She was amused by his fanboy attitude. Leo was always so laid
back, like he didn't care about anything. Who knew he was such a
football fanatic? She wished she'd known earlier so she could have
gotten him into football.

Though she wasn't sure she would have agreed to it without
Grant's influence and suggestion. She still thought it was a rough
sport.

And now she could see all the players up close—though they

were in a club box, so it wasn't like they were on the field or anything. But still, it wasn't like watching it on television. She was seeing it live, and those guys were so big, so muscular, and as she shifted
her attention to her little brother, she couldn't fathom how he could
compete with men like that. To her, he would always be that vulnerable five-year-old, confused about where Momma had gone, and
looking to her for love and guidance because she was all he had left.

Maybe she'd been a little overprotective of him and Anya, but
they were all she had, too, and she wasn't about to let anything
happen to them.

"Aren't these seats great?" Anya asked, plopping down in one
of the cushioned seats in the skybox. "I can't believe we get to sit
here and watch the game. Free food, too."

Her sister had a plate filled with all kinds of interesting foods.
Leo pulled up a seat next to his sister, food in one hand, a can of
soda in the other.

"Glad you two are settled. I guess I'll find myself something
to eat."

"Oh, and a woman I met up there said this was one of the boxes
where team family members sat, so you should introduce yourself
as Grant's wife." Anya snickered at her.

Katrina rolled her eyes. "You're so funny."

She went over to the food table. Anya was right. There was an
amazing array of delicacies to be had. She couldn't decide, so she
stood there, surveying everything.

"It's hard to reconcile what your stomach wants with what your
common sense and waistline tells you not to eat."

Katrina turned to find a gorgeous blonde standing next to her.
"I might just say the hell with common sense and my waistline."

The woman held out her hand. "I'm Savannah Riley. And you're
Katrina Korsova."

"I am. Nice to meet you."

"I've seen your pictures like . . . everywhere, and I've caught a few of your runway shows. I'm a big fan."

"Thank you." Typically women didn't like her. This was a surprise.

"I didn't know you were dating one of the Traders."

"I'm not. I only recently met Grant Cassidy. We did a photo shoot together. He offered my brother and sister and me tickets to the game today."

"Oh, Grant. I like him. Where are your brother and sister?"

"Stuffing their faces over there on the back row of seats." She pointed them out.

Savannah looked over where Katrina had gestured. "I see them. Teenagers, huh? Such a fun age."

"Yeah, unless you're in charge of raising them."

Savannah arched a brow. "You're their guardian?"

"I am."

"Oh, Katrina. We need some wine. And some of this great food, too. You have to tell me your story."

At Katrina's hesitation, Savannah laid a hand on her arm. "Trust me, I'm not press. I'm an image consultant, and I'm married to Cole Riley, wide receiver for the Traders."

"Image consultant? That must be a fascinating job."

"It's a great job. I love it. Now let's go get some wine."

They found the bartender, who poured them glasses of wine. They settled on a spot where she could keep an eye on the kids, who were busy watching all the pregame activities and chatting with the people around them, clearly not at all interested in where she was. No surprise there. But she had them in her sights from where she and Savannah took seats.

"Okay, now that we're settled, I want to hear all about you," Savannah said. "You are so famous. All the traveling you do to fun locations? What's that like?"

She always had guys hitting on her. Women tended to avoid her, and she never understood why. She found Savannah charming, beautiful, and friendly. She instantly liked her.

"The travel is great. I can't complain about it."

"But we do complain, don't we? I get to travel a lot for my job, and it's awesome. I love the work I do. But I find myself missing home."

Right away, Savannah understood. "Yes. I almost feel ashamed for resenting this amazing career I've been given." She looked around to make sure no one was within hearing distance. "I mean, I'm twenty-seven years old and I've made more money than I'll ever need in a lifetime."

Savannah took a sip of her wine. "But? You're tired of the travel? Burned-out? Lonely?"

Katrina blew out a breath. "It's like you took the words right out of my mouth, the ones I never say out loud."

"Oh, sugar, I think most career women feel that twinge of guilt. We have major successes, and maybe some women never have regrets. Me? I love my job. I'm living my dream. But when I've been traveling for two weeks straight there are times I'd give it all up just to be able to spend a month at home."

"Right. Until you spent a month at home."

Savannah laughed. "Isn't that the truth? Then I'd go crazy and I'd be dying to get back on a plane. Do you think men go through this?"

"I have no idea. Probably not, because they're not emotional like women are."

"You might be right about that. My husband Cole travels all the time during the football season. I never heard him say he's tired of it. He just says it's part of his job and he's used to it. On the other hand, after a week on the road I start missing my husband, my bed, and my favorite pillow. And our dog that we just adopted recently."

"Awww. That's like having a baby around."

"I know. Right now I'm missing Luther so much." She pulled out her phone and showed Katrina a photo of an adorable mixed breed.

"He looks like maybe some golden retriever?"

Savannah nodded. "Yes. Mixed with Labrador and the vet said likely something else. He's a year old and Cole and I are madly in love with him. Right now he's staying with my in-laws. I was here in New York on business, so I decided to stay over the weekend to see Cole's game. We're both headed home after the game and I can't wait to see our baby."

Katrina laughed and handed the phone back to Savannah. "That's awesome. With that little guy, travel's going to be even tougher for you."

"I know. I'm branching out my business and hiring two consultants, so my travel should start easing up a little. I'd like to stay put a little more in the future. We bought a house, just got married in May, and now with the dog, I need more stability and less flying around the country. If my husband and I never see each other, it's going to make marriage a lot tougher. He travels enough during the football season. We can't have both of us on the road all the time."

Katrina leaned back in her chair and took a couple sips of wine. "Do you think you'll miss it?"

"The extensive time in airports? No. And I'll be busy enough training new staff. They can handle the heavy travel workload, which will free me up to expand my business."

"Sounds fun."

"I hope it will be." Savannah shifted her gaze to the field. "Still doing pregame stuff, so we have time for you to tell me all about yourself. You've been modeling for a while now, haven't you?"

Katrina nodded. "Ten years."

"And successfully, too. Congratulations."

"Thank you."

"Is it all exotic locations?"

Katrina laughed. "No, not always. Sometimes it's urban, and a lot of times it's studio."

"But always an adventure, I'm sure."

"It is."

"And you've shot with some extremely sexy men."

The funny thing is, she'd never paid attention to them before. To her, they were props.

Until Grant. He'd been the only one she'd had a reaction to.

"Yes. The men are certainly fun."

"Any romances? Or am I being too intrusive?" Savannah asked.

"No romances. We're usually too concerned with lighting and position. It's always very professional."

Savannah studied her. "Yet here you are—with Grant. So maybe something there?"

Oh, Savannah was good at this. "We're just friends."

Savannah gave her a knowing look. "Of course you are. Now we're going to pause and go get some of that glorious food, and then I have more questions for you."

Since she was enjoying herself immensely, Katrina was game for anything, so she followed along, filling a plate with more food than she should. But since she didn't have another shoot for at least a week, she felt like indulging. They made their way back to their seats and their waitress refilled their wineglasses.

After devouring the food, Savannah wiped her lips with the napkin and took several sips of wine. "Now tell me about how you met Grant."

"We did a photo shoot together in Barbados for a swimsuit edition of a sports magazine."

"That sounds like fun. Was it fun?"

Katrina shrugged. "For me the shoot was work. Grant seemed to be having fun."

"I'm sure he did. He got to shoot with you."

"Thank you for that. He did seem to enjoy himself."

Savannah studied her. "And? Any sparks? On your side, I mean. Grant would have to be dead not to be attracted to you. For goodness' sakes, I'm attracted to you and I'm totally heterosexual."

Katrina laughed. "Thank you again. And yes, there were definite sparks. I don't tend to get involved with men, though."

Savannah arched a brow. "Oh. So you're into women?"

"No. Not at all what I meant. It's just that with my work and my siblings, my life is kind of full."

"Oh, honey, life should never be so full that you don't have time for some fun. I imagine Grant would be all kinds of fun. I mean, just look at him." Savannah's gaze strayed out over the field where Grant took warm-up snaps.

Katrina studied him. She had to admit, in his uniform he was something to behold. Tall, muscular, and he looked so commanding as he threw the ball.

"You're right. I'm sure he would be fun." She remembered the other night, the way he'd held her and kissed her. She'd definitely like to have some fun with him, but at the same time, she had responsibilities, and fun wasn't on that list of things she felt were important.

"Then go for it."

"I have the kids to think about."

Savannah swirled her wine around in the glass. "So . . . you feel you're not entitled, or that your needs should come last?"

Funny how someone she barely knew had nailed it so well. "Maybe."

"Sugar, give up on that notion right now. You work hard, and from what I can tell from here, those kids look well taken care of. Why don't you take some time for yourself and live a little?"

She might just have to do that. As long as she didn't take it seriously or get involved. "It sounds to me like you've had to learn to put yourself first."

Savannah nodded. "Admittedly, it wasn't always that way. But I've learned over the years that my needs are important. And my husband has helped me recognize that."

"He sounds like a pretty wonderful man."

"That he is. Though he wasn't always as perfect as I make him out to be. We met when I was hired to make over his image."

Katrina's lips ticked up. "Is that right?"

"Yes. He was kind of a bad boy."

"And you . . . reformed him?"

"Oh, no. I would never want to do that. I like him a little bad. But his public persona? It's as white as snow now."

"Of course. Just the way you want him, right? Good in public, bad in private?"

Savannah gave her a devilish smile. "Definitely."

They eventually made their way to the seats in front of Leo and Anya.

"About time you sat down. I thought you were gonna miss the game," Anya said.

She looked over her shoulder at her sister. "Wouldn't dream of missing it. Football is my life."

Anya rolled her eyes. "You're such a cynic."

Savannah laughed.

The Traders kicked off to New York. Katrina knew she should support her home team, but for some reason she found herself hoping the Traders would get the ball. So when New York punted after their first drive, her pulse raced with excitement. And when

Grant came out and took command of his team, she found herself leaning forward to watch him.

Football had always been something that she'd barely paid attention to. Leo and Anya watched it, and she watched it because they did. But it wasn't something she took an active interest in. She knew the game—sort of—at least the basics of it. She wouldn't claim to be an expert on it.

But now that she was at a game, she could see the appeal. This was much different. The crowd noise was something close to deafening, and the people in the club box were so into the game, laughing and cheering and standing up when there was a good play. It was fun to be part of this. Even for someone like herself who didn't know much about football, the enthusiasm of the people around her was infectious.

She tensed as Grant took the ball and backed away, looking for his receivers. She saw the field as a whole, where she was certain he had a specific play in mind. And in a split second, one of his receivers had made a catch and had the ball in his hands.

"First down," Savannah said with a wide smile. "That was my husband, Cole, who caught the ball."

"Oh, great. Good for him." Katrina made a mental note of Cole's uniform number so she could keep an eye on him.

"Cole's a wide receiver," Leo said. "Want me to tell you what they do?"

"I understand the positions," she shot back, then looked over at Savannah. "They think I know nothing about football."

"She really doesn't," Anya said. "She reads a book while we watch the games."

Katrina rolled her eyes. "I see more than you think. And I'm able to multitask."

"Sure you are," Anya said.

Savannah laughed. "I'll bet you do. Sometimes I'll catch up on work stuff while I'm watching the games. But don't tell Cole I said that. He thinks I'm riveted to the television the entire game."

"See? Someone who understands me. I can hear the game and still read my book. And then if something exciting happens, I look up."

"But you miss all the subtle nuances of game play if you aren't watching the entire time," Anya said.

"Such as?"

"Even a play where nothing happens still has importance," Leo argued. "I'm sure that's what Anya is talking about. Say they play first and second down and gain no yardage, or very little. Where are they on the field? Are they on their own twenty-yard line, or are they charging toward their opponent's goal? If they're closer to their opponent's goal, then third down becomes a critical play. What play are they going to call? Is it going to be a run or pass? If you're only paying attention to the cheers of the crowds, you're missing out on a lot, Kat."

Her brother knew a lot about football. Clearly a lot more than she did. She understood the plays and how the ball moved down the field, but it was obvious she was going to have to start paying closer attention.

"Okay, you've got me there."

She watched the series of plays made by the Traders with a lot more interest. On one play, New York backed them up several yards on what Anya called a busted run. But on the next play, Grant threw a pass for a thirty-yard gain and everyone cheered. They ran the next two plays for another first down. She leaned forward, watching each play with keen interest. Before she knew it, the Traders were very close to the New York goal line and everyone was standing.

It was third down, and the Traders were on the seven-yard line. Now she understood what Leo meant by critical plays. Her heart was racing as Grant took the snap. He took several steps back, defenders from New York were coming at him and she simply couldn't breathe.

It felt like minutes, when she knew it was only a few seconds until he launched the ball in the air.

One of the receivers caught it. It wasn't Cole because she'd memorized his number. But whoever caught it was in the end zone and it was a touchdown.

Everyone in the club room stood and screamed. She screamed. It was madness and the most exciting thing ever. They were all high-fiving and she'd never had so much fun watching a football game. What an adrenaline rush.

Now she was really into the game, and she probably asked Savannah and everyone around her a million questions. She learned more about football during that game than she ever had before, and by halftime she felt like she had a pretty good handle on the different plays. The Traders were up by seventeen points. The hometown crowd wasn't happy at all about that, but the club room was.

They got up to stretch, and Savannah introduced Katrina, Leo, and Anya to several of the people in the room, some of them wives and relatives of the other players. Leo and Anya decided to go out and wander around. She told them to stick together.

"Should we hold hands, too?" Anya asked.

Katrina rolled her eyes. "Just don't wander too far."

"We're going to ogle the souvenirs. That's it," Anya said. "We'll be back in a bit."

As they walked off, she turned to Savannah. "I probably smother them."

Savannah shrugged. "I'm horrified at the thought of someday having teenagers. Or children. I wouldn't have the slightest idea what to do. I think you handle them well. You don't seem like you're smothering them at all."

"Thanks. We've all grown up together, so I'm doing the best I can."

"It's all you can do, really. They seem like awesome kids. And hey, they both know football, so a point in their favor."

Katrina smiled. "They know a lot more than I do. They're constantly educating me. I wouldn't know much about pop culture, the latest hot music, or social media if it wasn't for them. Sometimes it helps having teenagers in the house. I feel so old sometimes, even though I'm only twenty-seven."

Savannah laughed at that. "I did an image makeover for a very young entrepreneur last year. He was a software developer and I spent quite a bit of time with him. I learned a lot of things I wasn't aware I didn't know about. I might know clothes and image and presenting yourself to the public as a professional, but Twitter and Instagram and Tumblr and the different types of music streaming and . . . God, I don't even remember the rest of it. Everything that's now and cool and other things I don't have the time or the energy to delve into. He was on top of it all and deeply immersed in it. Talk about feeling old. How can we be so young and be so out of the mainstream?"

"Because we spend all our time working and not enough time playing?"

"I guess. So, see, you're learning a lot just having teens."

"I suppose I am."

"Besides, they can program a new phone for you. Plus, they know way more about how to find things on the Internet than we do. That's invaluable."

Katrina laughed. "You're so right about that."

The kids came back and everyone settled in for the second half. New York came back and scored twice, but so did the Traders, with a field goal and a touchdown.

Grant didn't play the second half, nor did the other starters like

Cole. She wondered if he was hurt or if there was some kind of problem, but everyone told her since this was a preseason game, the starters typically only played the first and second quarter.

"It's just a preseason game, remember," Leo said. "I mean the coaches are watching, sure, but a lot of the second- and third-string players come in later in the game, so it's not like any of this means anything in terms of standings or anything. They're really evaluating players at this point."

"They also look at what plays work and what doesn't," Savannah said. "It's a chance to try out some plays that they'll use during the regular season."

Katrina was learning so much about football. It was like she was getting years' worth of information in one game.

Katrina found herself missing Grant. He really did have an imposing presence, a command of his team, and a knowledge of where his players were. The game didn't seem as exciting without him in it. But with the help of Leo and Anya as well as Savannah, she learned even more in the second half of the game about offensive as well as defensive plays. Once the Traders were up by fourteen points, the defense came into play as the Traders tried to hold the lead deep into the fourth quarter, when New York pushed down the field.

Katrina found herself alternately watching the clock and the play on the field, hoping the clock would move faster. When the clock wound down to the two-minute warning and New York was on the five-yard line, she felt the hard thump of her heart.

"This is agony," she said to Savannah. "What if they score? They'll be within a touchdown."

"New York will probably try an onside kick so they have a chance to get the ball back," Leo said.

New York had pulled all of their starters after the first half. And now there was a critical play coming up, and their backups were doing the heavy lifting.

Still, it was so interesting to watch, even if she didn't know the players.

But then, wonders of wonders, New York's running back fumbled the ball and the Traders recovered. There was more elated cheering in the club box, because the game was basically over.

The Traders offense took control of the ball, and the backup quarterback whose name she didn't remember threw to the tight end for a first down on the initial play.

"Woo!" Anya stood and pumped her fist in the air.

After that they let the clock wind down. The game was over, and the Traders had won. Katrina didn't feel at all like a traitor for being happy about it.

The kids didn't seem to mind, either. They both sported wide grins.

"Did you enjoy the game?" she asked.

"Are you kidding? It rocked," Leo said. "Can we do it again sometime?"

Savannah came over to them and smiled. "I'm sure you can. Going to the games is so much fun, isn't it?"

"Totally," Anya said. "This was so much better than watching them on television."

Katrina grabbed her purse. "Well, we should probably go."

"Aren't you meeting up with Grant?" Savannah asked.

"We didn't have plans to."

"Come on. I'll take you down to the locker room with me. I know he'd want to see you and the kids."

She wasn't certain that's what he'd want. He'd just sent tickets over for the club room, which had been a lot more than she'd expected. He likely expected she and the kids would go home, not that they'd show up outside his locker room.

"Uh, that's probably not a good idea."

Savannah stopped and stared at her. "Honey, he wants you there. Trust me."

"I want to see all the reporters and all the guys. So I'm going," Anya said.

"Me, too," Leo added.

Katrina sighed. "I guess we're all going."

She only hoped Grant wouldn't be pissed to see them there.

They could go and say hello and congratulations, and then they'd leave. She supposed it would be the polite thing to do.

ELEVEN

THEY'D WON. DAMN GOOD GAME, TOO. THE TEAM WAS shaping up. Grant felt good about his game play. He had some tweaks to make here and there, but overall, pretty decent. His offensive line was solid. The off-season trades the Traders had made had firmed up the holes in the line, and he was grateful for that. The rookies were looking good, too. He was confident this was going to be a great team this year.

Coach was positive about all the changes, too, and had told them after the game they had beat a tough team and that their individual coaching staff would meet with them next week to go over their game play. After that they'd had media interviews, Grant had hit the shower, then got dressed.

He checked his phone as he finished packing up. Several texts—one from his dad, of course. Praising him for the game, then telling him everything he'd done wrong.

He smirked. Typical.

Another text from his mother telling him she loved him and he'd played well. That made him smile.

Texts from his brothers, too.

Flynn texted: *You sucked. Surprised you won that game. Good thing the second string came in and won it for you.*

And from Barrett: *Damn good thing you have a solid defense. Otherwise you'd have had your ass handed to you.*

From Tucker: *Too busy playing baseball to watch your game. Did you win?*

He laughed at that because he knew Tucker would never miss one of his games.

He missed his brothers. Though he'd never let any of them know it. They'd never let him live it down.

Finally a text from his sister, Mia: *You rocked it. Can't wait for the regular season to start.*

Leave it to Mia to be the only one of his siblings to be encouraging. She knew the guys always gave each other shit, so she was the peacemaker.

"Reading your fan mail?"

He grinned up at Cole Riley. "Family criticisms."

"Aren't they the best?"

"Yeah. I imagine you get a lot of that as well from your family."

"Constantly. But I give the same to them so it evens out."

"Yup. Same here." In fact, Tucker had a home series in St. Louis next week. He was going to have to catch one of the games, that way he could be a lot more critical. In person.

He grabbed his bag and headed out the locker room door, surprised and happy to see Katrina, Leo, and Anya standing beside Savannah Riley. He'd meant to text her about meeting after the game, but his head had been filled with game prep so he'd forgotten. He figured he'd stop by their place after the game and see about taking them out to eat.

Cole swept Savannah up in a kiss.

"You played great," she said.

"I'm glad you were in town so you could be here for the game."

"Me, too. Cole, this is Katrina Korsova and her brother and sister, Leo and Anya. They live in New York and are friends of Grant's."

He shook her hand. "I know who you are. I've seen a lot of your photos." Then he shook Leo's and Anya's hands. "Sorry we beat your team."

Leo shrugged. "It's okay. It was a good game."

Cole slanted a look in Grant's direction, but Grant wasn't about to say anything to Cole. He figured he'd get a lot of questions about Katrina at the next practice, though.

"I hate to rush off, but I have a plane to catch," Savannah said.

Cole turned to them. "Hate to greet and run, but I'm going to head out with my wife."

"Very nice to meet you, Cole," Katrina said. "And you too, Savannah."

Savannah hugged Katrina. "I'm calling you the next time I'm in New York. Or if you're ever in St. Louis, we'll have lunch or dinner."

"Actually she's—" Anya said, but Katrina cut her off right away.

"I'll definitely call you. I'd love to get together."

"Great."

Grant wondered what that was all about. He'd have to ask her later.

"So, how about something to eat?" he asked after Cole and Savannah left. "I'm starving."

"We've eaten tons in here," Anya said. "Besides, I'm spending the night at Leah's, so if you can drop me off at her place, that would be great."

"I'm staying over at Bobby's."

Katrina looked at both of them. "How did I not know about these plans?"

"You do now." Anya gave her a sweet smile. "I promised Leah a rundown of the game. And we're going shopping tomorrow."

"There's an all-night video-game tournament going on. There are five of us playing, and I'm already late," Leo said.

Katrina looked at Grant. "Sorry. But if you're hungry, I'll be happy to go with you."

"Sure."

He had a car waiting for them, and they dropped Leo off first since their apartment was closer.

"Thanks, Grant. I hope I get to see you again."

"You will."

Anya was next.

"Don't you need overnight stuff?" Katrina asked.

"Already took care of that this afternoon when you were out running errands."

Katrina shook her head. "The things you do that I don't know about."

"Sorry, warden. Next time I'll file an agenda in advance. Thanks for the game tickets, Grant. Hope to see you soon."

"You're welcome. See ya."

"Oh, and my sister will be in St. Louis next week for a photo shoot. You two should get together." With a grin shot Katrina's way, she was out the door in a flash.

That's what Katrina had cut Anya off about. She was trying to avoid Anya telling Savannah she was going to be in St. Louis. Or, she was avoiding having Grant find out she was going to be in town.

That was more likely.

He leaned back in the car. "So . . . you're going to be in my home city, huh?"

Katrina looked a little flustered about that. "Well, yes. I just got a call this morning about it."

He wondered why she'd had no intention of telling him about it, either. He had no idea why she was so reluctant to be with him. He knew it wasn't because they didn't get along, and he knew damn well it wasn't because they didn't have any chemistry together. He was going to have to push the issue. "You have to let me show you around."

"I . . . well, I do have to work."

"Sure you do. So do I. But not twenty-four hours a day. You'll have some downtime, right?"

"I suppose."

"Then we should hang out. I promise it'll be fun. Besides, your sister kind of ordered us to, didn't she?"

She quirked a brow. "You really think I do whatever my little sister says I should?"

"No. But I'd like to spend time with you."

She didn't answer, because the car arrived at a restaurant Katrina had suggested to the driver.

"This place is open late, plus the food is really good," she said as they climbed out of the car.

He laid his hand at the small of her back. "I trust your judgment."

It was a French restaurant. Really nice, with a lot of mirrors, dark corners, and sexy ambiance. His kind of place.

The hostess smiled and said Katrina's name. Obviously she was well-known here, because a waiter came over and also greeted her by name, then led them to a table against the wall. Since it was late, they weren't crowded and had some privacy.

The menu was good, too. He zeroed in on something he wanted. Hell, he was hungry. Everything looked good.

The waiter handed them a wine list.

"Would you like some wine?" she asked.

He shook his head. "Not really, but you can have some if you want."

She handed the wine list back to the waiter, whose name was Claudio. "Just sparkling water with lime for me, Claudio."

Grant ordered regular water, and they placed their dinner order. Claudio left to get their drinks.

"Do you come here a lot?" he asked.

"On occasion."

"You know it's open late, so you must eat here after your late-night dates."

She laughed. "No dates. It's more like late-night photo shoots. It's a good place to come when everything else is closed and the entire shoot team is hungry."

"Uh-huh."

Her gaze met his, and in the muted light, her eyes sparkled like sapphires. It was amazing how the color of her eyes changed depending on the lighting.

"I told you, I don't date. I'm too busy. But I do have a tendency to want to eat, especially after a grueling day of shooting. Just like you, tonight. You worked hard. You're hungry."

"And you're barely eating. You only ordered a salad."

"I ate plenty in the club box tonight. Thank you again for the amazing seats. Leo and Anya really enjoyed themselves."

"You're welcome. Did you have a good time?"

"I did. I spent a lot of time with Savannah Riley. She's charming."

"Yeah, she is. She keeps Cole on his toes."

"I could see that. She seems very organized."

Claudio brought their drinks.

"Thank you, Claudio."

"You're very welcome, Miss Katrina. Your food should be up shortly."

Their waiter politely disappeared again.

They were sitting on the same side of a booth, looking out toward the restaurant. He turned to her. "I don't want to talk about Cole and Savannah. Tell me how you liked the game."

She half turned to face him. "It was fascinating, actually. Having never been to a football game, I realized there was so much to learn. And of course, Leo and Anya felt it their duty to educate me."

He picked up a lock of her hair, rubbing it between his fingers. "Of course."

She was squirming, but she didn't pull away. A good sign.

"So you learned a lot about football today?"

"Yes. A lot more than I knew before. It was quite an education."

"And you like learning new things, I take it."

Her gaze was glued to his. "Yes, I do."

"Any questions you want to ask me?" He paused for effect. "About football, that is. I'm a good teacher."

He'd lowered his voice.

She hesitated, swallowed. He watched her throat work, then moved his attention to her mouth. He really wanted to kiss her right now, but the restaurant wasn't that empty, and he didn't want to break the spell. He liked the silky feel of her hair between his fingers, even though he wanted to cup the back of her head and draw her closer.

"You don't play the entire game."

"Not yet. I will soon. The coaches like to put in the rookies and the free agents who haven't played for the team yet, see how they fit."

His fingers brushed the top of her breast. She drew in a deep breath. Was that so his knuckles would linger on her skin? Either way, he sure as hell enjoyed the sensation. Katrina didn't seem to mind it, either, because she leaned in a little.

"Do you evaluate them, too? When you're on the sidelines?"

He felt her heart pumping faster against his hand as he continued to play with her hair. But outwardly she maintained such calm.

"Yeah. Especially any of the new offensive linemen and the receivers that weren't in when I was playing. I want to see how fast the receivers run their routes, how accurate they are, and whether they're where they're supposed to be. With the linemen, how tough are they? Can they beat the defensive linemen off the mark, or are they getting pushed off the line? If they can't protect me when I'm in the pocket, then I'm going to end up on my ass and they're of no use to me."

There was fire in her eyes, a desire he read and knew well. His dick was getting hard, and so far all he had in his hands was a lock of her hair. What would it be like if he held her body against his, if they were naked? If he could run his hands down her back, cup her breasts, feel her breathing against him?

"Katrina."

She pulled back when Claudio arrived with the meal.

"I brought baguettes as well. Hot and fresh from the oven," Claudio said.

Their waiter looked at them both and wished them bon appétit, exclaiming that their dinner should be excellent.

The spell was broken, and Katrina spent a minute or so talking over their meal with Claudio. Then, hunger took over and Grant dove into his food, which, true to Claudio's word, was damn good.

"Do you like it?" she asked, motioning to his steak.

"It's perfect. How's your salad?"

"Amazing."

"Would you like a bite?" He sliced off a piece of steak and held it up for her.

"I would, actually."

He fed it to her, and liked that she didn't mind eating off his fork. He slid it between her lips and she chewed, her eyes closing.

"Mmm, so tender. You're right. It is very good."

When she licked her lips after, his cock tightened.

And that was just food she liked. There was something about her mouth that mesmerized him. Of course he had kissed her before, and remembering that made him want more. But there was an innocence about her, a hesitance in their interactions that intrigued him. She was twenty-seven. Surely she'd been with guys before, even if she did say she didn't date. She just meant she didn't date a lot, right?

He was going to have to ask her about that, and that wasn't a subject easily brought up. A guy didn't just ask a woman how many men she'd fucked, especially a woman he wasn't really dating.

He'd like to be dating her, though, but she always seemed so reluctant. And it wasn't because she didn't like him. He was good at reading signals, both on and off the field. And Katrina's signals said she was interested. But they also said back off, which confused the hell out of him.

Maybe she'd gotten burned badly by her last boyfriend, and she was gun-shy. He understood that. He just needed to know how to approach her. He could take things slow, but he needed to know the score, and the only way to do that was to ask. He preferred to take an upfront approach with women, and appreciated women who did the same. He didn't mind being shot down as long as they were honest with him about why.

They finished their meal. Katrina declined dessert, and so did he, so when Claudio brought the check, he took out his credit card and paid. He flagged down a taxi and they climbed in.

"Thank you again for inviting us to the game. We had a great time."

"Anytime. I'm glad you came."

When the taxi stopped in front of his hotel, he turned to her.

"I thought we might have a little more privacy here. We could go to the bar, have a drink and talk, and you wouldn't have to worry about the kids popping in. What do you say?"

Katrina hesitated. Just what kind of expectations did Grant have? What kind did she have? She wasn't ready for this. Or was she?

It was just the bar, right? And she could go home whenever she wanted to.

So why was her pulse shooting out of the stratosphere?

She'd barely survived dinner with Grant, and all he'd done was hold on to a strand of her hair.

This man was not good for her. He made her think about things. Hot, sexy things she had no business thinking about.

Still. Just a drink. Play it cool, like he didn't matter. She was very good at this.

She shrugged. "Sure, but then I'll have to leave. I have a lot of details to iron out and I have to fly out tomorrow."

He smiled, his hand at her back. "Me, too."

As they walked through the doors of the hotel, she asked, "Details to iron out, or flying out?"

"Both."

He motioned with his hand to the left, toward the bar. It was very late, but the bar was well attended. Vacationers, maybe some business travelers. Perhaps people in town for the game? One of the things she'd always enjoyed about travel was guessing the reason for people's destination.

Their waiter came by and she ordered a cognac. She felt wound up, and she figured that would relax her.

Grant ordered whiskey.

While waiting for their drinks to arrive, she looked around at the people populating the bar.

"Looking for someone?" Grant asked.

"No. It's a game I play whenever I travel. I try to figure out what people are in town for."

Their waiter arrived with their drinks. She took a sip and let the warm liquid slide down. Sweet, sultry, she felt herself relax after a couple swallows.

Much better.

"Is that right?" he asked. "Okay, tell me a few of your guesses."

She held the glass in her hand, but motioned with it toward the couple in the corner. "She's in a short dress, he's in nice slacks and a button-down shirt. Obviously not here on business, but not dressed as tourists, either. My guess? Honeymoon."

He studied them, too. "Why honeymoon and not anniversary?"

She shrugged. "Just the way they're looking at each other, like a massive hole in the ground opening up between them couldn't separate them. It's new love, not mature love. Plus, they're young. And look at the way he's rubbing her back, touching her hair. It's like he can't keep his hands off of her."

She nodded, reaffirming her initial thoughts. "Definitely honeymoon."

"Or they're having an affair."

She shot him a glare. "Hey, cynic. Don't ruin my imagined young-love honeymoon here."

He laughed, then took a sip of the whiskey. "Maybe they're just getting to know each other and they're in those initial stages of hot lust. When you know you really want someone, and you can't wait to get your hands on them, get them naked, and explore their body."

He dragged his gaze away from the couple and planted it firmly on her, those gray eyes of his turning stormy dark with desire. He laid his arm across the rear of her chair, his fingers lightly teasing the back of her neck.

And then he leaned in to whisper in her ear.

The contact was electrifying.

"That's why he can't keep his hands off her, Kat. He wants her.

This whole touching and leaning thing in the bar is foreplay. He wants to get her up to the room as soon as possible so he can take her clothes off and run his hands and mouth over every inch of her skin, to see if she tastes as delicious as she smells."

Katrina's breath caught.

"You smell like something exotic, a musky, enticing scent I can't quite put my finger on."

He pressed his lips to the side of her neck. She let out a small gasp, and shivers popped up on her skin.

"But I'd like to put my mouth on you. All over you, Kat, until you screamed my name."

She swallowed, her throat gone dry. She lifted her glass to her lips, her hand shaking as she did, then took a sip to coat her throat.

"Do you want that?" he asked.

"I . . . no. I don't."

He kissed the side of her neck again. "Okay."

Then he straightened, picked up his glass, and downed the rest of his whiskey in one shot.

"Point out someone else and tell me what you think."

He seemed calm and together, whereas she was an utter wreck. Her nipples were tight points of aching, screaming need, her clit was throbbing and her panties were damp. She was turned on and ready to straddle him right there in the bar, ready to beg him to give her the orgasm she so desperately craved.

And he, Mr. Oblivious, calmly watched everyone else in the bar, completely out of tune with her needs.

Or was he? She casually glanced downward and saw one very impressive erection.

Which only made her own dilemma worse, especially when she pulled her gaze back to his face and caught his knowing smile.

Damn man.

"I have to go," she said.

"Do you?"

"Yes. I have to pack and . . . things."

"Okay. Don't want to keep you from your . . . things." He signaled for the waiter, who brought the check. By the time Grant had signed off on the bar tab and stood, whatever impressive hard-on he'd sprouted had dissipated, much to Katrina's disappointment.

He stood, and so did she, following him outside the bar.

In the lobby, he stopped and turned to her. "Come up to my room. Spend the night with me."

For a fraction of a second, her spirits soared. She'd been surprisingly deflated when he'd cut off their teasing banter so easily in the bar. She appreciated his being a gentleman and all, but at the same time, she'd been disappointed, too.

Conflicted much, Katrina?

No. She knew where her responsibilities were, and they weren't in Grant Cassidy's bed. She forced herself to remember the reason she was independent. And all the reasons she didn't want a man in her life.

"I can't."

He nodded, then slid his hands up her arms. "I understand. Can't say I'm not disappointed about that."

She wanted to say she was, too, but those were dangerous waters, and she wasn't about to wade into them. She was in way over her head already.

"Thank you again for tonight."

"I'll walk you out and hail you a taxi."

"It's not necessary."

He shook his head. "Come on."

He slid his fingers in hers, and she was surprised to find how much she liked the feel of his big hand in hers. She was tall, and she dwarfed most men. With Grant, she felt . . . small. A bit unusual, but she had to admit she liked it.

He signaled for the valet to hail a taxi.

"I'll see you next week in St. Louis?"

"I'm going to be awfully busy with work and—"

Before she could finish, he'd slid his hands around her neck and his mouth was on hers. It was a soft, but demanding kiss, and she fell into it easily, her hands resting on the solid warmth of his wide chest.

It only lasted a few seconds, but God, she wanted so much more. When he pulled back, she licked her lips, tasting whiskey.

"Think about me when you're at home doing . . . things."

His lips curved as he tucked one of her curls behind her ear.

He walked her to the taxi and leaned in after she got inside.

"And I will see you next week in St. Louis, Kat."

He shut the door and the taxi pulled away.

She wanted to turn around and look to see if he was still standing there watching, but for some reason, she knew he was.

She had no idea what she was going to do about Grant Cassidy.

Keeping him out of her thoughts and out of her life was proving more and more difficult all the time.

TWELVE

KATRINA HAD SPENT THE PAST TWENTY-FOUR HOURS making care arrangements with the au pair to watch over Leo and Anya, who'd argued they were far too old for a babysitter and could handle spending a week alone.

Ha. She could only imagine the parties and the trouble those two could get into unsupervised. Once Cerissa showed up, Katrina had packed, taken her flight to St. Louis, and gotten settled into her hotel. First thing Monday morning she'd met with the photographer and the rest of the team.

They were doing a wedding shoot at the Jewel Box for one of the bridal magazines. She had the cover photo, and would be showcasing some of the features inside the magazine, so it was a pretty big deal, and she'd have several dresses to wear. Typically she didn't give much thought to the outfits, but she rarely had the opportunity to model bridal wear. It was going to be a fun shoot.

Plus, the location was gorgeous. The Jewel Box was a greenhouse in one of the parks in the city, and her manager told her it was listed on the National Register of Historic Places. She'd looked it up while she was in her hotel room last night, and couldn't wait to start the shoot today.

When she arrived on scene, she was whisked over to hair and makeup and spent a couple of hours there having makeup applied and her hair curled. They started out with her hair down, which went well with the strapless designer gown. It was an ivory satin full ball gown, luxurious and a striking complement to the gorgeous Jewel Box, with its Art Deco cantilevered design. They did the first pictures outside. It was the perfect day from a production standpoint. Though quite hot, little to no breeze helped to keep the dress and other paraphernalia in place. They had to stop in between the shots though, to keep patting her down to erase any sheen. The dress was ultra heavy and not at all suited for outside August weather in St. Louis, but she handled it just fine.

Fortunately, the photographer was quick, and before Kat knew it, she was out of that dress and into the next, this time a lovely white lace A-line with sleeves. She was lucky this series of photographs would be taken inside, next to some of the most beautiful flowers she'd ever seen. They'd redesigned her hair for these photos, pulling it up so it was off her shoulders. After all, the lace on her shoulders and down her arms had to be seen.

After a couple of hours of various poses in that dress, they were finished for the day.

She went back to her hotel and showered off the heavy makeup, washing the excess product out of her hair. She let her hair air-dry outside on the balcony of her hotel room while she talked on the phone to Cerissa, who told her everything at home was fine. Leo was working out a lot and Anya was, as typical, always on the phone or with her friends.

At least she didn't have to worry about the kids. After she hung up, she grabbed a book she'd started in the middle of her flight to St. Louis and spent about an hour reading. When her phone rang, she put the book down and looked at the display.

It was Grant. She thought about ignoring his call, but that would be rude. Not that she wasn't an expert at rudeness, but he'd been so nice to her and the kids, so she at least owed him an answer to his call.

"Hello, Grant."

"Hi. How was your shoot today?"

"It went well, thank you. What did you do today?"

"Not much. Day off, so I worked out and cleaned my garage."

She tried to get a mental visual of him working in his garage. All sweaty, maybe his shirt off.

More dangerous thoughts.

"I see. Sounds relaxing, I suppose."

"I was thinking of barbecuing some chicken for dinner and wanted to invite you over."

She couldn't imagine him doing that, either. "Oh, well, I have an early call tomorrow, so . . ."

She wanted to let him off easy. She'd thought a lot about him—about that kiss he'd given her the other night. She was attracted to him. Too attracted.

It was time to back away.

"I promise to have you back to your hotel in time for curfew. Whatever time that is. I'd really like to see you, Kat."

Well . . . crap. And the problem was, she wanted to see him, too. Wasn't that *the* problem?

She should say no. End this, before things got even more complicated than they already were.

But the words spilled out of her mouth before she had a chance to pull them back. "Sure. What time?"

So much for listening to her inner voice.

"How about I pick you up . . . uh, let's say about four o'clock?"

"That sounds fine. I'll be outside so you don't have to park."

"Okay. I'll call you when I'm close so you don't have to linger outside too long. See you then."

She hung up, then stared at her phone.

Clearly, there was something wrong with her. Normally, she had no problem saying no to men. She said no all the time, because she got asked out all the time. She'd said no politely, and not so politely, depending on who was asking. She was an expert at turning men down.

But for some reason, she hadn't yet figured out how to say no to Grant Cassidy.

Maybe she should stop thinking of all the reasons to say no. Maybe she'd let her fears guide her for too long. Grant was gorgeous and hot, and of all the men she'd ever been tempted by, he was the most—

Tempting.

She'd thought a lot about her conversation with Savannah, about having some fun.

Grant could definitely be fun. Not a forever thing, but a temporary fling. Or at least a gorgeous man to hang out with.

There was absolutely nothing threatening about that.

THIRTEEN

AFTER HE'D GOTTEN OFF THE PHONE WITH KATRINA, Grant had spent the rest of the afternoon cleaning his house.

The place was a wreck. As a bachelor, he didn't much care what it looked like on most days, unless his parents were coming for a visit. Then he usually brought in a cleaning service to scour the place from top to bottom, because if there was one thing his mom didn't stand for, it was a messy house. When he'd lived at home, as soon as you were old enough to hold a broom in your hand, empty trash, or do dishes, you had a chore, and it didn't matter if you were a guy or a girl. Mom wanted everyone to grow up and be able to fend for themselves. Even cooking.

He was grateful he'd been taught to cook, though he'd sworn when he'd stood at the stove and was taught to make pasta sauce that someday he was going to eat takeout every single night for the rest of his natural life. That lasted until he'd eaten takeout for two weeks straight. Didn't take him long to figure out that fast food every night got boring fast and maybe his mother was smarter than he'd ever given her credit for.

But he'd never really grabbed the virtue of keeping the house neat. He had a cleaning lady come in once every two weeks so mold didn't grow in places it wasn't supposed to. Otherwise, he threw his dirty socks on the floor and dishes tended to pile up. When he ran out of usable dishes, he washed them. It was a system that worked for him, and unless he had someone coming over, who cared, right?

Like today, with Katrina. It had been a week since the cleaning service had been to the house so he was going to have to do it himself.

So he'd scrubbed the toilets and wiped down the counters in the bathrooms, loaded the dishwasher, and thoroughly cleaned the kitchen, then vacuumed the entire house, picking up everything that he'd carelessly tossed in all the wrong places.

It had taken him a couple of hours, and by then he was a sweaty filthy mess, which he'd already been after working in the garage, so he'd taken a shower and put on a pair of jeans and a T-shirt, then hopped in his car to pick up Katrina at her hotel.

He called her on his way over and she was waiting outside as they'd arranged. Her hair was down and she wore a sundress that showed off miles of gorgeous leg, and he was struck again by how beautiful she was. She was leaning against the valet desk, casually smiling and chatting with some dark-haired kid who couldn't be more than eighteen or nineteen.

The kid was obviously trying not to swallow his tongue as Katrina tucked her hair behind her ear. It was a simple gesture, yet the kid's gaze tracked the movement like it was the most fascinating thing he'd ever seen in his young life.

Grant understood the appeal. Everything about Katrina was pretty damn riveting, and she did have an ear he'd like to tug on with his teeth.

He got out of the car and waved off the valet, no doubt crushing the kid's dreams.

Too bad. He could go get his own girl. This one was his date for the night.

Katrina turned when Grant approached.

"Sorry. I was talking to Gregori here. He and his family emigrated from Russia just two years ago. I was practicing my very rusty Russian on him. Thank you again, Gregori. And best of luck to you in college."

Gregori nodded, and Grant watched the kid swallow nervously, smile, and walk away.

Poor kid. He might not ever recover from meeting Katrina. Then again, it might be something he remembered forever. Grant gave the kid a wink and a smile.

From the same country or not, the kid was still ogling the hell out of her.

He led Katrina to his car, opened the door and waited for her to slide in.

He put the car into gear and pulled away, onto the street, heading onto the highway.

Katrina was quiet, looking out the window, so he told her a little about the city.

"You're not from here," she said.

"No. My family's from Texas. My parents have a ranch there. I grew up in Green Bay, where my dad played football. In the off-season we lived on the ranch."

"I see. But you live here, right?"

"Yeah. When I signed with St. Louis during my rookie year, I fell in love with this city. I bought my house the year I made the team."

She pulled her gaze from the window. "How long ago was that?"

"Six years ago."

She nodded. "From what I've seen, it's a very nice city. A lot of space here."

"I'll show you around this week."

"That's not necessary. I'm sure you're very busy."

His lips curved. "But I want to. This is where I live, Katrina. I want you to see it."

"Oh, of course. Then thank you."

He wasn't certain her hesitation was just politeness. He should find out before he took this any further.

"Do you have a boyfriend?"

Her gaze snapped to his. "No."

"Okay."

"Why would you ask that question? I wouldn't be seeing you if I did. I wouldn't kiss you if I did. I would never—"

"Calm down, Kat. I only asked the question because you're always so reluctant to spend any time with me. And I know it's not because you don't like me."

She let out a laugh. "Of course. Because what woman wouldn't like you? You being so irresistible and all."

He shot her a grin. "I know, right?"

"No problem with your ego, is there?"

"None that I'm aware of."

He pulled off the highway and drove several blocks toward his neighborhood.

"This is a very nice area," she said. "I love the seclusion of it, and all the trees."

He pulled onto his street. "There was something about this area I liked a lot when I was out looking at houses to buy," he said. "There were a lot of families in the neighborhood. Plus there's a park and a lake and it's in a very good school district. And then when I saw the house, I knew I had to have it."

When he pulled up into the driveway and parked, she turned to him. "You talk about kids and stuff. Is there something I should know?"

"Like?"

"Like maybe an ex-wife and some kids you haven't told me about?"

He laughed and unbuckled his seat belt. "No. Just thinking about the future. I don't intend to house hop. I figured at some point I'll get married and have some kids. This seems like a good place to do that."

Katrina gaped at the house, the big front yard and the impressive neighborhood. Living in Manhattan, space was always at a premium. She loved her apartment, and it was spacious by New York City standards, but this was spectacular.

It was a two-story stone house with a dark roof. There were a lot of windows flanked by gorgeous white shutters. It was huge, yet welcoming at the same time. The front yard was immense, with a lot of lush green grass, tall trees, and shrubs.

"Did you do all this landscaping?" she asked as he walked with her to the front door.

"Some of it. My mom suggested the flowers after I moved in. She said the front landscaping needed some color or something like that. She and my sister ordered them and had them delivered, and my dad and brothers and I put them in."

"Your mother is right. It would have looked barren without some color."

"Yeah, so they told me—repeatedly." He hit the button on the garage door, which lifted to reveal a big truck in the garage.

She looked at the truck, then over at him. "Yes, you strike me as a truck guy."

"What exactly is a 'truck guy'?"

"Manly. Testosterone. That kind of thing."

"I'm going to take that as a compliment."

She smiled. "You do that."

He led her through a door into the house, which was so much cooler than outside.

It smelled like cleaning products—piney and lemony. He must have cleaned today before coming to pick her up.

How sweet.

And utterly unexpected.

Inside was spacious and light, with a lot of windows and very cool tile. The kitchen was magnificent—definitely a cook's paradise, with a large island and a six-burner stove.

The living area was the same, with amazing dark hardwood floors, and windows overlooking a woodsy backyard.

And, oh, God, a pool.

She turned to him, grasping his arm. "You have a pool."

"Yeah."

"Can we go see it?"

"Don't you want to see the rest of the house first?"

"No."

With a quirk of his lips, he nodded. "Okay. Let's go out back and see the pool. There are two entrances out back. One through the living room, which is actually a side yard. There's another way, down the stairs and through the laundry slash mudroom."

He took her down the stairs and, dear God, this room was as big as the entire main living area in her apartment. It was a laundry room, but also a prep area for the pool. The floor was tiled, and there were open cupboards holding beach towels and a vast array of pool paraphernalia, with a laundry prep area as well.

"Wow."

"It was a big selling point for me. People can come in here and use the bathroom, and it doesn't muck up the rest of the house. Plus lots of storage for the pool stuff."

"It's amazing."

"Thanks. I agree."

They went out the door and it led onto a huge covered patio. He had a few tables and chairs, but there was potential for so much more.

The pool, however, was magnificent, surrounded by smooth rocks, with a waterfall and a slide. There was an attached hot tub as well, which was simply gorgeous.

The pool was huge and inviting. The yard surrounding and beyond was lush and green with mature trees farther back in a wooded area. She wanted to strip and dive into the pool, then spend the remainder of the day there.

"I forgot to mention the pool so you could bring your suit. We'll do that tomorrow."

She wanted to tell him she wasn't coming over tomorrow, but after seeing this pool, how could she not? It was entirely too tempting. Like the man who lived here.

"It's really lovely out here. I imagine you spend your entire summer in the pool."

"Yeah, it's pretty great. I enjoy it a lot. But you have a pool at your apartment, don't you?"

"It's an indoor pool. Not even close to being the same thing. This is outside, where it's warm. And just steps from your house. It's so private." Whereas she had to share their pool with everyone in the building. No privacy. No sunshine. No fresh air.

If she lived in a house—and really, what must that be like—she'd be out here first thing every morning with her coffee, watching the birds and the butterflies and listening to the sounds of nature, then swimming a few laps before breakfast.

"You could take a dip now if you want to."

He had moved behind her, and laid his hands on her shoulders. The warmth of them seared through her.

She tilted her head back to look up at him. "No suit, remember?"

"Oh, I remember. But I have a lot of privacy. No one will see you. Except me, of course. And it's not like I'd complain."

The thought appealed, especially since she'd want to swim with him.

Naked. Which caused her to entertain visuals of the two of them entwined in the water, her legs wrapped around his waist, his hands sweeping over her body.

Her nipples tightened, her sex becoming all too aware of her needs.

And that was dangerous territory. Light and easy, remember? Not naked and passionate. That would only lead to trouble.

She shook her head. "Not gonna happen. Let's go see the rest of your house."

Upstairs were four bedrooms, all well decorated, as well as the master, which was huge and had a great deck overlooking the yard and pool. She could well imagine waking up in the morning and spending more leisure time out there, or having a last glass of wine before bed talking over the day with—

Well, it wasn't like that was going to happen anyway, so no point fantasizing about it.

"You have a lovely home, Grant," she said as he led her back down the stairs toward the kitchen.

"Thanks. Would you like something to drink? I have tea, soda, water, wine, and beer. Or I can make a mixed drink."

"Aren't you just a regular bartender?" She went for a glass of white wine, and he told her to select from his wine fridge. She picked a chardonnay and he opened the bottle and poured her a glass, then pulled a beer from the refrigerator for himself. They headed outside and sat on the deck overlooking the pool.

It was hot, yet there was a breeze. She didn't care. It was beautiful out here and that pool still tempted her. So did his suggestion to swim in it.

"How did the shoot go today?"

She liked that he was interested enough to ask.

"It was good. We shot at the Jewel Box."

"Great place for a wedding shoot. It's beautiful there."

"So you know it."

"Sure. I've been there a few times."

She took a sip of her wine, leaned back and studied him. "Been married a few times?"

He laughed. "No, but I've been in a few friends' weddings and photos were taken there. Pictures turned out pretty good. I imagine yours will be better."

"I don't know about better. Just different, since these are bridal gown shots for a magazine, as opposed to wedding photos. Though they are bringing in some other models tomorrow to do actual wedding party photo shots. Those should be fun."

"Ah, so tomorrow you get a groom, huh?" He took a long swallow of his beer and arched a brow. "Some hot stud that will perfectly complement the gorgeous bride?"

She laughed. "Something like that. I have no idea who it is. Likely someone I've worked with before."

"And maybe dated before?"

She wrinkled her nose. "God, no. I don't date models."

"Why not?"

"Well, for one thing, and as I mentioned before, I don't date. And the other is that there's too much potential for conflict. Models tend to weave in and out of each others' lives all the time. If you have a relationship with one and it ends badly, then you have to do a shoot with them, that animosity is going to be reflected in your work."

She shrugged. "It just makes it harder to do our jobs, and our jobs are difficult enough as it is. The last thing I need is to be half-naked, sweating, and body to body with someone I can't stand."

"I agree. That's why I don't date any of my offensive linemen. I need them to protect me on the field, and if I broke one of their hearts, they might just let the defense knock me on my ass a few times for payback."

Katrina laughed. "Yes, I'd steer clear of them if I were you."

"I do. Besides, wide receivers are more my type."

She snorted, then pushed her empty wineglass away. "I think one glass will be enough for me."

He picked up the glass. "Oh, no. You need another. We're just getting started."

Grant went inside and refilled Katrina's glass, then grabbed another beer. He was enjoying seeing her unwind—even laugh. He wanted her relaxed.

And in his pool tonight.

He'd have to figure out how he could get her there.

He brought out the drinks and laid them on the table, then pulled up the chair next to her. There was a slight breeze blowing the tips of her hair across her bare shoulders. He wanted to press his lips to her skin, to start there, then explore her neck, her collarbone, and work his way down her back. He remembered from their photo shoot just how soft her skin was, and he wanted to put his hands on her again. He wanted to kiss her, get her naked, and slide inside of her.

He was getting hard, so it was probably time to stop thinking about all the things he wanted to do with her.

Or maybe it was time to step up the game, and see if she wanted to play.

"Are you hungry?" he asked.

She was taking a sip of wine, so she swallowed then set the glass down. "Not at the moment. I'm enjoying the wine, the view, and being outside."

"Okay. You let me know."

"I'll do that."

That's when the idea came to him. "Let's go sit closer to the pool."

"Sure."

He picked up her glass and his beer, and she followed him to the pool's edge. Since he had on board shorts, he kicked off his shoes, then laid their drinks down. He held her hand while she slipped out of her sandals and sat. He grabbed a spot next to her, handed her drink to her, and dipped his legs in the water.

"The water feels so good," she said as she took another drink of wine.

"It does, doesn't it?" It was a perfect night. Hot, a slight breeze, the kind of night that made you want to—

Then Katrina shocked the shit out of him by untying her sundress and lifting it over her head. She wore matching navy blue and white polka-dotted cotton bra and bikini underwear.

She turned to him and smiled. "You knew I wouldn't be able to resist, didn't you?"

"I was kind of hoping."

She slid into the water feetfirst, letting it swallow her up. When she came up, her hair was wet. She hadn't worn makeup, but then again, she didn't need to. She swept her hair away from her face and looked up at him. Water glistened off the curves of her breasts, a hard gust of wind sweeping through and causing her nipples to harden against the cotton of her now-soaked bra.

He'd never seen anything sexier.

"Coming?" she asked.

He damn near had.

FOURTEEN

KATRINA HAD NO IDEA WHAT POSSESSED HER TO strip off her sundress and dive into the pool in her underwear.

Inability to resist the lure of the water, she supposed. She'd always loved to swim and had wanted a pool of her own for as long as she could remember.

An outdoor pool all to herself, not the indoor pool like she had at her apartment. And now she stood in this amazingly cool water with the sun beating down on her and no one else was around.

Except Grant, who drew his shirt off, giving her only a brief glance of his very attractive, tanned torso before he slid into the water and disappeared under it. He came up, shaking his head back and forth, and sprayed her with droplets, making her laugh.

It wasn't like he hadn't seen her near naked, anyway. A lot of men had seen her near naked. She wasn't shy about her body. At least as far as her job, anyway.

Grant reached for her, but she pushed off the side of the pool

and swam to the other end, not realizing until she got there that
he'd been right on her the entire time.

Since they were at the deep end, she pulled her arms up to the
edge of the pool.

"You're a fast swimmer," she said. "Want to do some laps?"

"Not particularly, but I'll be happy to watch you do them."

She shook her head, smiled at him, then pushed off the side. She
swam, dipping her head in the water and enjoying the movement of
her body through the pool. It was so freeing, feeling weightless in
the water. She could have done this for hours, but it was selfish of
her to use Grant's pool this way, so she finally came up for air.

Grant was leaning against the side of the shallow end, his
elbows resting on the tile. He was watching her, his gaze so intense
it was overwhelming, and also more than a little exciting.

She didn't want to be excited. She wanted to be not in the least
interested in him. The problem was, she *was* interested. A lot interested. She found him extremely hot and utterly charming. Two
lethal combinations.

She needed to distract herself with something else. Like this
great pool.

She looked around at the woods surrounding the yard. All this
privacy. The peace it afforded. "If I had a pool like this—outside—
I'd swim every morning."

"It's a little cold in the winter."

She laughed, and swam over to him. "Okay, every morning,
weather permitting. Besides, it's heated, isn't it?"

"Yeah. I can usually swim well into late October."

"Perfect. And with the attached hot tub, you have year-round
opportunities to enjoy it."

"This is true. Though those mad dashes from the hot tub back
to the house in January can be an adventure."

"Oh, but the amazing feeling of being surrounded by all that heat when it's so cold outside? I once did a photo shoot in Iceland, and took a hot tub outside. It was breathtaking."

"Yeah, and the frigid cold shrinks your balls to the size of peas."

She laughed. "Well, I wouldn't know about that part. But cold is good for your skin."

"Whatever you say. I'm not a fan."

"Baby."

He shot her a glare. "Hey. I'm a tough guy. I can play three hours of football in New England or Green Bay—in January. You try that."

She rolled her eyes at him. "Please. Try posing in nothing but a skimpy bikini for six hours on a boat in Nova Scotia with below-zero windchills. And then you have to give the camera hot, smoldering looks while you're covered in goose bumps and your lips are turning blue, but you can't shiver because the photographer will get pissed and you know damn well if you screw up the shot he'll make you stand out there an hour longer just to make you suffer. And he doesn't give a shit because he's all wrapped up in warm winter gear."

He stared at her. "Okay, you win."

"Damn straight I win."

"That really happened?"

"Of course it happened. People think modeling is all glamour shots and beaches, when it's anything but that. Sure, we get to do some great location shoots like the one in Barbados, but for every one like that there are five more in remote, uncomfortable locations. I do a lot of winter shoots because I work all year long."

"You give a good insight into what it's like being a model. You work your ass off, but you're right—people think it's all glamour."

She appreciated that he understood how hard she worked.

He dipped down into the water, then came up and dragged his fingers through his hair.

Could the man possibly look any sexier? Water dripped over his shoulders and torso, making her want to draw close to him and swipe her hands over him. Maybe rub against him a little.

Good God, what was wrong with her? She saw sexy, wet men all the time on the job. Grant was nothing new.

Except she wasn't at work, and every time she was around Grant she had some weird chemical response to him. Her nipples tightened, her feminine parts clenched, and all she could think about was sex.

Maybe that wasn't so bad. She'd never thought about sex much. Wasn't it high time she did?

No. It wasn't. She had way too much going on in her life to think about herself. But then Grant moved into her and swept her hair away from her face, and every part of her tingled with awareness. They were alone. The kids were back in New York, and she had free time tonight.

She could have anything she wanted.

She could have him.

But if she did, it would change everything.

Was she ready for this? Would she ever be ready for it?

"Do you want to get out of the water now? I can make us some dinner." He slid his hand down her arm. Touching her came so easy to him. Why wasn't it easy for her?

She was as confused as ever. She knew what she wanted, and it had nothing to do with dinner. All she had to do was reach for it—for him—and she knew she could have him. The way he looked at her, the desire she read in his eyes was so clear.

Being with him was so simple. It should be simple, yet the difficulties it represented were monumental, at least to her. She felt frozen with indecision.

Until Grant tipped her chin with his fingers, forcing her eyes to meet his.

She read such certainty in his eyes. He knew exactly what he wanted as he dipped his head and paused, their lips only a fraction of an inch from each other.

"Tell me what you want, Kat. Tell me what you want and I'll give it to you."

He hovered so close his breath sailed across her lips. She wished she had that level of confidence, wished she could just fall into this so easily, without her mind going off in a million directions and thinking of the consequences.

Her nails dug into his arm and she tossed those consequences aside. "I want this. Kiss me."

His lips met hers and she sank into the sweet sensation of his mouth moving over hers. She breathed him in and let her hands snake up his arms, enjoying the feel of a very tall, powerful man pulling her against his body.

They stood in the water, torso to torso, her heart beating a crazy rhythm as her pulse rate flew out of control. Grant swept his hands down her back and she moaned as he deepened the kiss. When he cupped her butt, she knew right then that whatever he wanted, she wouldn't deny him.

This was what she'd dreamed about for so long, what she'd held back from out of fear and a sense of responsibility. All these years it had been everyone else's needs taking a front seat. Now it was her turn and she wanted this.

She really wanted this.

She clutched his shoulders and allowed herself to really feel for the first time in her life, suddenly wishing they were out of the pool and naked so she could have what she so desperately needed.

When Grant broke the kiss, she was left shaking and needy. But he only climbed out of the pool and in one swift move hauled her out, too.

"Let's go inside."

She looked down at herself, at her soaking wet underwear and dripping body. "I'm all wet, Grant."

His lips tipped up into a wickedly sexy smile. "God, I hope so." He took her hand and led her to the side door, then shut it behind them.

The air conditioning inside gave her an immediate chill and she shivered.

"Let's get you out of those wet clothes."

It was all moving so fast. Not that she had a problem being naked, but this was different. It wasn't a photo shoot, and he wasn't a photographer. There wasn't staff around and in this, she wasn't modeling. They were a man and woman, about to become intimate together.

She was in over her head, but she wasn't about to back down. Not when the endgame was something she wanted so much.

She undid the clasp on her bra and pulled the straps down, letting the bra fall to the floor. Then she shimmied out of her panties and left them on the floor as well.

Grant stared at her. "You are beautiful, Kat."

He dropped his shorts and she took a moment to admire his chiseled body. Broad shoulders and chest, narrow waist and slim hips and a sizable erection that made her throat go dry.

He grabbed an oversized towel and came over to her, wrapping it around her and himself, bringing their bodies in contact.

"Better?" he asked.

The contact was electrifying. She could stay like this forever, body to body with him. She tilted her head back to look at him. "Much."

He rubbed her body with the towel, the motion causing a rush of warmth that did nothing to quell the desire running rampant through her. She was flushed with a heat that had a lot more to do with desire than the friction from the towel.

She pushed the towel off and slid her hands across his shoulders. "Kiss me," she whispered.

"I'll do a hell of a lot more than that. But not here in the laundry room."

He swept her up in his arms and stalked out of the room.

"I'm heavy," she protested.

He laughed and looked down at her. "No, you're not. But you're goddamn sexy like this."

He paused in the hallway and his mouth came down on hers—hard and passionate, his tongue sliding against hers and making her weak with all those unspoken needs that had been swirling around in her head for too long. She twined her hand around the back of his neck, wanting more of what he gave her.

"Goddamn," he said when he pulled back, licking his lips.

And then he carried her up the stairs to his bedroom, nudged the door open and laid her on the bed. She barely had time to take a breath before he was on top of her, covering her body with his, kissing her until she couldn't breathe, couldn't process all these signals her body gave her.

She was swamped with sensations she'd never felt before, had never allowed herself to have before. There were things she wanted to tell Grant. Slow down. Don't slow down. She wanted it all right now, but wanted to savor everything in slow motion.

This was all so new to her, almost embarrassing that she'd waited so long to allow herself to have it. But now that she was, she intended to fling herself into it all, taste it all, experience it all and not look back. There would be no regrets because she knew she was in it for the fun, for the experience, and nothing more.

Then she'd finally walk away a woman.

Something she'd waited seemingly a lifetime for.

FIFTEEN

GRANT COULDN'T GET ENOUGH OF KATRINA'S TASTE, the silk of her skin gliding along his hands. He felt the fast beat of her heart along her chest, took in her soft moans as he kissed the column of her throat and nibbled at her earlobe.

And the way she touched him made him so goddamn hard he couldn't wait to slide inside her wet heat and lose himself, ride them both until they both came.

But as he lifted up and looked into her gorgeous violet eyes, he read something there that made him put on the brakes.

An innocence, a wariness he couldn't quite believe he saw there.

He rolled to his side and took a slow taste of her lips, caressed her rib cage, and gave himself a minute to ogle the perfection of her body.

She was breathing in and out, hard. And she wasn't aggressive, didn't roll over on top of him to demand he continue. She hadn't once grabbed his cock and stroked it. It was almost as if she had no idea what to do. Like she'd never—

Nah. That wasn't possible.

He snaked a fingertip up her stomach. She turned her head to watch his face.

"Tell me what you like," he said, letting his fingers dip lower.

He caught her nervous swallow. "I like . . . everything."

He changed direction, moving up her body to cup her breast. She gasped when he brushed a thumb back and forth over her nipple.

"Hard or soft?"

She frowned. "What?"

"Do you like it soft, like this?" He demonstrated by using featherlight touches of his fingers over her nipple. She seemed to like that.

"Or a little harder, like this." He increased the pressure. She moaned, and when he bent over and sucked the bud between his lips, she arched upward, feeding her nipple into his mouth.

Oh, yeah. He flicked his tongue over her, loving the soft areola and hard bud against his tongue. And when her fingers slid into his hair to hold his head in place, he knew he had her, that she was enjoying the pleasure he gave her.

But she still wasn't saying anything, so he added his fingers, traveling over her lower stomach to cup her sex, playing with her clit and her pussy.

She was wet, and as he dipped his fingers inside her, he realized just how damn tight she was.

He lifted his head and watched her face as he slid his fingers in and out of her. Her eyes were closed, her teeth clamped down on her lower lip. Her face was flushed and she lifted her hips against his hand.

"Are you going to come for me, Kat?"

Her eyes flew open, her gaze meeting his. Her hips relaxed and it was as if she'd lost the drive, the need.

"You're watching me."

His lips curved. "Yeah. It makes my cock hard looking at you. Does it bother you?"

"I don't know. Yes. I don't know, maybe."

"It would be kind of hard for me to make you come if I'm not in the room."

"Of course. I understand that. But . . . this is a little . . . personal."

He let out a soft laugh. "Sex is all kinds of personal. You have done this before, right?"

When she didn't say anything, he had his answer. He withdrew his fingers.

"Katrina. You've had sex before, haven't you?"

She shifted and pushed her way up, leaning against the pillows. "Technically, no."

Reality came tumbling down on top of him like a landslide. He avoided the knee-jerk reaction of wanting to ask her how the hell she could be twenty-seven and still a virgin. There was obviously a reason for it and he needed to get to the bottom of it. "Okay. You need to talk to me about this."

She shrugged and looked down at her hands. "I've had . . . responsibilities. The kids. My job. There wasn't time. Or the right guy. The right moment."

And she thought *he* was the right guy and this was the right moment? Christ. That was loaded with responsibility. Responsibility he didn't know if he was ready for. He'd never had a virgin in his bed. What was he supposed to do with her?

He looked over at Katrina and saw the disappointment on her face and felt an instant stab of guilt that he'd even, for a second, felt like this was a problem.

Okay, it wasn't like they were sixteen—like she was sixteen. She was twenty-seven, and he sure as hell wasn't a kid. He needed to be an adult about this. So she hadn't had sex before. This wasn't a problem. It was an opportunity. Looking at the embarrassment on her face made him realize this was no easier for her than it was for him.

And he'd be goddamned if he'd turn this into something less than monumental for her. She'd chosen him, and he felt damn good about that.

"You think I'm stupid," she said, barely able to make eye contact. "Or naïve or something."

He tipped her chin with his fingers, forcing her to make eye contact with him. "Hey, I don't think you're anything like that. I admire you for what you've done for your brother and sister. You've made a lot of sacrifices. But now it's time to think about yourself and what you want."

She didn't say anything.

"But you have to be really sure, Kat. Is this what you really want? And now is when you want it?"

She gave him a quick nod. "I'm an adult, Grant. Not a child. I'm perfectly capable of making adult choices. This is definitely what I want. I've waited long enough and I want to be here with you."

He felt relieved, and a lot of pressure to do this right.

He picked up her hand and twined his fingers with hers. "Okay, so tell me what kind of experience you have had. With guys. Or with yourself."

"Well, I definitely know my own body. I mean technically I'm not really a virgin anymore. It's more that I haven't been with a guy."

He smiled at that. "Which means you've used your own hands to get yourself off."

She nodded. "Right. And vibrators."

He sucked in a breath. "I'd like to watch you do that sometime."

Now she gave him a sexy smile. He liked seeing her relax a little. It was time to get the topic back on sex, where it belonged. He wanted her confidence high again, where it had been before.

"You would?" she asked.

"Hell, yes. There's nothing hotter than watching a woman make herself come. And you could watch me jack off."

Her breasts rose and fell with her deep breath. "That would be interesting. And probably quite fun."

He laid his hand on her leg, let his fingers do a light dance across her kneecap, then up her thigh. "Babe, you have no idea. Okay, tell me what experience you've had with guys."

"Not much, really. I haven't had a lot of exposure. Some kissing, a little under the shirt action. Nothing down here."

She pointed to her sex.

Okay, so he had to educate her—and himself as well. Other than the early teen years when he and girls had fumbled around with each other, he'd only been with experienced women before—women who knew what they wanted and knew how to ask for it.

Katrina wasn't going to be the only one experiencing something new today.

And he owed it to her to do it right, because a woman's first time with a guy should be something special.

He didn't intend to fuck this up.

SIXTEEN

KATRINA HAD BEEN MORTIFIED. SHE'D PLANNED TO get this sex thing over with before Grant had any inkling she'd never done this before. Leave it to someone as masculine and filled with confidence as him to read right through her. He'd known almost instantly that she had no idea what she was doing.

But he'd handled it so well. He hadn't laughed at her, and he'd asked all the right questions. Now they could get down to business and make her lack of experience a thing of the past.

"Okay, so what do we do?" she asked. She had a gloriously hot and sexy naked man in bed with her, and she wanted to move forward with that.

His hand lay on her thigh, and as his fingers crept forward, that flush of heat surrounded her again, making her breasts feel swollen and heavy, and her clit tingle with anticipation.

But he didn't move. Instead, he teased the inner curve of her thigh. "We do whatever feels good. I don't know about you, but

I'm not in any hurry. I want to explore your body. I want to kiss you and lick you and make you come. I want your bones to turn to jelly and make you quiver all over. And then when I fuck you, Kat, you're going to scream my name over and over again."

She shuddered out a breath at the fantasy of it all. She read a lot of books, many of them romances. She got the fantasy. She'd masturbated to a lot of very explicit erotica many times. But that's all it was—a fantasy. She was smart enough to know real life wasn't like that.

"You're giving me a look like you don't believe I can make it happen for you."

Her lips curved. "I'm very open-minded and eager to learn. But I highly doubt that real sex is all I've read about."

He stood, tugged on her ankles, and pulled her down the bed, laying her flat. "I'll accept that challenge."

He climbed onto the bed and laid next to her, using his hands to sweep over her body.

"Sex should never be rushed. I did that a lot when I was younger." He used the palm of his hand to rub a spot just above her collarbone. "I learned after a while that you miss out on some great stuff."

She met his gaze. "Such as?"

"Such as learning what spots on a woman's body drive her crazy. And that you need to relax and enjoy the journey. It isn't all about fucking, you know."

To her, it was. But she'd take his word for it since he was the one with all the experience.

"We're going to take our time to explore, Kat. We've got all night."

He cupped his hand on her jaw and kissed her. Lightly at first, but oh, the man had an amazing mouth, coaxing her to open. He slid his tongue inside to tease hers. Without the mind-numbing hard passion, she fell into the kiss, an array of sensations that, coupled with the light touch of his fingers across her skin, made her dizzy with pleasure.

Who knew that a lazy, soft kiss and a tangle of tongues could be so erotic? Especially when a man took his time mapping her naked body with the tips of his fingers.

She couldn't help but arch against him when he found that spot on her inner hip that she'd never realized caused a zing of awareness. He didn't press in, just circled the spot with his fingertip.

And then he kissed his way over her jaw and down to her neck, moving over her like he'd just been given a new toy to play with. And who knew the right side of her neck was so sensitive? The left side felt good, too, of course. But the right side caused chill bumps to skitter across her skin and when he sucked that spot . . .

"Oh, my God." She was unable to resist exclaiming out loud as he slashed his tongue across the side of her neck and licked her. A slow, deliberate lick that drove her out of her mind with desire.

She grasped his head and brought his mouth to hers, and now it was her turn to explore. She deepened the kiss this time, sucking on his tongue. Her body was on fire from his explorations and she wanted an orgasm.

Now.

But Grant hadn't been joking when he said they had all night to explore. While she was in the throes of quaking need, he skimmed his fingers across her rib cage, then over her breasts, teasing her nipples until they were tight, hard peaks just begging for his mouth. And when he bent and captured one of her nipples between his lips, she thought she might explode from the shooting arcs of pleasure.

"I need . . ." She couldn't form the words, but there was so much she needed. His touch, his mouth on her—everywhere. His cock. She couldn't wait for his cock. She'd waited a lifetime for this and she wanted him inside her right now.

"Shh," he said, letting his hand slide down her belly to cup her sex. "I know what you need."

His touch inflamed her. Her hips arched, seeking the magic of his fingers, needing them inside her. And when he slid them into her, she cried out from the deepest pleasure.

This wasn't her touching herself. It was Grant, his fingers smooth and sure as he pumped inside of her, as if he knew just what to do. She'd never felt anything like it, a sweet pressure that filled her. And with every thrust of his coaxing fingers, he pressed the heel of his hand against her clit. It felt like the Fourth of July across her sex, and she was the fireworks ready to explode.

No man had ever made her come before. She'd had plenty of orgasms, all self-induced. Always alone, creating fantasies in her head of what this might be like. And now, Grant brushed his thumb over the knotted bud and she was ready to go off.

"Let go," he whispered against her ear. "Relax and let go. I'll be right here."

It seemed so easy. She knew her own body so well, she could get herself off in a few minutes. But this was new, and so intimate. He lay against her, touching her in such a familiar way, watching her as she helplessly drew ever closer to a release she wanted so damn bad it made her entire body shake.

She finally grabbed hold of his wrist, needing to take some control back.

"Here?" he asked, going where she led him, changing the pace and making it faster. "Like this?"

"Yes. Oh, yes," she said, her voice ragged and breathless. She focused on his hands, on her body's reaction, and let go.

Her orgasm rushed through her, as out of control as the ever-changing winds. It knocked her senseless. Grant took her mouth in a kiss, deepening every sensation, connecting her to him, not just the orgasm. She wrapped her hand around his neck and held on for dear life as she trembled with the force of it, tuned in to his mouth and his tongue and the way his hands and fingers continued to move over her. She quaked, endlessly, as her orgasm wracked her, seemingly going on forever.

Finally, she came down. He'd gentled his movements, but he was still connected to her, his fingers still inside of her.

She shuddered at the intimacy of it. And when he broke the kiss, his gaze met hers and she smiled up at him.

"Well, that was good."

He laughed. "Just good?"

"Okay. Really good."

"It'll get better. I'm shooting for great. Awesome. Amazing."

She loved that he was so easy about this, that he made her feel no embarrassment. "I like a goal-oriented man."

He slid off the bed "I'm going to get us something to drink. Then I'll be back to show you just how goal oriented I can be."

She shook her head, but the smile had yet to leave her face.

Technically, she supposed she was still in virgin territory, but with Grant, she felt assured that was going to be taken care of soon enough.

He'd made her feel so good about herself, and hadn't made fun of her for being a twenty-seven-year-old virgin. So many men would have backed off, or run like hell, not wanting to waste time with an inexperienced woman.

Not that she was all that inexperienced. With men, definitely. With sex—well, she was a reader. She knew a lot about sex. And she watched plenty of movies. It wasn't like she was completely in the dark. She only needed some practical application.

As Grant walked back into the room, she couldn't help but notice his erection.

He had two glasses of ice water, and he looked down at his cock, where her attention had been riveted.

He grinned. "I was thinking about you when I was in the kitchen."

She turned on her side to face him. "You were? And what were you thinking?"

He set the glasses on the nightstand, then climbed on the bed. "About how lucky I am to be with you."

She hadn't anticipated that. "You're lucky to be with me."

"Sure." He laid his hand on her hip. "You could have chosen any man to be the first man to be with. You chose me. Now I get to teach you all the fun stuff. That makes me a very lucky guy."

"Not every man would think that."

He frowned. "Why not?"

"While you were off getting us drinks, I was thinking that some guys would have run in the opposite direction when faced with a virgin."

He grunted. "Oh, come on. It's not the fucking dark ages anymore. Now if you and I were sixteen or something, then yeah, we'd be having a different conversation right now. But you're a very smart, very adult woman who knows exactly what she wants in the way of sex. And what she doesn't want."

She liked that he put the decision making in her hands. And he called her smart, not for the first time. She liked that about him as well.

"Thank you for realizing I'm capable of making sound decisions."

"Of course you are. You chose me after all."

She laughed. "Yes, well, I chose you for a night of hot sex. It's not like we're dating. Or getting married. Or anything like that."

He gave her a sad look. "What? But all those promises you made to me."

She laughed. "I'm serious here, Grant. No strings. We're not getting into a relationship here just because we're having sex."

He squeezed her hip. "Got it. No relationship. Just sex."

"Okay. I just don't want you to get the wrong idea."

His eyes twinkled, and she saw the teasing glint there. "So I shouldn't be upset if you don't call me in the morning?"

She shook her head. "Very funny."

He slid down the mattress, his mouth where his hand had just been, this time kissing her hip bone. He lifted his gaze to her. "But you'll still respect me, right?"

That teasing, oh-so-hot look he gave her made her breathing harder, especially when he turned her onto her back and spread her legs.

"Definitely."

He shifted, moving between her legs. "Good. Because I'd hate to think you were just using me for my superior sex skills."

If his skills got any better, she wasn't sure she'd survive the night. But this was the night of her education, and she intended to learn and experience everything.

Like the feel of Grant's mouth against her sex. Heat and wetness, moving over her clit. Down, then back up again. Nothing she could do to herself could match this. It was overwhelming in the best kind of way.

She raised up on her elbows, needing to see what he was doing to her. The sensations were mind blowing. She didn't think she could come again so soon, but what he was doing to her unraveled her.

He had a very talented mouth, and used it in creative, relentless ways. She spiraled out of control faster than she expected, her body tingling as her clit and pussy quivered under the mastery of Grant's lips and tongue. Before she could even gasp in surprise, she was coming, lifting against his mouth, never wanting this to end.

Suddenly he was above her, taking her mouth in a kiss that tasted of her. It was erotic and hot and she wrapped her hand

around his neck to hold him there, licking at his lips as she continued to come down from that incredible high.

Her gaze met his when he pulled back. She was out of breath,
her mind more than a little blown by all these firsts.

"Thank you," she said.

"It was my pleasure. You taste like hot, salty cherries."

She shuddered, then rolled with him as he went to his side. He
handed her a glass and they each took several long drinks of water.

She swept her hand over his shoulder, still unable to believe she
was lying in bed naked with a man. With Grant, who wasn't just
any man, but a hot, built, extremely sexy—no, wait—that wasn't
even the right word for him.

Extremely *sexual* man.

She laid her water on the table, then rolled over onto her back
and stretched, raising her arms above her head.

"You look satisfied."

She tilted her head toward him and smiled. "I do, don't I?"

He grinned, then finished his glass of water and set it down.
"Yeah, and we haven't even gotten to the best part yet."

"No, we haven't." She rolled back over and skimmed her palm
over his chest. "I have to tell you, Grant, that you're a very good
teacher."

"Thanks."

She walked her fingers down his chest and over his abs, loving
the rock-hard feel of him, especially when she got to his cock. She
fisted it in her hand.

"So how about we get to the best part now?"

SEVENTEEN

GRANT PRIDED HIMSELF ON HIS SELF-RESTRAINT. BUT the past hour with Katrina had been a test of that restraint. She was beautiful, her scent drove him crazy, and the way she responded to his touch and his mouth had nearly put him over the edge.

She might not have done this before, but her hand on his cock told him she'd done her research.

"I like you touching me," he said.

"I like feeling you. You're hard, but the skin is soft. And hot. You're really hot."

"You have no idea how hot I am right now."

"Am I doing it right?"

"Anything you do with your hand on my cock is right."

She lifted her gaze to his face. "No. Seriously. Teach me."

He laid his hand over hers, closed his fingers, and directed the pace. "A little harder. You won't break me. Short, fast strokes, then shift to longer, slower ones. Mixing it up feels really good."

He let go once she got the hang of it, because he wanted her hand on him, not his own. Katrina learned fast, and damn if she wasn't an expert at jacking him off.

Maybe too much of an expert. He finally grasped her wrist.

"That's enough for now."

"Why?"

"Because if you keep doing that I'll come."

She gave him a very hot smile. "Isn't that the idea?"

"Generally, yeah, but I want to come in you, while I'm fucking you."

"I like that idea. How about we do that now?"

Her eagerness to explore excited him. And he couldn't deny he wanted to fuck her. Hell, he'd wanted her since the first time he'd laid eyes on her in Barbados. Now she was naked and in his bed.

What he hadn't expected was her lack of experience.

He was going to take care of that now. But he was going to take it slow.

He rolled over and pulled the box of condoms out of his bedside drawer, lifting a packet out.

"Glad you're prepared," she said. "Also, I'm on the pill. Not that I expected to have sex tonight—or any night, for that matter. It's to regulate my periods."

She paused, then stared at him. "You so didn't need to know that, did you?"

He caressed her leg. "It's a good thing to know. We're doubly covered that way. But either way, I'm always safe."

She wrapped her arms around her knees. "I like knowing that. It makes you more attractive."

"So, I was less attractive before I whipped out the condoms?"

She laughed. "I don't think it's possible for you to be less attractive."

He pushed her back onto the bed. "I'm glad you think so."

He pressed his lips to hers, moving his body on top of hers to test how she'd feel about that. She opened her legs and he nestled his body between them, letting his cock ride against her sex.

It felt good to be there, to feel her legs wrap around his hips. He thrust against her, letting his erection tease her clit, warm her up as he deepened the kiss and threaded his fingers into her hair.

He wanted her relaxed, not tense and thinking about what was going to happen, so he took his time teasing her mouth with his, listening to her moans, connecting with the movements of her body.

She was turned on and into what they were doing. So was he, and it was damn hard not to thrust into her, to feel her heat wrap around him, especially when she arched her pelvis against him.

He wanted to feel her come when he was inside her, to feel that grip of her pussy squeezing him when she climaxed. Just the thought of it, of how that would send him reeling into his own orgasm made him thrust against her sex.

"Grant," she whispered, her fingers digging into his shoulders. "I need you inside of me now."

He knew that urgency. He pulled away from her to open the condom wrapper.

"Now that's sexy," she said as she watched him apply the condom.

He'd never thought so, but having her watch him so intently? Now that made his dick twitch.

He spread her legs and slid into her, easy and slow.

"Tell me if it hurts."

"I told you I'm not really a virgin. I've had other things in there."

"Things. Tell me what kinds of things." He inched in a little more. She was tight, hot, and wet, and he wanted to drive in deep. But he held back.

"Dildos. Vibrators." She breathed in and out and lifted against him. "I even tried a cucumber once."

"Fuck, Katrina." Unable to resist anymore, he shoved to the hilt, burying himself in her.

She gasped. "I had to know what it felt like to get fucked."

He scooped her butt in his hands and tilted her pelvis up, needing to angle her so he could feel her—really feel her. God, she felt so good.

"Well, now you know what it feels like to get fucked." He withdrew, then thrust again.

She planted her feet on the mattress and met his thrusts with one of her own, giving as good as she got. "Yes, I do. It feels good. Really good. Now give it to me hard. And don't hold back."

She was going to make him explode. His brains were going to leak out his ears and he was going to die fucking this woman.

And he didn't think he'd care.

KATRINA HAD NEVER FELT ANYTHING LIKE THIS. OF course she'd never felt anything like this, because this was a man. A living, breathing, human male and not a toy.

It was an amazing feeling having Grant's cock moving inside her, his body sliding over hers, his chest rubbing against her breasts.

And, oh, God, he knew just how to maneuver his body so that he rubbed her clit.

"You feel good," he said, his lips brushing against her ear. "Hot. Tight. Wet. Do you know how that squeezes my cock, Katrina?"

The way he spoke to her, his voice husky and dark as he moved within her, made her body tighten around him.

"You make me want to come," he said. "And when I do, I'm going to push deep inside you and fill you."

She'd dreamed about this, about what it would be like to have a man fuck her. But never in her wildest imaginings had she thought it would be this . . .

Amazing.

He didn't just use his cock on her. He kissed her neck, her mouth, teased her earlobe with his teeth. And he swept his hands down her rib cage to grasp her hip, to raise her leg so he could sink deeper inside her.

He talked to her, told her how it felt for him, about how she felt to him.

It was sensory overload of the best kind. She was swept away, her mind and body both trying to process everything she was experiencing.

And when she tightened around his cock and came, she tilted her head back and expressed herself with a loud cry. In response, Grant gripped her tightly and groaned against her neck, laving her neck with his tongue and shuddering against her.

She never knew that experiencing a man's orgasm could extend her own, but it did. She wrapped her legs around him and held him deep within her, riding out the waves of pleasure that fully swamped her.

Breathing was difficult after that. They clung together, their bodies attached by sweat and tangled limbs. The ends of her hair stuck to his chest.

She'd never known anything more perfect.

Or more terrifying, because now that she'd had this, self-induced pleasure was never going to be adequate again.

Grant caught her attention by pressing his lips to hers. "You okay?"

"I'm . . . perfect."

He grinned down at her. "Yeah, you are."

She laughed. "No, seriously. That was awesome. You were amazing."

"See? I told you I'd get to awesome and amazing."

She laughed. "You did, didn't you? Well, you succeeded."

He rolled away and disposed of the condom, then held out his hand to her. "Come on. We both need a shower."

He was right about that. She followed him into the bathroom, where he indulged her even more in his oversized shower. He soaped her back—and her front—which she found all kinds of fun. Plus she had the opportunity to touch him by soaping him up. She liked having free rein to run her hands over his body, and wasn't at all surprised when he got hard again.

"If I didn't feel like I'd already used you enough tonight, I'd want to be inside you again."

"I'm not a fragile flower, you know."

He gave her a hot look, turned off the shower and tugged her out, barely giving her time to dry off before her threw her on the bed.

He was inside her again before her feet were off the floor.

Grant was apparently a master at condom application, because he'd done it so quickly she'd hardly noticed. She had no complaints about that, because having her hands all over him in the shower had done erotic things to her thought processes, and all she'd wanted was to feel him buried deep.

This time it was quick and dirty. He sucked her nipples and fucked her hard, rubbing his pelvis over her clit.

She didn't think she could come again.

She was wrong. She came hard and fast and bit his shoulder when she did. He groaned against her and took her mouth in a deep, wholly satisfying kiss when he came, leaving them both out of breath.

When he lifted his head, his eyes looked dark and dangerous, his hair still a little damp. She brushed it away from his face.

"We might need another shower," he said.

Her lips curved. "I can do this song and dance all night."

He rolled her over on top of him. "So can I. Should we see who gives in first and passes out?"

"I've done all-night shoots on two hours of sleep, Cassidy. You might be surprised which one of us gives in first."

Around four a.m., they both fell asleep in the middle of sex.

Katrina would call that a joint victory.

EIGHTEEN

KATRINA'S MAKEUP ARTIST HAD GIVEN HER THE EVIL eye the entire day, making harsh comments about the dark circles under her eyes.

Yeah, she'd screwed up.

Grant had driven her back to her hotel at seven that morning. And okay, maybe three hours' sleep wasn't such a great idea the night before a shoot, but despite his comments, Carlos had put cucumber slices on her eyes before he'd applied makeup.

It wasn't like she hadn't gone without sleep before a shoot. She'd done late shoots the night before an early shoot and she'd always managed just fine. Maybe not three-hours-of-sleep fine, but she'd done okay.

Today, though, she was sore and tender, and Carlos had asked her about a couple of suspicious "marks" on her body he'd had to cover up with body makeup.

"Is that a hickey on your neck?" he'd asked with mock horror and a knowing smile.

She'd slapped her hand to her neck. "I do not have a hickey. Don't be ridiculous."

Though she had recalled, in the fuzzy part of her brain that was semi functioning, that maybe Grant had sucked on her neck while he was moving deep inside of her.

She hadn't minded at the time. In fact, she recalled that particular maneuver had made her come pretty hard.

Just the thought of it had her tightening all over.

"Quit flushing," Carlos had said, which had gotten him started all over again about staying up too late and how hard he was going to have to work to mask the effects of her partying.

"I assure you, I was not partying."

"Well, whatever you did into the wee hours of last night, it's all over your face. And, apparently, your neck."

She knew he was baiting her for details, which would not be forthcoming.

The shoot had gone well so far, despite her exhaustion. She was a professional. It didn't matter if she was tired or sick or whatever, she'd suck it up and do her job. They'd done two sets of shoots today—one by herself and one with bridesmaids. Next up was a change of outfits and they were going to do a shoot with her and a groom.

"I'm looking for—oh, there you are. They said you'd be in here."

She looked up at the sound of Grant's voice.

She was shocked to see him there. "What are you doing here?"

"Practice ended early today, so I thought I'd pop in and check you out."

He looked good in jeans and a white short-sleeved T-shirt. He was tan, his hair looked freshly showered, reminding her of their escapade—okay, more than one—in the shower last night.

"Your face is flushing again, Katrina," Carlos said. "And who might this be?"

"Carlos Zenera, this is Grant Cassidy."

Grant came over and shook Carlos's hand.

Carlos gave Grant an up-and-down critical examination.

"Are you the hickey guy?"

Grant frowned, then glanced down at Katrina. "I gave you a hickey?"

Carlos stepped behind her. "No use denying it now, honey. Hot stuff has confessed."

She was mortified.

"Also, oh my God," Carlos whispered at her back. "Well done."

Now everyone was going to know about her and Grant, because when you sat in the makeup chair, Carlos gossiped about everyone he knew and what and who they were doing.

"So you came to see Katrina?" Carlos asked Grant. "How do you two know each other?"

Katrina got up. "I need to go get dressed. Take a walk with me," she said to Grant. She kissed Carlos on the cheek. "Thank you for the makeup fix. We'll chat later."

"You can bet on it," Carlos said, giving her the fingers to the eyes and back as she walked away.

Grant laid his hand on the small of her back as they walked, his touch burning through the thin material of her silk robe.

They walked down the hallway toward the dressing area.

"So . . . a hickey, huh?"

He couldn't look more pleased with himself.

Men.

"You cannot tell anyone about us."

He arched a brow. "Yeah? Why not?"

"Because you just . . . can't. That's why."

He folded his arms over each other. "So I'm okay to fuck, but not bring out in public?"

She hurriedly looked around. "Oh, my God. Why would you think that?"

He laughed. "Relax. I know you're working. I just wanted to watch since I had some free time. If you need me to leave, I can cut out."

He was taking this so well. Probably a lot better than she would have if he'd said to her what she'd just said to him. She took a deep breath, then exhaled. "No. It's okay. You can stay. Though frankly, I think you'll find it boring. There's a lot of standing around and resetting for the shoots. Well, you know. You've done this kind of thing before."

"I don't mind. And if I get bored, I'll take off."

She nodded. "All right. I have to go get dressed. My next shot is by the building. You'll see us."

"I think I can handle it."

She went and met the staff, who dressed her, then her assistant led her outside.

"We're ready for you, Katrina," the photographer said. "I need you and Elliott here."

She'd worked with Elliott before on other shoots. He was professional, always showed up on time and he sometimes brought his wife along to the exotic locations to take vacations. He was a really nice guy.

She smiled at him. "How's it going?"

"Good. I just have the shoot today, then Sharma and I are heading out to St. Thomas."

"Oh, such a great place for a shoot. I'm jealous."

He grinned as they turned to face each other according to the photographer's directions. "Yeah. We're finally ready to settle

down and make a baby, so I figure that's the perfect place. I only
shoot for three days, then we're taking a week extra for 'us' time."

She couldn't help but smile at the thought. She laid her hand on
his arm. "Aww. I hope it's a great baby-making spot for the two
of you."

He grinned. "Me, too."

The shoot went well. She and Elliott fell into an easy rhythm,
laughing with each other as they posed together. She had on a hel-
laciously tough dress with a corset, so bending was difficult. Showcasing the dress was paramount, of course, as was setting a
romantic mood. Elliott was as helpful as possible, and she was glad
she had him as a partner for this segment.

All in all, it took about an hour and a half. By the time they
were finished, her back was aching and she couldn't wait to get out
of the dress.

She kissed Elliott on the cheek and wished him and Sharma
well on their baby-making vacation, then moved off toward the
dressing area.

It was only then that she noticed Grant standing in the shade.
He had put on dark sunglasses, which made him look tall, dark,
and oh so dangerous.

She'd totally forgotten about him.

"You're still here. I'm so sorry. I got caught up with work."

"That's what you're supposed to do, isn't it?" He picked up her
hand and kissed the back of it. "You look beautiful, by the way."

"This dress is a pain in the ass. The corset is tight as hell and I
can hardly breathe. I don't know why some woman would want to
wear it on her wedding day."

He laughed and walked with her toward the building they were
using for dressing and makeup.

"So you're more a get married in the courthouse kind of woman?"

She shrugged. "I've never given it any thought, to be honest."

"Really? I thought wedding day stuff was something all women thought about from the time they were little girls."

Weddings made her think of marriage. Which made her think of her mother. Then her father. Him leaving, making promises he hadn't kept. And why she never wanted to get married or be tied to a man.

She stood at the door to the dressing area. "Not me. All I've thought about from the time I was seventeen was making sure my brother and sister had food, a roof over their heads, education, and that they never felt abandoned like I did."

Once again, she'd opened her mouth and all these truths spilled out. She had no idea why she kept doing that with Grant. Now he stood there, studying her, and she felt exposed. And it wasn't because of the clingy, tight-as-hell dress. No, she felt emotionally vulnerable. And that scared the hell out of her.

"I . . . have a few things to finish."

Fortunately, he didn't ask her to expound on her truth-telling. He simply said, "I'll wait for you."

She didn't know what else to say, having said too much already, so she nodded and slipped away.

NINETEEN

KATRINA CONSTANTLY SURPRISED HIM. NOT ONLY WAS she fun and sexy, but she was also serious.

Maybe too serious sometimes.

Oh, sure, she took her job seriously. He admired that about her, because he did the same thing. There was always plenty of time for play, but when it came time to work, you had to focus. He had no time for people who didn't respect their work. He already knew Katrina did, because he'd seen it firsthand.

She had plenty of professional goals. But he had no idea she didn't have personal dreams.

Not that every woman needed to have dreams of getting married, or that some dude on a white horse holding a sword over his head would swoop in and save her. He was starting to learn a little more about her every time he was with her, though, and it was becoming more and more apparent to him that she'd sacrificed a lot for her family.

Her youth, and all the fun that should have been associated with that. When he was seventeen, he'd been partying his ass off. Yeah, football and college had been a priority for him, and he'd been damn serious about it, but he'd also found time for partying and girls and doing all those fun things a young guy should be doing.

Katrina, though? She'd landed a job as a model, and as far as he could tell, she hadn't partied anything off. She'd had a laser focus on making money, establishing her career, and making sure Leo and Anya had been taken care of.

Admirable as hell. And really sucked for her.

Maybe it was high time she make up for that lack of fun.

He could definitely help in that area.

So when she finished talking to the photographer, he grabbed her hand.

"Hungry?"

"I'm actually more tired than hungry. Someone kept me up late last night."

"Yeah, I noticed that when you passed out before I did."

She tugged on his hand. "I believe it was you who gave out first."

He studied her, loving her competitive spirit. "Let's call it a draw."

"If that's what you need to feel better about yourself."

He smirked. "Okay, food first, then I'll let you get some sleep, since I'm sure you had a full day of work and barely ate anything."

She sighed. "You're right about that. As much as I'd like to fall face-first on the hotel's bed and sleep, I do need to eat something."

He waited outside while she went and changed clothes. When she came out, she was wearing a light blue sundress and her hair fell down her back in soft black waves.

He'd like to lose himself in her hair, tangle his fingers in it, bury his nose in it while he was buried inside of her.

His cock twitched just thinking about it, so he figured he'd better think about something else. He walked up to meet her.

"You look pretty."

"Thank you. I feel like a wreck."

He led her to his car, opened the door for her and waited while she slid into the seat, then went around to the other side.

"What are you hungry for?" he asked as he started up the car.

"About ten hours of sleep."

"Okay. I was going to take you to a nice restaurant to eat, then show you the sights of the city, but I don't think you're up for that. How about we grab some pizza and go back to my place, instead? We can kick back and relax."

"Sounds perfect."

He made the call to the pizza place from the car so it was ready when he pulled into the lot. He dashed in and picked it up, then made the short drive to the house.

They set up in the kitchen. Katrina put out plates, while Grant poured drinks for them.

"I didn't get a chance to ask you how your day went," she said as she grabbed a slice of pizza.

"Practice was fine. We're ready for the game this weekend."

"Still preseason, right?"

"Yeah. You should stay the weekend and watch the game. In fact, we should fly Leo and Anya out for the game. You all can hang out here at the house."

She paused, mid-bite. "Oh, I don't think so."

"Why not?"

Her brain was fuzzy and she couldn't think up a legitimate excuse. It was summer, nearing the start of school. Camp was over, and the kids had nothing going on. "I . . ."

He grinned. "Great. I'll make travel arrangements for them. We'll fly them out tomorrow."

She blinked, feeling like she'd just been bulldozed. But she was too tired to fight it. The kids would enjoy seeing another game. Plus, they'd never been to St. Louis. "All right."

They finished their pizza.

"Would you like to take a swim?"

Normally she'd jump at the chance, but as she stifled a yawn, she shook her head. "I don't think so."

He nodded. "How about we sit on the sofa and watch a movie instead? I can make travel arrangements."

"Okay. I'll call the kids."

She made a quick phone call, talking to both Leo and Anya, who were very much on board with the trip. She wasn't surprised at all about that. Anya barely spent three minutes on the phone with her before saying she had to pack, so she turned her over to Leo, who then gave the phone to Cerissa.

Katrina peeked over at Grant's laptop as he finished up the travel arrangements. She gave him Cerissa's e-mail, and Grant forwarded the information to Katrina, copying Cerissa as well so she'd have the pertinent information when she took the kids to the airport tomorrow.

She finished her phone conversation, then laid the phone on the table.

"All set. Wasn't that easy?"

Surprisingly, it had been. "Thanks for this. Leo and Anya are very excited."

"I am, too." He turned the television on, and scrolled through the movie selections. "See anything you like?"

"I like comedies. Action movies. Suspense. You choose. I'm fine with anything."

She leaned back on the sofa, kicked off her sandals and put her feet up.

He settled on a channel where a movie was just starting. "Here's a suspense."

"Perfect."

She didn't make it ten minutes into the movie before she yawned again.

"Lay your head in my lap."

She wasn't going to say no to that. It was much more comfortable lying down.

And then, when he started rubbing her back, she knew she was a goner. His hand glided over her skin, not rubbing hard. Just gentle, soft, strokes.

She was asleep in minutes.

TWENTY

ONCE AGAIN, GRANT TOOK KATRINA BACK TO HER hotel, but this time it wasn't after only a few hours' sleep. Sometime after she'd fallen asleep on the sofa, he'd picked her up and carried her to his bed. She remembered him lifting her dress over her head, and he'd helped her unhook her bra.

And that was it, because she'd slid under the cool sheets, her head had hit the pillow, and she'd been out for the entire night.

Some hot date she'd been.

She'd apologized for that the next morning, but he'd laughed and said he'd been pretty tired, too. He'd even admitted to falling asleep on the sofa with her, and that he'd awakened around midnight to put them both to bed.

So maybe she wasn't the only dud in the bunch. But they'd both had a very exuberant, very late night the night before, so now they were both very well rested.

Unfortunately they both had to work today, so he dropped her off at her hotel with a quick brush of his lips across hers, and then he was off to practice. She took a quick shower and headed out again. At least they only needed her for half a day, because they were shooting with other models.

In the afternoon she was meeting the kids at the airport and they were going to Grant's place.

The photography went fast, which she was grateful for. This had been a great photo shoot. The director knew exactly what he wanted, which meant there hadn't been a lot of waiting around, which could be interminable hell on models. Clothing and hairstyle changes had gone quickly, and, when they'd finished, she'd thanked the entire production team and her fellow models.

After scrubbing off her makeup, brushing out her hair, and changing clothes, she'd grabbed a taxi to the airport. She picked up Leo and Anya, and at the baggage claim there was a driver who had her name written on a large white card.

"I'm Katrina Korsova," she said.

"Mr. Cassidy sent a car for you and your party."

"Ooh, we're a party," Anya said over her shoulder. "Let's rock this."

They took their bags and followed him to the limo. Really, Grant didn't have to send a limo when she and the kids could have grabbed a taxi.

"Sweet," Leo said, sliding in and putting on his earbuds.

She tried to never spoil the kids. They took cabs or they walked in the city. This was extravagant and a little over the top, but Anya seemed to be enjoying it, while Leo tuned into his music, though they both looked out the window at the sights.

"I want to see the Gateway Arch if we have time," Anya said. "I've heard the view up there is amazing."

"We'll see if there's time."

The limo pulled up to the house. There was an older woman at the open front door.

"You must be Katrina," she said. "I'm Gail Josephs. I'm Grant's next-door neighbor."

"Oh. Hello."

"I have a key to his house and he asked me to let you in."

He'd texted her earlier and told her about Gail, since he wouldn't get out of practice today until about five.

"Very nice to meet you, Gail. This is my brother, Leo, and my sister, Anya."

"Hello. You have a beautiful family. And speaking of families, my daughter is coming by shortly, so I have to run. Do you need anything?"

"No, we're fine. Thank you."

Gail ran off, so she led the kids inside.

"This house is big," Leo said.

"And this kitchen. Wow." Anya took a look around, her gaze gravitating to the back door. "Plus, a pool. I'm going to take a dip. Where do we change?"

She hadn't even thought to ask Grant about what rooms, but fortunately there was a note from him on the kitchen counter.

Tell the kids to pick any room they like—other than mine, of course.
You can put your things in my room.

—G

She wrinkled her nose at that. Staying in Grant's room with the kids here? She didn't think that was a good idea.

"Grant said to pick any room you want—except his."

"Imagine that," Anya said. "I think with the two of you in there, it'll be crowded enough."

Katrina gaped at her. "What makes you think I'm staying in Grant's room? With him?"

Leo rolled his eyes, then looked at his sister. "She thinks we're naïve."

"Right? Come on, Leo. Let's choose our rooms."

And just like that, her brother and sister completely assumed she was sleeping with Grant.

Maybe she was the old-fashioned one. Though she was hardly old-fashioned.

Whatever. She gave up trying to shelter them. Maybe they were right. They weren't babies anymore and they knew what was what. She picked up her bag and carried it upstairs to Grant's room, then changed into her swimsuit and cover-up.

When she came downstairs, she found the kids outside, both of them already in the pool.

Nothing like making themselves at home. She shrugged and made herself a glass of iced tea, then headed outside.

"This place is great," Anya said, swimming over to the side of the pool.

Katrina took off her cover-up and slid into a chair. "It is, isn't it?"

"I can't believe some hot babe hasn't scooped up Grant and married the hell out of him."

"Your language, Anya."

"Okay, whatever. But you know what I mean. He's a catch, Kat. He's good-looking, obviously makes great money based on the house and all the land here. Plus, he plays sports. What's there not to like?"

What indeed, if a woman was looking to settle down with a man.

Which she decidedly was not. She liked her life just fine. She was single and independent, and needed no man to complete her already complete lifestyle.

Though the sex was an added plus.

She didn't need to be married to have sex, though. She just needed to alter her current lifestyle to accommodate having sex more often. Now that Grant had introduced her to it, she definitely wanted more of it.

But monogamy? Or, God forbid, marriage? So not for her. She'd seen how that had worked for her mother, who'd been dedicated to a man who'd abandoned her—and his children—when they'd needed him the most. And then Mom had died, and her children had been left alone.

No, thanks. She'd made sure to put away enough money so that Leo and Anya would never have to depend on anyone.

And neither would she.

They spent time lying in the sun and swimming in the pool. Grant showed up about an hour later. She hadn't heard him arrive home, because he came out back shirtless and in his board shorts.

"I see you all made yourselves at home."

"That's us," Anya said, floating on a mat in the center of the pool. "Thanks for inviting us, by the way. Your house is great."

"You're welcome." He pulled up a spot at the edge of the pool next to Katrina. "Everything going okay? Kids' flight on time?"

She nodded. "Fine. How was practice today?"

"Intense. And hot as hell. I need a dip. You look like you could use one, too."

Before she could say anything, he'd grabbed her by the waist and dumped her in the pool, following her in. Then it was a free-for-all as Leo, who'd been listening to music in a chair, dove in, and Anya dunked herself.

They spent the next hour or so hanging out in the water playing volleyball, which was all kinds of fun, especially for Katrina to watch.

Grant was so great with the kids. And he was ruthless with Leo, picking him up and throwing him around whenever he missed a shot since it was women versus men.

Leo loved it. Why wouldn't he, since he had no father or uncles to roughhouse with him. He was in heaven. She'd never seen her brother so unguarded, laughing out loud and giving as good as he got. There was just no way Grant was going to allow her brother to be sullen and introverted.

She liked that part a lot.

Finally, Grant pulled himself out of the water. "I don't know about the rest of you, but I'm hungry. I stopped on the way home and bought some stuff to put out on the grill."

Katrina got out of the water as well, and with one look at Anya and Leo, they were out of the pool, too. "We'll dry off and help."

"You don't have to," Grant said, grabbing one of the towels nearby. "I can handle this."

"What kind of guests would we be if we allowed you to do all the work?" Katrina finished drying off, then put on her cover-up. "Besides, the kids and I love to prep food and cook."

"Just try to keep me and Katrina out of that awesome kitchen," Anya said.

Grant nodded. "Okay, then. Let's get started."

They did the prep work for the chicken kabobs in the kitchen. Grant rinsed and sliced the chicken and carved the pineapple, then Leo sliced the pineapple into chunks while Katrina and Anya took care of the other vegetables.

"I have an amazing teriyaki sauce recipe for this," Anya said.

Grant looked at Katrina, who nodded at him. "Go for it," he said to Anya. "My kitchen is yours."

She hunted down the ingredients she needed, then mixed the sauce and set the kabobs into the marinade. "Twenty minutes should do it."

Katrina had dug out the rice maker, so she started the rice cooking. By then it was time to take the kabobs outside and put them on the grill. Grant was already out there with Leo.

While he cooked, Katrina looked around.

"You know, you have enough room in this patio area for a complete outdoor kitchen."

Anya squinted, then nodded. "That's a great idea. Built-in oven here, outside the overhang so you can cook here. Maybe separated by a stone wall to keep the heat away from guests. Plenty of room for ceiling fans, too, to cool the area down and keep the flies away. Prep area over there. Big eating and entertainment area here."

"Yes. With a huge multiple burner grill for cooking, with storage space underneath. And in the yard area to the west between those two giant trees, a hammock," Katrina added, then turned to face Grant. "You could do some serious entertaining back here. God knows you have the space."

Grant closed the grill and watched Katrina and Anya talk, verbally renovating his patio. Obviously they were having a great time, and their ideas weren't bad, either.

"Oh, you know what?" Anya said. "I have a template for room renovations on my tablet. Let me go grab it real quick. Then we can move stuff around, really visualize."

Now it was getting serious.

Leo shrugged. "They do this a lot. You get used to it."

"Obviously they enjoy it."

"They do. But they're right, you know. You could do so much more with your space back here."

He tried not to smile. "So you have some ideas of your own?"

"Maybe."

"Hit me."

Leo pointed. "A zip line from the far tree over there in the woodland section to the one over there."

Grant arched a brow. "Huh. That's an interesting idea."

"Are you insane, Leo? A zip line?" Katrina cast a horrified look in their direction.

"What's wrong with a zip line?" Grant asked.

"Think of the liability issues. My God, the amount of insurance you'd have to carry—and what if someone fell? Someone could get hurt. You could get sued."

They all stared at her.

"You are seriously no fun, Kat," Anya said, coming back with her tablet.

"What Anya said," Leo added.

"I didn't say I was going to hook up a bungee cord today, Katrina, so don't worry. I just said it was an intriguing idea."

"Well, un-intrigue yourself. It's a terrible idea."

Leo leaned into him. "A zip line from the woods directly to the house would be even better. People could drop into the pool along the way."

"I heard that, Leo," Katrina said.

Leo threw a smirk Grant's way.

The kid's sense of humor mirrored his. He liked this kid. He enjoyed them both.

He liked their sister an awful lot, too.

They ate dinner inside because it was brutally hot outside. After they cleaned up, everyone dashed upstairs to change out of their swimsuits. When they reunited downstairs, he had a surprise for the kids. He led them to the basement, waiting for their reaction when they saw what he had down there.

"Holy crap," Leo said, marveling at the media room with its wide screen and comfortable, leather theater seats. "And there's gaming stuff here, too."

Anya turned to him. "See? This is why you need to expand your outdoor entertainment area. That plus this? Your guests would never want to leave."

Grant looked over at Katrina. "I'm not sure that's such a good idea."

She laughed.

The kids amused themselves that evening playing video games for a while. Even Grant got in on the action, and before long, they'd convinced Katrina to join them. She had to admit, it was fun, though she obviously wasn't as well versed in whatever universe they were playing in, and got her butt kicked frequently. But she enjoyed a nice relaxing evening with her siblings, laughing as they hunted her down and killed her more than once.

"You guys are ruthless," she said.

"Hey, don't blame us if Grant doesn't have your back on the battlefield," Leo said.

"Not my fault," Grant said, keeping his eyes on the screen. "She keeps going in the wrong direction. I can't protect her if she's heading the opposite way."

"There's too many buttons on this controller. I can't figure out what to do with them all."

"That's because you don't play enough," Leo said.

She decided to take a break from the carnage, letting her soldier—or character, or whatever—die, much to Grant's dismay. She went upstairs to refresh her drink. When she came back down, she didn't reenter the game, just watched for a while, and surveyed the rest of Grant's unfinished basement. It was cool down here, even in the hot summer. Which gave her even more ideas. Taking some time to amuse herself while the rest of them finished out their battle, she grabbed Anya's tablet and used her sister's home decorating app to flesh out some thoughts that had popped into her head.

She curled up on one of the side sofas and lost herself in her ideas.

"What are you working on over here?"

Grant's warm breath tickled her neck. "You'll laugh."

"I doubt it. Looks like you're renovating the basement now." He came around and sat next to her. "Show me what you've got."

"Well, you've done this amazing media room, but people have

to go upstairs for drinks. It's nice and cool down here, and you have plenty of space for a wine cellar, plus a wet bar over here."

He studied the plans she'd created, then looked over the space in the basement.

"Definitely doable. I've been wondering what to do with the unfinished part of the basement."

She fiddled with the design. "Then you could soundproof this room, close it off from the dressing room and laundry area, but both areas would still have doors leading to the stairwell so people could get upstairs."

He glanced over at her. "I really do like this idea, Katrina. Plus the outdoor barbecue. You and Anya are good at this."

She shrugged. "Just playing, really."

He laid his hand over hers. "No, I'm serious. Can you e-mail this to me? I want to talk it over with my contractor. I think this is something he could get started on right away. We could do the outside entertainment area before the cold weather sets in, and they could work indoors this winter."

He was taking this way too seriously. "You know we did not mean for you to spend money renovating your house. We were just throwing out silly ideas."

His lips curved. "That would be fun if the ideas were crazy. But these are realistic and would add value to the house. Why wouldn't I take them seriously, especially if it's something I want to do?"

She stared at him. "You are taking this seriously."

"Well . . . yeah. My mom's been after me to finish the house for a while now—especially the basement. I haven't given it a lot of thought. Now I am."

Anya flipped around and faced them. "So you're going to do it?"

Grant gave her a grin. "I think so."

"Very cool. I want to come back when the outside kitchen is

finished. I think it's going to look awesome." She turned around and went back to the game.

Until Leo paused the game again and turned around. "The zip line, too?"

Grant laughed. "I don't think that one's gonna fly, buddy."

Leo faced the game again, shaking his head. "Too bad. You could be really popular if you did the zip line."

"I think Grant is popular enough without it," Katrina said.

Grant called an end to the game and they agreed on some epic movie watching, though everyone argued over what to watch. Anya wanted a romantic comedy. Leo picked a horror movie, and in the end, Katrina and Grant won out with an action flick, which Anya and Leo grudgingly accepted.

They made popcorn, everyone refilled their drinks, and they settled in to watch the movie.

The sound was amazing, and Katrina was convinced that once the room was enclosed and soundproofed, it could be even better. The movie was pretty fantastic, too, with nonstop action. Even the kids admitted to liking it.

Once it was over, though, Katrina and Grant headed upstairs, leaving the kids to watch the movies they wanted.

"Don't stay up too late," Katrina said.

"Or what?" Leo asked. "We'll be tired for school tomorrow?"

She pinned him with a look.

"He's kind of got you there," Grant said, then turned to Leo. "You should stay up all night. Then when I wake you around eight, you'll really enjoy it."

Leo frowned. "Why would you wake me that early?"

Grant arched a brow and gave Leo a smug smile. "Wouldn't you like to know?"

"Fine. I'll go to bed after the next movie's over."

"Good plan." Grant turned to Katrina, winked at her, then followed her upstairs.

"Why are you waking him at eight?"

"And wouldn't you like to know, too."

In the kitchen, she pivoted to face him. "Actually, I would like to know."

"I'm taking him to practice with me tomorrow. If that's okay with you."

She thought maybe he was trying to teach him some kind of football discipline, like getting up early, even in the summer. She hadn't expected this. "Oh, Grant, he's going to love that."

"Thought he might. He won't be able to run drills or anything, but he can watch a pro team practice."

"He'll enjoy every second of it. Thank you."

He shrugged. "It's not a big deal. I cleared it with the coaches, and they're fine with him hanging out. But it'll be a full day."

"That's fine. I was thinking of taking Anya with me tomorrow."

"Yeah? What are you two going to do?"

"I have to meet with the photographer and review the final photos, make sure everything's set. Maybe do a couple more shots. After that, I thought we'd go up to the Arch since she wanted to see it."

"I'm sure you'll enjoy that. Oh, and the Rivers are playing tomorrow night."

She gave him a blank look.

"Baseball team. My brother plays for them. I thought we'd all catch a game."

"Sounds great. The kids will like that."

He brushed his fingertip across her lower lip. "You will, too."

"If you say so."

He caged her between him and the counter. "So, I'm getting kind of sleepy. How about you?"

She wasn't tired at all, but she got the gist of his suggestion. "Maybe a little."

"I saw your stuff in my room. You okay staying there with me with the kids here?"

"I wasn't at first. They seemed to be matter-of-fact about it, like it would be ridiculous for me to stay anywhere else."

"Kids are a lot smarter than we give them credit for. I think they probably know we're sleeping together."

"I guess so. And it's not like they're my children. I don't know. They confuse me sometimes. I'm confused about it. About us. I don't want to give the kids the wrong idea."

"About us? I don't think they're all that concerned about what's going on between you and me. I think they're more involved with themselves and having a good time. Don't worry so much about it. Besides, they're not babies anymore, Kat. They're practically adults."

She sighed. "Don't remind me."

His eyes glittered with amusement. "I assume you've had the talk with them—you know, about sex."

She pushed at his chest and freed herself. "I think they probably know more about sex than I do."

He took her hand and tugged her toward the stairs. "Then let's fix that."

"Hey, I was just kidding." But she allowed herself to get dragged along.

Though she really wasn't all that reluctant.

Grant thought she had a lot to learn. She might not have a lot of practical experience, but she knew a lot more about sex than he might imagine.

She might as well put that book knowledge to good use.

On Grant.

TWENTY-ONE

GRANT HAD THOROUGHLY ENJOYED SPENDING TIME with Leo and Anya today.

But that meant he had to be on his best behavior, which meant keeping his hands off Katrina, and that had been damn hard to do.

Coming outside this afternoon and seeing her lounging by the pool in her bikini had been a lesson in restraint. All he'd wanted to do was put his hands—and his mouth—on her.

Now that they were alone and in his room, with the door firmly shut and locked, and the teenagers two floors below them, he intended to touch and kiss her until he had his fill, and until she got everything she wanted.

She sat at the foot of his bed, eyeing him with a mixture of wariness and expectation as he approached.

"So, Kat, tell me your fantasies. What have you been studying up on, sex-wise, that you'd like to experience."

Her lips curved, and damn if that wasn't one of the sexiest

expressions he'd ever seen. It made her violet blue eyes smolder darker.

"I have a long list."

"We have all the time in the world, and we don't have to get to it all tonight. Pick something from your list."

"How about we start in the shower—together?"

He liked where this was going.

"Sure."

She got up, took him by the hand and led him into the bathroom.

"After all, we need to wash off all that chlorine." She lifted her tank top off, then popped the clasp on her bra and let it fall to the floor, baring her gorgeous breasts.

"Of course." He drew his shirt off and added it to the pile, watching her shimmy out of her shorts and underwear while he shed the rest of his clothes.

He turned on the shower, setting the water temperature, then stepped in, taking her hand and drawing her in with him. There were jets on both sides of the wall, so they were both getting wet.

Katrina tilted her head back, wetting her hair. Grant grabbed the bottle of shampoo and poured some in his hand.

"Turn around."

She did, and he slid the shampoo in her hair, coating the strands before moving back up to massage her scalp.

"Mmm, that feels good."

What felt good was the sound of her voice as he washed her hair. Just touching her like this—even in a nonsexual way—got him hard. Slipping his fingers through every strand of her hair, rubbing his fingers across her head, everything about her turned him on.

"Rinse."

She did, and he grabbed conditioner, coating the strands of her hair with it, rubbing it into the ends of her hair.

She half turned to look at him. "I probably shouldn't ask this, but how do you know so much about washing and conditioning a woman's hair?"

He gave her a half smile. "I have a little sister. I got stuck baby-sitting now and then when she was small and had to give her a bath. Conditioner doesn't go on the top of the head."

She nodded. "It's good for guys to learn these things."

"That's what my mom said."

She rinsed her hair, then turned around. "Now it's my turn."

She soaped up her hands, and washed his hair. This was something new for him.

"I don't think a woman has ever washed my hair—other than when I go to the hair place and they cut it."

"Then the women you've been with are stupid."

She was tall, so he only had to bend a little for her to get the shampoo on his head. And oh, man, he liked her hands on his head and in his hair. She knew not to treat his head gently. She massaged his head hard, really digging in and it felt great, especially when she used her thumbs at the back of his neck.

"I might have to ask you to give me a massage," he said. "You have very good hands."

"I think we could arrange that. As long as we're naked." She slid her soapy hand around and stroked his cock, making him suck in a breath. Now that she could do for a very long time and he wouldn't complain at all.

"Yeah, that kind of a massage. It feels good to have your hand on me."

"Like this? With long strokes?"

He swallowed, lost in the feel of her hand wrapped around him. "Yes."

"We'll get back to that in a minute. Rinse your hair."

He enjoyed this side of her, when she was relaxed and playful.

He rinsed his hair, and when he opened his eyes she had the bottle of body wash.

"How about you wash me now?"

Grant was looking forward to this. He poured body wash onto his hands and rubbed them together, forming a lather. He started on her back, massaging her muscles as he soaped her up, taking in the sounds of her moans, which only made his dick throb harder.

And when he slid one finger between her buttocks, she leaned forward and palmed the wall of the shower, letting out a low moan.

"That feels good," she said.

He moved in closer. "Does it?" He moved one hand around and cupped her sex, rubbing back and forth until her breath caught, while teasing her anus with his finger.

"Oh. Oh, God, yes. Keep doing that. Keep touching me there."

Now they were getting somewhere. He was learning what she liked, what turned her on, and she was driving him crazy. He wanted to be inside her so badly he was ready to explode.

But right now he wanted her to explode.

He kept up the movements of his hands, sliding a finger inside her pussy while using the heel of his hand to make contact with her clit and using a gentle back and forth motion across her anus.

"I want—"

She didn't finish, but he knew, so he slid the tip of his finger into her ass.

"Oh, yes. That's what I want. All the way in."

He loved that she gave him direction, that she told him what she needed.

He pushed his finger inside her anus, while thrusting his finger into her pussy and increasing the pressure on her clit.

"Oh, I'm coming." Her body tightened around his fingers as she came with a hard orgasm. He felt every part of her shudder for a good long minute that left him ready to go off as well.

When he withdrew, he washed his hands, turned her around, and kissed her, needing to take her mouth, her tongue, envelop her in the passion that had overtaken him. She wound her hand around the nape of his neck and wrapped her leg around his hip.

He needed a goddamn condom and he needed it now.

Breathless, Kat broke the kiss, her body still quivering from the orgasm that had left her weak and shaking.

Katrina had never experienced anything like that, had been so focused on what Grant had been doing to her that she'd lost all sense of time and place. She might have screamed. She couldn't remember, and right now, she couldn't care. All she knew was she wanted more.

And from the heated looks Grant gave her, she knew he was ready as well. He quickly grabbed soap and washed his body, then turned the shower off. They climbed out, dried off, and headed to the bedroom.

"I need to fuck you," he said pushing her onto the bed. "Right now. I need to come hard in you."

Having a man nearly shaking with need for her was a heady realization. What he'd done to her in the shower—the heights of pleasure he'd taken her to—had shattered her.

She spread her legs. "Do it to me again, Grant. Make me come like that again."

With a low growl, he grabbed a condom and tore the wrapper open. She expected him to thrust inside her, but instead he went lower, kissing her inner thighs before burying his face in her sex.

Oh, the things the man could do with his tongue. He lapped at her pussy, then moved up to her clit, sliding his lips and tongue over her until she was ready to scream again. She was shaking all over, so close to an orgasm she had grasped his hair and was arching her pussy against his face.

Only then did he climb up her body, kiss her deeply, then put on the condom and thrust into her.

He raised himself up on his arms. "Now we'll come together. I want you to squeeze the come right out of me, Kat."

She reached up and slid her fingers over his lower lip. "Make me."

Again, that animalistic growl that never ceased to make her sex flutter. He dropped down on top of her and cupped her butt with his hand, tilting her pelvis up so he could grind against her.

"I'll make you. I'll make you come so hard you won't even know your own name."

He kissed her, his tongue doing delicious things to hers. The kiss was deep and heady and she lost all sense of herself as he seduced her with his mouth and with his cock. And when she exploded, he was right. She was gone, an out-of-body experience, and she had no idea who she was. She knew only pleasure, only the slide of her hands across hard muscle, the feel of her pussy clenching his cock as stars exploded behind her eyes. She heard his loud groan as he went with her, felt them both shuddering together, then collapsing, holding on to each other like a lifeline in a storm of ecstasy.

He'd taken her breath away, exceeded all her expectations as to what sex was all about. And now, as he lay next to her, rubbing her back and kissing her shoulder, she realized she'd waited entirely too long for this sex thing.

Or maybe she'd waited just the right amount of time. Because Grant was pretty damn good at this. So maybe she'd just been waiting for the right guy to introduce her to it.

"Tired?" he asked.

"Mmm-hmm."

He brushed his hand over the top of her head, then kissed it and tugged her against his chest. "Sleep, Kat."

That sounded like a really good idea. "Okay."

TWENTY-TWO

GRANT WAS PRETTY GOOD ABOUT SWITCHING FROM play mode to game mode.

Last night with Katrina had been all about play. Today, it was getting into game mode. There were three days until the game, and even though it was still preseason, with every game, they drew closer to finalizing the team and the start of the actual season.

He worked with the offensive coordinator and the backup quarterbacks, trying to confirm the plays they'd use this year. He spent time trying out the rookie receivers to see who would make the team, who was going to fit with the organization this year.

All in all, there was a lot going on right now, especially for those who were busting their asses to make the roster.

Grant was the starting quarterback. His job was set. But he knew there were other guys on the bubble. His job was to help the team figure out which guys would stay, and which would go.

He'd explained all this to Leo as they'd driven in this morning.

He was pleasantly surprised to find Leo up and ready when he'd come down at seven-thirty for coffee.

"It's not even eight a.m. yet," he'd told him.

"I figured whatever you had in mind for me today, I'd better be early," Leo had said.

Katrina might be worried all the time about these kids, but she'd done a fine job giving them the right tools they'd need to succeed. Leo had the work ethic in place. Now it was up to Grant to tap into it.

When Grant had told Leo he was taking him to practice today, Leo's eyes had widened. He was so excited, even though Grant had told him he couldn't work out with the team or anything.

"It's just watching, ya know?"

"I don't care," Leo said. "I'm excited just to be there to see the team go through practice. It's the closest I'll ever get to seeing a pro team do this."

Grant slung his arm around Leo's shoulders. "At least until you make a pro team yourself."

Leo let out a snort. "Yeah, like that's ever gonna happen."

Grant had stopped him there. "With an attitude like that, it never will. If you don't believe in yourself, how do you expect anyone else to? How will a college coach believe you've got what it takes to make the team?"

Leo had looked embarrassed. "Okay, you're right. I'm fast and I'm good enough. I know it. I'm just getting a late start, is all."

Grant slapped him on the back. "That's better."

Grant introduced Leo to all the guys in the locker room, then placed him with one of the assistant offensive coaches, who promised Grant he'd explain everything there was to know about football.

Grant was certain Leo was going to get one hell of an education today. There would be yelling and cussing, and if Katrina knew that, she'd likely be horrified. But this was a player's world, and Grant was confident Leo could handle it.

In fact, during one of their drink breaks, Grant spotted Leo glued to the coach's side as the coach was screaming obscenities at one of the wide receivers. Leo was doing his best to suppress a grin.

Yeah, the kid was doing fine.

So was the team. Rookies looked acceptable; the few guys they'd signed during free agency were a good fit. They'd shored up holes in the defense, and JP McClellan was back on the offensive line after an injury last season. Grant felt confident in his team this year.

Grant had been studying the playbook when Cole Riley came over.

"How's it going, Cassidy?" Cole asked.

"It's going so great that I think you're going to have a good year, because I'm going to be throwing to you a lot."

Cole grinned. "Of course you are, man. Because I'm a superstar wide receiver. And you're the superstar QB."

Grant laughed. "Yeah."

"Isn't that Katrina Korsova's brother? The one you introduced me to the other day?" Cole asked, tilting his head toward the sidelines.

"Yeah. He's interested in playing football, so I brought him along with me today to give him some insight."

"Cool. So you're dating Katrina? Since when?"

"Since, I guess that shoot I did with her in Barbados."

Cole nodded. "She's hot."

"She's smart and funny and beautiful. A lot more than just hot."

Cole held up his hands. "Hey, you don't have to convince me. I married smart and funny and beautiful."

Grant laughed. "How is Savannah?"

"She's great. She's in Los Angeles right now, working on an image rehab for a basketball player."

Grant slapped Cole on the back. "You got lucky getting her to marry you, since you're such an asshole."

"Don't I know it."

He and Cole met up with the other receivers and quarterbacks to go over a few plays with the coaches, then it was back to practice. The drills were going well, and they had a game plan for this weekend.

When practice ended, he fetched Leo from the coach.

"How did it go?" he asked as they left the locker room and headed for the parking lot.

"It was fantastic," Leo said. "I mean, I mostly stayed out of the way and watched, but Coach asked me some questions. And when he found out I haven't played football yet, but that's what I want to do—like really wanna do—he gave me some tips on how to bulk up, and what I should be doing to prep for the upcoming football season. And he said if I really wanted to make the team, I should start working out at least four days a week and keep running."

Grant smiled. Coach had given Leo sound advice. He wasn't blowing smoke up Leo's ass by saying it. "That's great."

"Yeah. And then he made me run drills with the receivers. Did you see that?"

He had, but he figured Leo would want to tell him all about it. "Is that right? How did that go?"

"They smoked me, of course. But Coach said I was fast." Leo turned and started jogging backward. "Can you believe that? He said I was lightning fast. That's good, right?"

"That's really good. He thinks you have potential."

Leo was beaming. Grant was glad he'd invited him along today. The kid needed a lot of big boosts in his self-esteem, especially as it related to football. He really wanted Leo believing in himself, that he could do it.

Today helped.

"So, you like baseball, too, right?" Grant asked Leo after they'd pulled out onto the highway.

"Sure."

"My brother, Tucker, plays for the Rivers."

Leo nodded. "I know. He pitches."

"Yeah. I thought we might catch a game tonight, since the Rivers are finishing up a home series."

"No shit. I mean, yeah, I'd love to go. Kat doesn't really follow baseball. You think she'll let us?"

"I already talked to her about it. She said it sounded like fun."

Leo shook his head. "You're a good influence on her. At least sports-wise. Before you, she would have never gone to a baseball game."

Grant laughed. "Good to know."

They headed back home. The girls weren't back yet, so Leo went up to his room to take a shower and change clothes. Grant made a few calls and went through his mail. He had given Katrina the code for his garage door and keys to one of his cars, which she was a little unsure about, but he'd told her it had GPS, so she could plug in addresses, and she and Anya could go wherever they wanted.

Anya had been excited about having a day to explore and Katrina had seemed happy to have the freedom of his Camry, even if she was a little nervous about driving in a strange city. He hadn't been worried. He knew Katrina would be fine.

When he heard the garage door open, he went to greet them.

They were carrying packages. A lot of packages.

"Let me take those," he said, grabbing the bags from both Katrina and Anya. He set them on the counter. "Did a little shopping today, huh?"

"Yes," Anya said. "We found a great mall. And you'll be happy to know Kat didn't hit anything with your car."

Grant laughed. "I wasn't worried about it at all."

"I was," Katrina said, laying her purse on the counter next to the bags. "I don't have an opportunity to drive all that often. I was a little rusty."

"Well, now you've had practice."

"Maybe you could teach me to drive, Grant," Anya said. "It's a major crime that I'm seventeen and don't have a license yet."

"You live in New York and don't need to drive," Katrina said.

"You live in New York, too," Anya shot back. "Yet you have a driver's license."

Katrina shrugged. "I figured at some point I might need to drive a car, so I took driving lessons a long time ago and got my license."

Anya looked to Grant. "See? Which means at some point I might need to know how to drive."

Katrina sighed.

Grant laughed. "She has a point."

Katrina slid Grant a look, then directed her attention to Anya. "Fine. We'll see about taking care of that this year."

Anya grinned. "Awesome."

"So what did you all buy?"

"Kat and I both got new capris. I love mine and I'm definitely wearing them to the game tonight. Kat bought pillows for your sofa. I helped pick them out. We argued for a good twenty minutes over which ones. She won, but only because she has the credit card."

He looked over at Katrina. "You bought pillows for my sofa?"

"Yes." Katrina went to the counter and pulled two pillows from the bag. "I thought you needed something extra on your sofas. They'll add a nice design element and be extra comfortable."

He didn't know much about decorating, but the pillows were a tan with black and looked nice on his couches. What he really liked was that she'd thought about him.

"They look great. Thank you." He put his arms around her as she surveyed the sofas. "It was so thoughtful of you."

She shrugged. "It's not a big deal."

"It is to me."

"Before you two make out or something, I'm going upstairs to change," Anya said, scrunching her face up and grabbing her bags.

Grant grinned as she left the room. But she winked at him as she walked by.

He got the idea Anya approved of him.

For some reason, that meant something to him.

He turned Katrina around in his arms and brushed his lips over hers. She melted against him, so he deepened the kiss, intending to take just a quick taste. But she felt good, her body warm and pliant. He was getting hard, and he didn't know when the kids would be back downstairs, so he pulled back.

"Did you have fun today?"

"We did. I only had to do a quick reshoot, so we were out of there within a couple of hours, which left us the entire day to go sightseeing and shopping."

"Did you visit the Arch?"

She shook her head. "We were going to, but we ran out of time."

He nodded. "Maybe we can fit it in tomorrow. I could take you."

"Don't you have practice?"

She palmed his chest, her nails digging in just a little. It made his blood rush. He wondered if there was time to sneak upstairs to his bedroom. The idea of a quickie appealed.

"I'll have time to take you all to the Arch tomorrow."

He was just about to tug on her hand, to lead her upstairs, when Leo came down.

"Oh, hi, Leo," Katrina said. "How was your day with Grant and the team?"

Time was up. He left Katrina and Leo to talk. He ran upstairs and changed clothes. When Katrina came up and closed the door behind her, he turned to face her.

"Everyone ready to go?"

She nodded. "It'll only take me a few minutes to get ready."

"Don't worry about it. We have plenty of time."

He was going to head downstairs, but then Katrina asked him to help her unzip her sundress.

That got his attention. He walked into the bathroom.

"Turn around," he said.

She did, facing the mirror.

"Pretty dress."

Her gaze met his in the mirror, her lips turning up into a smile. "Thanks."

He drew the zipper down, his knuckles brushing bare flesh. He couldn't resist as he bared the skin of her back, so he leaned in and pressed a kiss to her shoulder.

"Do we have time for this?" she asked.

He gently pressed on her back, bending her forward. "Absolutely not."

Moving into her, he was already hard when his crotch met her butt, rubbing his body against hers. He closed his eyes and allowed himself to feel her, the heat of her, breathing in the scent she gave off.

It was heady, and he wanted her.

"If you're going to fuck me, you should unzip, and I should get out of this underwear."

He opened his eyes, saw the passion reflected in hers, and dropped down on his haunches, reaching under her dress. He found her panties and pulled them down.

"I wish I had time to eat you, make you come," he said, lifting her dress and pressing a kiss to her hip bone.

She let out a breath. "I do, too."

He stood, opened the center drawer and took out a condom from the box there. "I'll make you come another way. With my fingers, when I'm inside you, fucking you deep."

"Grant."

His name floated from her lips like a sexy whisper. He unzipped his pants, put the condom on, then lifted her dress over her butt. Damn, she had a pretty ass. He took a minute to let his hands roam over her, slid his fingers between her legs.

"You're wet," he said.

"I'm ready for you. Just you talking to me, touching me . . . I'm ready."

He pulled the straps of her dress down over her shoulders, taking her bra with it, baring her breasts. He cupped a handful of her, rolling her nipple between his fingers as he slid into her pussy.

"Oh," she said, pushing against him as he thrust.

He let his hand roam down, palming her sex, rubbing her clit as he drove into her again and again.

"Yes, there," she said, giving him momentum.

He'd been consumed by her since that kiss downstairs. Looking at her, breathing her in—she made him want her in ways that were inexplicable to him.

She tightened around him, gripping him, making this pleasure unbearable. He needed to come in her, but first, she was going to come.

He played with her clit, listening to the sounds she made as he moved within her. He was learning her body, finding out what hit her hot buttons. She liked him to move his hand fast and easy against her, and as she clenched around him in orgasm, he shoved deep in her and let go, shuddering as he came, feeling her body unravel around him in deep, rhythmic waves.

He was sweating against her back, out of breath and had never felt anything so good.

She lifted up and leaned against him. "I'm going to need a quick shower now."

"Yeah, me too."

They both jumped in the shower and did a quick rinse off. He got dressed, then got out of Katrina's way and headed downstairs.

"What is she doing up there?" Anya asked. "It usually takes me twice as long as her to get ready."

Grant just shrugged. "No idea. I think she might have changed her mind about what she was wearing. Or . . . wait. I think she said something about hopping in the shower."

Anya rolled her eyes. "Whatever."

She went back to scrolling through her phone, so he figured they had managed to skate by without the kids figuring out what had happened upstairs. Or maybe the kids were smarter than he gave them credit for and they simply didn't care.

Either way, Katrina came downstairs a short time later, looking gorgeous in her new black capri pants that hugged her curves. She wore a hot pink tank and tennis shoes and looked absolutely edible.

How could a woman dressed so casually look so damn sexy? He wanted to undress her and lick every inch of her.

He filed that thought away for later.

They drove to the ballpark and made their way to the ticket window, where, thanks to his brother, tickets were waiting. He'd texted Tucker yesterday after he'd gotten the idea to take Katrina and the kids to the ball game.

That had been a fun conversation.

I need four tickets to tomorrow night's game.

Tucker had texted him back with: *Asshole. Next time give me more notice when you want four seats. You'll be lucky if I can get you bleachers. We're popular, ya know.*

Grant had texted back with: *But you can get me box seats anyway, right?*

Tucker had ignored him for about an hour, then texted back with: *Probably. And fuck you.*

Grant grinned when he opened the envelope with his name on it and found four box seat tickets.

Because that's what the brothers did for each other. They gave each other shit, then they pulled through when necessary.

They went through the gates and Grant led them through the crowd and up to the stands.

"Wow," Leo said as they found their place. "These are great seats."

They were along the first-base line with an excellent view.

"Tucker's having a good season," Leo said, reviewing his brother's stats on his phone. "He's twelve and three so far on the season, with a two point three earned run average. He's also got over a hundred strikeouts. He's like a beast out there."

Grant smirked. "Yeah, he's doing good."

And then Leo proceeded to lean across him and explain to Kat what all that meant.

She listened intently and nodded, and he had to give her credit for at least appearing to act interested.

"So Tucker's a pitcher," she said after Leo focused himself elsewhere.

"Yes."

"And the rest of your brothers play football?"

"Yeah."

"So why did Tucker decide on baseball?"

Grant leaned back in the seat. "We're not sure if it was because he loved this game more than football, or if he did it just to piss off Barrett."

At Katrina's curious stare, he said, "Barrett and Tucker are twins. Barrett plays safety—that's defense—for the Tampa Hawks. He's one mean, tough, sonofabitch and I've never known anyone who loved football more than Barrett."

"More than you?" she asked.

Grant laughed. "Yeah, probably. Though I think my dad loves football more than all of us."

"So was your dad upset when Tucker decided to play baseball?" Leo asked.

"Not at all. Dad just wanted us all to do what made us happy. The fact that all of us ended up in sports was a bonus. He would have been just as happy if we'd been accountants. He didn't care."

Katrina focused her gaze on the pitcher's mound, where Grant's brother, Tucker, was taking warm-ups.

He was tall, like Grant, and had dark hair he wore a little long. But he also wore black glasses, which Katrina had to admit didn't detract from his attractiveness at all, at least not from what she could tell from this distance. And the pitches he threw were fast. Like, wow fast.

"Did you ever play baseball?" she asked Grant.

He nodded. "I played Little League when I was a kid. By the time I got to high school, I realized I wanted to focus on football. That's when Tucker moved strictly to baseball. He got a scholarship to play ball at Oklahoma."

"So he's really good."

"Yeah, he's really good."

"He's not only a good pitcher, he can hit, too," Leo said, still apparently studying his stats. "He's hitting three twenty-nine with runners in scoring position."

"Impressive." She didn't know all that much about baseball, but she did watch it some when Leo was catching the games on TV. And she liked statistics, so when he'd talk about hitting percentages and averages, she paid attention. They'd discuss the players, who was good and who was struggling at bat.

As a result she knew hitting three twenty-nine was amazing. Okay, maybe she knew a little more about baseball than she'd thought.

"Who's hungry?" Grant asked. "Hot dogs and beer? Soda for you kids, of course."

"You're no fun," Anya said, then winked. "I'll go with you."

That was a surprise, but she was glad Anya had a male figure to bond with. Having grown up without a father, she knew Anya hungered for a dad. Not that she'd missed anything with their own father, who'd been absent for most of Katrina's childhood, busying himself with work during the day and womanizing at night.

Katrina's mother thought she didn't know about the other women, but once she'd gotten old enough, she'd heard the whispered phone calls and had snuck out to follow him one night, curious about where he was going. She'd seen him with another woman, had watched him kiss her at the front door of her apartment before following her inside.

It had broken her heart. She'd never said a word about it to her mother, but she'd seen the sadness in her mother's eyes, and knew her mother was well aware of what her father had been up to.

And then Mom had gotten sick, and Dad had permanently disappeared. No doubt because he couldn't deal with Mom's illness and three children who so desperately needed him.

Coward.

Anya was much better off without a father like that. Though she'd never tell Anya or Leo about Dad. They only know he disappeared. They thought he went back to Russia. It was a story she told everyone. Or that he was dead. She'd made up various versions over the years to cover for his disappearance.

Whatever. Much better for everyone to think that instead of him shacking up with some woman. No one else needed to know what she absolutely knew was truth. That her father hadn't loved them enough to stay.

Hearing the sound of Anya's laughter, she looked up to see her sister and Grant making their way down the stairs, the two of them leaning into each other while juggling sodas, beer, and hot dogs.

Her sister had a serious case of hero worship going on. Katrina wasn't sure that was a good thing. She didn't want either Leo or Anya to form too close an attachment to Grant, since her relationship with him was, at best, a temporary thing.

Not much she could do about it now, though, since it appeared both the kids had bonded with him.

Then again, school would be starting up soon, and Grant would be forgotten once they got involved in their friends and activities again, so maybe she was worrying for nothing.

Grant handed her a hot dog and a cup of beer.

"Ballpark staple. It's like a ritual," he said. "Besides, hot dogs and beer taste like an expensive bottle of champagne, plus caviar, when you eat them at the ballpark."

She gave him a dubious look. "Seriously. You tried this on me in New York, and I have to tell you, the hot dog tasted like a hot dog."

"This is different. Would I lie to you about something this sacred?"

He had a serious look on his face, so she shrugged. "Of course you wouldn't. I'm certain this hot dog and beer will be a truly religious experience."

"See, now I want a beer," Anya said.

"And you can certainly have one."

Her sister's eyes brightened.

"In four years, when you turn twenty-one."

Anya pouted her lips, then looked to Grant. "See how abusive she is?"

Grant laughed. "Yeah, I can tell you're regularly tortured."

The teams were introduced, and Katrina ate her hot dog, which, again, tasted like a regular hot dog to her. Clearly she was missing something about hot dogs.

It was really hot out tonight, though, and the beer was refreshingly cold. Not exactly a life-changing moment, but she wasn't going to say that to Grant, who looked at her with a hopeful expression on his face.

"Good?"

"Amazing."

He looked suspicious. "Somehow I think you've had better dinners."

"Well, yes, of course. But as ballpark fare goes, this was good."

"And how many ballpark meals have you actually had?"

"Uh . . . not a lot. But this ranked right up there. Seriously, it was a good hot dog. And remember, I live in New York. I have very discerning taste in hot dogs."

"This is true," Anya said. "It's a great dog. Though I can't really state how good the beer is."

Anya gave Katrina a hopeful look.

Katrina shook her head. "No beer for you."

Anya huffed out a sigh, and then it was time for the game to start.

Tucker was pitching first, so Katrina had someone to focus on besides the very good-looking man sitting next to her and her constantly chirping siblings.

She studied his mechanics, the velocity of his pitches, while

Grant explained the types of pitches his brother threw. Apparently he had several, including what Grant described as one very nasty curveball.

"I know nothing about the different pitches," she admitted, which led Grant, Leo, and Anya to explain them to her every time Tucker threw one. Grant even demonstrated how one would hold the ball in his hand for the curveball.

"Tucker's got a unique spin on his, too," Grant said. "I've never seen one like it."

Next time Tucker threw a curve, she noticed the downward dive of the ball. And the way the hitter swung and missed.

"His curves are hard to hit," Leo said. "When he throws them perfectly, they're impossible to hit."

"Plus, a lot of hitters are fastball hitters," Anya said. "The curve is their nemesis."

By the end of the game, the St. Louis Rivers had scored three runs. Los Angeles had scored none and they'd only had six hits. Tucker was impressive.

Grant had been extremely patient, explaining the subtle nuances of baseball to her. She'd found herself thoroughly enjoying the game—a lot more than she'd expected.

As they filed out of the stadium, she leaned into Grant. "Will we get a chance to meet your brother tonight?"

Grant shook his head. "Unfortunately, no. He has to catch a flight to Houston for his next series."

"That's too bad. I wanted to congratulate him on such a good game."

"Yeah, I'm sure he would have enjoyed that. Maybe some other time."

She had no idea when that would be since they were heading home soon. But it had still been a great night.

They got back to Grant's place, and Leo and Anya immediately scattered. Anya headed outside toward the pool with her phone, no doubt to text her friends, and Leo went downstairs. He'd asked Grant on the way home if he could play a game, which of course Grant said yes to.

They found themselves alone in the kitchen. She lifted her gaze to Grant.

"Thank you for taking us to the game."

"You're welcome."

"I'm sure the kids will thank you once they catch up with their friends."

He smiled. "Hey, I was a teenager once, too. I know the priority. Don't worry about it."

"I worry about them being polite and they should have thanked you."

"They did. Anya thanked me when we went to get the hot dogs, and Leo did when we were talking stats before the game."

"They did?"

He moved into her, slipping his arms around her waist. "Yeah, so quit worrying."

"It's my job to worry. I have to make sure I'm not raising assholes. There's already too many of those out there."

He swept his knuckles against her cheek, the action gentle and calming. "Yeah, I know. But Leo and Anya aren't assholes. They're awesome, so take the night off from being the anxious parent, okay?"

She sighed. "Okay."

"Good."

Anya came in from outside, her face buried in her phone as she was deep in conversation with a friend.

"Uh, hang on a sec, Leah." She tucked the phone in her neck, went to the fridge and grabbed a bottled water, then made her way over to Kat and kissed her on the cheek. "Heading up to my room for the night. Oh, and thanks again for the game, Grant. I had fun."

"Me, too. Good night, Anya."

She waved her hand above her head as she disappeared up the stairs.

Grant looked at her. "See?"

Katrina exhaled. "I guess you're right."

"Of course I am. Now, how about some wine?"

"I'd rather have beer. It's so hot tonight."

"Works for me." He went to the fridge and pulled out two cans of beer, handing one to her. "Now you can really relax, right?"

"Yes." He was right. She had to let it go. At least for tonight, anyway.

She started to pull up a seat at the kitchen island, but he shook his head.

"Come with me."

She expected him to take her upstairs, but he surprised her when he led her out back.

"Stop here, first. It's summer, and I don't want you bitten up by mosquitos."

She arched a brow. "Where, exactly, are we going?"

"You'll see."

He pulled a bottle out of one of the cabinets. "This stuff doesn't stink, but it'll keep the bugs from biting."

"Good to know." She stood still while he sprayed the exposed parts of her body, then did his own. He took her hand and they walked outside.

She thought they were going to sit by the pool, but he surprised her by walking around it and heading toward the wooded area behind it.

"Kind of dark back there at night."

He squeezed her hand. "Yeah, but I know where I'm going."

"You do? And where might that be? Don't forget I read crime thrillers."

He laughed. "Trust me."

"Oh, sure. That's what every serial killer says. Right before he chops the poor victim up in small pieces."

"Damn. And I forgot my knife. I'm doing this all wrong."

She slid a glare at him, though it was ineffective in the darkness. "So not funny."

Then he gave her an evil laugh, and she was even less amused. She tried to pull her hand away, but he put his arm around her. "I promise I have only good intentions—mostly."

She didn't know whether to laugh or cry. But since she was already in the woods with him, she supposed she'd go along for the ride—or walk.

Besides, she was alone in the dark with a very attractive man.

Somehow she got the idea he had more in mind than just a walk.

That she was very interested in. And like her favorite books, she couldn't wait to see what was going to happen next.

TWENTY-THREE

GRANT DIDN'T INTEND ON SCARING KATRINA, BUT HE could tell she took every step cautiously, as if she didn't quite trust his intentions. He didn't know whether to laugh or be insulted by that.

So he took his time leading her into the woods to the cabin by the pond.

"This is where you bring your victims, right?" she asked.

He turned to face her, unsure if she was really that scared. But then he caught the upturned corners of her mouth. Relief washed over him. For some reason it was important that she trust him.

"This is where I bring you. Only you. And sometimes where I go fishing. It was a big highlight of the property when I bought it."

He led her along the path. He knew it well enough he could see it in the dark, but he still took his time, pointing out fallen limbs and rocks so Katrina wouldn't trip over anything. When they got through to the clearing, he led her to the edge of the pond. There was just a sliver of moon tonight, enough for her to see the water.

"It's beautiful here," she said, her voice lowered to a whisper.

"Yeah. It's a nice peaceful place to get away on my own and do some thinking."

She tilted her head as she looked at him. "Do you have a lot to think about?"

"Sometimes. If I have a bad game or occasionally pregame, I'll come out here with my fishing pole and think about what went wrong or how I want to approach a game plan. It's so quiet with nothing to distract me, it helps my mind-set."

She stared out over the water, then nodded. "I can see that. It's a good meditation spot."

He'd always considered it a good fishing spot, but he understood what she meant. "Yeah."

"What's in the shack?" she asked.

"Fridge, sink, a small bathroom, and a bed. Not much, really. I've thought about tearing it down and building something bigger, like a guesthouse kind of thing."

"Can I see it?"

"Sure."

Since the property was well fenced, he never locked the door. He turned the knob and opened the door, waiting for Katrina to walk in before he closed the door and turned on the small light in there.

"This is interesting," she said, moving into the very small sitting area that only had space for a couple of chairs.

Immediately past that was what one would generously call a kitchen, with a mini fridge and a sink. No stove, though.

"There's a bathroom through that door on the right. Just a toilet and sink. No shower. And the bed tucked into this room."

She peeked into the room and saw the twin bed. "Yes, you definitely need to tear this down and build a guest cottage. You need more space and a full kitchen."

He could already see her mind whirling with ideas. "I assume you'll drag Anya out here tomorrow with her tablet, and the two of you will sketch out some ideas?"

She was still looking around. "Maybe."

He put an arm around her shoulders. "Good. I could use a few ideas, and so far the ones you've come up with have been great. Have at it."

She turned in his arms, then laid her beer next to the sink. "I have a few ideas."

He set his can beside hers and grasped her hips, enjoying the feel of her. "I'd like to hear those ideas."

"Well, it involves getting naked. Or semi-naked. I feel like we were just warming up before the ball game tonight and we didn't get to finish what we started. Being in such a hurry and all."

Just the sound of her voice could get him riled up, hard, aching and ready in an instant. "Oh, I can definitely finish what we started. Right here and right now."

He left her only long enough to turn off the light, shielding them in darkness. Not that anyone knew where this place was besides him, but he wanted the privacy.

Because she was wearing those pants, and he wanted her out of them.

"Shoes off."

She toed out of her tennis shoes, and he grasped her pants, peeling them over her hips and down her legs. He tossed them in the chair. Her underwear went next, leaving her naked from the waist down.

There was just enough light in the room to see her, to see how beautiful she was. He kneeled, grasping her ankles and letting his hands roam up her legs, shouldering between them to spread her thighs.

She was leaning against the small counter, so she had balance when he put his mouth on her sex.

He heard her breathe in sharply when he flicked out his tongue over her clit. He drew his tongue down, taking a slow, long taste of her. She was salty honey, pouring over his lips and tongue as he laved her sex until he felt her tremble.

He grew harder, and palmed his cock as he licked her over and over, listening to her breathing and her moans as he took her right to the edge.

"Yes, right there," she said. "That's going to make me come."

He moved his mouth over her clit and sucked, feeling her entire body shudder as she came. He grasped her butt and pulled her closer, licking her all over as she came down from her climax.

That's what he'd wanted, that climb of pleasure for her. Making her come. Taking her there never failed to rock his goddamned world. And now he was filled with the scent of her, the taste of her lingering on his lips. He was hard as hell and aching to fuck her.

She was breathing heavily as he kissed her hip bone, then stood. He grasped the hem of her shirt and pulled it off, then nuzzled her breasts, reaching behind her to unhook her bra. She was lax, her head resting against his shoulder as he removed her bra and tossed it in the pile.

When she lifted her head, she cupped the nape of his neck and pulled him toward her for a kiss. He was full, his balls heavy with come. He dove into the kiss, groaning against her lips as her tongue slid against his.

"Mmm," she said as she laid her forehead against his. "The things I'm learning about you."

"Yeah? What kinds of things?"

She brushed her index finger against his bottom lip. "You have a very talented mouth."

He smiled. "Glad you enjoyed that."

She took a deep breath and sighed. "Very much. Now how

about you go sit on that tiny little bed in there? Oh, and take off your clothes."

He was ready to be inside of her, to feel her tight pussy surrounding him. He headed into the small bedroom, jerking his shirt off and tossing it on the floor. He kicked off his shoes and undid the button on his jeans as Katrina entered the room. He had shrugged off his pants and boxers by the time she reached him.

He threaded his arm around her waist and tugged her close. Skin to skin, he felt a surge of heat surrounding them. It was hot in here, so he reached over to raise the window, letting the night air blow in.

But he really didn't care about the heat, not when Katrina pushed him down on the bed. He sat, and she grabbed the pillow off the bed and kneeled on it, then spread his legs.

"I've been wanting to try this. It feels so good when you do it to me."

He leaned forward and slipped his fingers into her hair. "Yeah, I want you to suck me, Katrina. I want to feel your hot, wet mouth around my cock."

It was all he could do not to grasp her mouth and shove his cock in there, to hold her head and fuck her mouth. His balls tightened at the thought of her sweet lips sucking him. But this was her first time doing this, and he wanted to use restraint, to take it slow and give her all the control.

He read the excitement on her face as she leaned her arms on his thighs and took his shaft in her hands. "You know I haven't done this. But I've read a lot of books. Some erotica that had some very enticing oral sex scenes."

Her talking about it only dragged him up the ladder of need one tortured rung at a time. "Is that right? You know doing isn't the same as reading about it."

"So I've discovered. So is there anything you particularly like—or dislike—I should know about?"

"Yeah. I like your hands on me. I'm gonna love your mouth on me."

Her lips curved—a sexy, deliberate smile that told him she was looking forward to having the control.

And he was looking forward to giving it to her.

Because as she bent and licked the head of his cock, he hissed. She scooped her hair out of the way so he could watch as she took his cockhead between her lips, swirled her tongue around it, then closed her lips.

"Christ," he whispered, wanting to put his hands on her, to thrust, to do anything to ease this torment. But he held perfectly still as she raised up and took more of his shaft in her mouth.

The heat and wetness of it sizzled, a sensual fire that threatened to burn him from the inside out. Sweat dripped down his forehead as he fought for control. He grasped the sheets and held on while she continued to experiment, using her tongue, her lips, and the roof of her mouth. She varied the pressure, squeezing, then licking him, slow and easy, like she was going to torture him the rest of the night.

Until she engulfed him, taking him deep.

It was perfect. She was perfect, and when she met his gaze, he felt like the top of his head was going to come off. He fought the orgasm for as long as he could, wanting this to last forever, yet wanting it to end right fucking now.

"I'm gonna come," was all he could say, because he was lifting into her mouth, enjoying the sweet heat of her and he couldn't hold back anymore.

She gripped his shaft and squeezed, pumping more of his cock between her lips.

His hips rocketed off the bed as he came with a roar, jettisoning what felt like a gallon of come along her tongue. He felt it throughout his body, saw her cheeks hollow and her throat work as she swallowed, and when he was empty, he was covered in sweat and was unable to form words. All he could do was lift Katrina up and drag her on top of him as he fell back on the bed.

"Your heart is beating fast," she said.

"I'm surprised my heart is still beating at all. You really did do some heavy reading on the topic."

She raised herself up on his chest, gracing him again with that sexy smile that, despite the epic orgasm he'd just had, made his cock twitch. "Indeed."

He tunneled his fingers into her hair and dragged her up for a kiss, rolling her to her side so he could cup her breast and tease her nipple as he kissed her. She slung her leg over his hip, arching her sex against his quickly hardening cock.

"I don't suppose you brought a condom with you," she said.

"Do I look stupid? Of course I did." He reached onto the floor and pulled the condom packet out of his jeans pocket. "The whole reason I brought you here was to get you alone and seduce you. Though I think I feel a lot more seduced right now."

She grinned. "You do? Excellent. My work here is done."

She rolled over and tried to get up.

"I don't think so. We're not finished here."

She laughed and lay back down, scooting close to him. "Don't I know it. I believe that's what they call foreplay."

"It was a hell of a lot more than foreplay, hot stuff." He raised up and she grasped his cock, stroking him to full erection. "I'm pretty sure you blew out a few of my brain cells with that blow job."

"Now you're going to make me blush."

"I don't think it's possible to make you blush. You might not have had any practical experience, but you know what the hell you're doing."

He spread her legs and dropped down on top of her, then shifted them to their sides again, bending her knee so he could position himself against her sex. When he entered her, she leaned back to watch.

"I wish I could see where we're connected."

All he could think about was doing just that. "Next time I'll make sure we're in front of a mirror. So we can both watch me fucking you."

She pushed on him, and climbed on top. "Or me fucking you."

He grasped her hips, rolling her forward, then back, giving her clit friction. "Fucking each other."

She gasped. "Yes. Like that."

He cupped her breasts, plucked and teased her nipples until she rolled herself out lengthwise fully on top of him.

He felt encased within her, and as he thrust, she tightened around him.

"Oh, that hits me right in the clit when you do that," she said, her nails digging into his shoulders.

"So you want me to do it again." Which he did, and she moaned, which made him thrust again.

"Grant. Please."

He knew exactly what she was asking for. The same thing he wanted. Within a few thrusts she was coming, and he'd held back long enough because the way she'd positioned herself squeezed his dick in the best way possible and he was ready to go off. He came, hard, powering into her as pleasure surrounded him.

After, they lay in silence listening to the crickets outside.

"If it wasn't so damn hot outside and this bed wasn't so small, we could hide out here all night."

Katrina didn't even lift her head. "We might have to. I'm not sure I have enough energy left to get dressed and make the walk back to the house."

"Okay by me. I like you right where you are."

She managed to lift her head. "Sweating on top of you?"

He smoothed his hand over her butt. "It's a good spot."

She finally sighed and climbed off. They got dressed and walked back to the house.

"Quiet in here," she said as they entered the living room.

"I'm going to go check on Leo," Grant said.

Katrina smiled. "Thanks for that. I'm going to head up and take a shower. I'll check in on Anya before I do."

He stopped downstairs. Leo was still playing games. Since it was nearing midnight, he told Leo he could play for another half hour. No more. Leo didn't even balk, just nodded and said okay.

Grant shook his head as he grabbed a couple of waters to take upstairs. He kind of felt like a parent there for a minute, which was a unique position for him.

He had no rights to these kids. They were under Katrina's care.

But he was beginning to care for them.

And for her.

They sure as hell didn't fit his lifestyle, though. He'd been single for a long time. He'd had a few relationships here and there, but nothing serious, and none of the women he'd ever dated had kids. He came and went as he pleased. He had a lifestyle that was all about travel during the season. He didn't have anyone who depended on him, and he liked it that way.

He was totally out of his element here, and yet the whole situation felt . . . normal. He was comfortable with Leo and Anya.

And he sure as hell felt good with Katrina.

But he knew better than to rush things, especially when kids were involved.

It was time to slow down a little, maybe reevaluate where things were in this relationship.

And he knew exactly what the next step was.

TWENTY-FOUR

KATRINA, ANYA, AND LEO SPENT THE FOLLOWING morning lazing by the pool. It was fun and relaxing and Katrina couldn't recall the last time she had done absolutely nothing.

She'd checked her e-mail and nothing was pressing at the moment. There were a few e-mails from her business manager about booking jobs in the fall, but she'd look into those more closely when she got back home. No reason to rush into that when she could take a day off and enjoy hanging out with her brother and sister. It wouldn't be long before they'd be headed back to school, she'd go back to work, and they'd see a lot less of each other. The time together today—and this whole week—was an unexpected gift.

She had Grant to thank for that.

He arrived home in the middle of the afternoon and told everyone to go change clothes because they were heading out to see the Arch.

The kids loved riding the elevator up to the top of the St. Louis

Gateway Arch, and Grant obviously enjoyed taking them to the historical portion, telling them about how it had been built and all the history behind the expansion into the western territories. Katrina was surprised Anya and Leo paid such rapt attention.

"Now for the fun part," he said after they left the Arch.

"What's that?" Leo asked.

"Well, Six Flags, of course."

Anya stopped. "Aren't we a little old to go to the amusement park?"

Grant shot her a look. "Do I look old to you?"

"A little," she said, offering up a saucy smirk.

Katrina was going to let the kids fight this one out with Grant.

He kept walking to the car. "I'll have you know you are never too old to go to an amusement park. I'm shocked. You mean you all don't love roller coasters?"

He stopped and stared at all of them, as if he dared any of them to object.

"I'm a huge fan of things that go around and around and upside down until I want to throw up," Katrina said, giving him a deadpan look.

Grant arched a brow at her.

"You'll get no complaint from me," Leo said.

Anya said, "Six Flags it is, then."

He put his arm around Anya's shoulders. "Promise, you're going to love it."

He was right. The amusement park was so much fun, and Katrina couldn't remember the last time she'd been to one. Maybe when Leo was about seven? That had been a long time ago.

This one had a water park as well, so Grant had stopped at the house on the way so they could all pack up their swimsuits. They rode every ride until Katrina thought she really might throw up. She also distinctly heard her sister laugh uncontrollably on the roller coaster—several times. And then Anya insisted they ride it again.

The water park was fun, too, and on a hot day it was perfect. Grant rented a private cabana at the water park, and while Leo and Anya had run off to the waterslides, the two of them sipped cool drinks. Until Grant grabbed her hand and they took a tube ride down the river.

"I don't know when I've had more fun," she said as they held hands and coasted along the water. Kids shuffled past, splashing water everywhere. She didn't care.

"It's good to have fun. You should have fun every day."

She didn't know about that, but she was definitely enjoying this week. And so were the kids.

"Thank you for taking the time to do all these things with us. I know you're so busy with football."

He linked his fingers with hers. "Can't work all the time, Kat. Gotta spend some moments on what's important, ya know?"

She knew what was important. She had always had her priorities straight. Work and her family. That had always been it.

Right? She'd done it all right, like she was supposed to do.

But maybe a little fun now and then wasn't a bad thing.

"Hey, you two." Leo bumped his tube into theirs.

"Hey, yourself. Where's Anya?" Katrina asked.

Anya brushed her tube alongside Katrina's. "Right here."

"How was all the water sliding and such?" Katrina asked.

The kids filled them in on their death-defying waterslide activities. When they were all sufficiently waterlogged and exhausted, they left the park and grabbed pizzas on the way home.

Katrina couldn't recall pizza ever tasting quite so good before.

"Do you have work scheduled for next week?" Grant asked her as they were all eating.

Katrina shook her head. "Nothing on the horizon for a while."

"Good."

She took a long swallow of ice water. "Why?"

"I was thinking. I have a game against Dallas next week, but I have a few days off before practice starts. I was planning to visit my parents' ranch down in Texas. It's my dad's birthday on Monday, so everyone's going to try and make it in. I thought maybe you and the kids would want to go."

Leo's eyes widened. "The Cassidy ranch? Where your dad lives? Can we go, Kat?"

"Never been to a ranch before," Anya said. "Are there horses?"

"Yeah, there are horses. And some cattle, too."

"No kidding. We should go, Kat," Leo said. "I really want to meet Grant's dad. He's like a legend in football."

Katrina really wished he hadn't asked her in front of the kids. "I'll . . . think about it."

"Think hard about it," Anya said. "It would be really fun."

Katrina looked to Grant, who just offered up a hopeful smile.

They finished pizza and everyone gathered downstairs in the media room to watch a movie. After, Katrina wanted to wash off the chlorine from the day, so she went upstairs to take a shower, then put on a pair of shorts and a tank top and sat on the bed to read a book.

But thoughts of Texas kept pulling at her.

The kids wanted to go, but she didn't think it was only because they'd never been to Texas, or that Leo wanted to meet Grant's father.

She knew the kids were pushing her at Grant, shoving her toward a relationship with him. Mainly because *they* liked him. She got that. Logically, she understood their rationale. But she shouldn't foster it. She couldn't, because it wasn't realistic.

They lived in New York, and soon enough it would be time to go back to school. She had her work. Her priority. Grant had his job as well. While right now she and Grant were having fun together, that's all they had. There was no permanence to this.

Even if he was smart and fun and hot and sexy and she did like spending time with him as much as the kids did. But she was an adult, and she could make the break easier than they'd be able to.

Was she hurting Leo and Anya by allowing this to go on any longer? Wouldn't it be better to break it off now instead of heading down to Texas to meet his family? That would only prolong the inevitable and make the kids' heartbreak even more painful.

She knew what she had to do.

The problem was, she didn't want to do it.

Not right now.

Which was so selfish of her. What was wrong with her, any- way? She always made the right decisions. She'd always sacrificed what she wanted in favor of what was best for the kids.

She heard a knock on the door. It couldn't be Grant. "Come in."

It was her sister.

"So I was thinking," Anya said, slipping into her room and climbing in bed with her. "Wouldn't it be easier to do some shop- ping along the way rather than flying all the way home to unpack and repack? There are stores in Texas, you know. And we've already done laundry here. We've actually bought more clothes when we went shopping the other day. We'd only need to pick up a few things."

"I haven't yet said that we're going."

Anya tilted her head up to meet her gaze. "Oh, come on, Kat. You know you want to go. You like Grant. We all do. Let's go to Texas."

Her little sister wasn't so little anymore. Katrina uncrossed her legs and stretched out alongside Anya on the bed, unable to fathom how long her sister's legs were now. She remembered a time when Anya would huddle with her in the bed, and they would read sto- ries together.

It wouldn't be long now before Anya would be going off to college. She wouldn't need Katrina anymore. She wouldn't be in her life as much.

That's what growing up was all about.

Maybe she was overthinking this whole thing with Grant. She had to constantly remind herself that the kids weren't little—or as impressionable anymore.

Maybe she wasn't worried as much about how the kids would feel after breaking away from Grant as she was herself.

She grabbed a piece of Anya's hair and gave it a gentle tug. "I'll . . . think about it."

"You keep saying that. But you know you want to go as much as we do."

She cocked her head to the side. "Really. And what makes you think that?"

"You like Grant."

This was a topic she didn't really want to get into with her sister. "Yes. I like Grant. But you do realize there's a difference between liking someone and having a serious relationship with them."

Anya rolled her eyes. "I'm not a kid anymore, Kat. Of course I know the difference. And you know I don't have a boyfriend. Who has time for that nonsense? I'm going to college after next year. I don't even want to think about the drama of boyfriends. Dating is one thing. Relationships are a whole other package of cookies."

Out of the mouths of babes. "Indeed they are."

"Not that you would know since I've never seen you bring a guy home before. Until Grant."

"I didn't exactly bring him home. He showed up at the apartment."

Anya shrugged. "Same thing. Why? Don't you like him . . . I mean like him, like him? Like in the boyfriend way?"

In some ways, she was having a very adult conversation with her sister. In other ways, she had to remind herself she was still talking to a teenager. "He's not my boyfriend."

"Oh, really. And how would you differentiate between some guy you're hanging out with and having a boyfriend?"

Then again, her sister was very perceptive. Very smart. And sometimes quite irritating. "I'm not defining my relationship with Grant with you. I haven't even defined it with him."

Anya picked up her hand and squeezed it. "Maybe you should. Maybe there's something there between the two of you. You know, it wouldn't be the worst thing in the world if you fell in love with someone."

Yes, definitely too deep now. She tapped her finger on her sister's nose. "And you should let me get back to my book."

"So . . . about Texas?"

"I'll get back to you."

Anya sighed and climbed off the bed. "Whatever. Let me know when you decide."

When she looked up to watch Anya leave, she saw Grant leaning against the doorway.

"Talk her into it, will you?" Anya said to Grant. "She's being stubborn and vague."

"Good night, Anya," Grant said.

"Night, Grant."

Anya left the room, and Grant shut the door. Katrina wondered how much of their conversation he'd heard.

"Second thoughts about Texas?" he asked. "Or is it just you and me?"

Obviously, he'd heard plenty. "I don't know. She wants me to define our relationship."

He came over and stretched out on the bed.

"Do you feel the need to define it? Because I don't."

She couldn't help but admire the wide shoulders, the incredible chiseled biceps, or his amazing legs. But she also realized there was a lot more than physical chemistry attracting her to him.

Maybe if it was just a sexual attraction this would be easier. They could have their fun, and then go their separate ways.

But there was such a depth to him that went beyond the hot body and physical talent. He was smart and funny and he not only liked her, he liked Leo and Anya, too. The bottom line was, she enjoyed being with him.

And for her, it meant a lot.

"I guess it requires no definition. We're enjoying each other's company at the moment. Isn't that enough for now?"

"I think it is. I'm fine with taking things slow, Kat. And it's nobody's business—including your sister's—what's going on between us." He cupped her foot, began to rub it. Just a simple gesture but it fired up the heat of pleasure, and also relaxed her at the same time.

Decision made, she supposed.

"I guess we're going to Texas, then."

He looked up at her and the fire she saw in his eyes flamed her. "Glad to hear it."

She wasn't sure if she'd just made a good decision, or a really bad mistake.

She supposed she'd find out in the next week.

In the meantime, Grant pulled her down and covered her body with his, his kiss smoldering hot, awakening the fire that was always barely banked around him.

Then all thoughts of anything but him went entirely up in flames.

TWENTY-FIVE

"TELL ME ABOUT YOUR FAMILY," KATRINA SAID AS THEY made the drive from the airport to the ranch.

Grant's game had been Saturday night, and they'd left town early Sunday morning, because Grant wanted to maximize the time they could spend at the ranch. It was a lengthy drive, but fun. Grant had talked a lot to Leo about the mechanics of football and how to get himself in shape. Katrina had enjoyed listening to their conversation. He and Anya chatted about music. The man had very eclectic taste.

They'd stopped at a mall so Anya and Katrina could do some shopping for more clothes, and they'd still had plenty of time left to get there, since the ranch was only about fifty miles from Austin.

"I already told you I have three other brothers. Flynn is the oldest. I'm second oldest. Then there's Tucker and Barrett, the twins. And Mia, the youngest."

"And your dad is Easton Cassidy," Leo said. "He went to school at Texas, was drafted in the second round by Green Bay, and played his entire career there as quarterback. Fifteen seasons. Won two Super Bowls, too."

Grant laughed. "You know your football, kid."

"Who wouldn't know about your dad? He's a legend."

Easton Cassidy was more than a legend, at least to Grant. He had always just been Dad, the guy whose shoulders he had ridden on when he was a kid, and the man who broke up the fights he'd had with his brothers.

When his dad spoke, everyone listened.

Okay, everyone but Mom. Because as powerful a man as Easton Cassidy was, Lydia Cassidy was even more formidable.

"Yeah, he was a great football player. He's an even better father. He set a strong example of responsibility and honor and how to treat a woman. I've tried very hard to follow his example. Of course it helped that he married one hell of an amazing woman, who set some pretty fine examples herself."

"Tell me about your mom," Katrina said.

"Her name is Lydia. She was an attorney. She gave up her career after the twins were born and Mom and Dad bought the ranch. She decided she was a lot happier running after us crazy kids than she was dealing with the courtroom."

"What kind of law did she practice?"

"She was a prosecutor. Damn good at it, too. But it demanded a lot of her time and Dad kept getting her pregnant."

Katrina laughed. "I'm guessing he didn't get her pregnant against her will, but that she likely wanted a lot of kids."

"Okay, yeah. She did. I think you'll really like her. She's super smart, like you."

"That's a very nice thing to say, Grant. Thank you."

"It's the truth."

As they made the drive through the Double C's gates, Grant felt a pull, as always. No matter where he lived, this was always home to him. It represented family.

The dirt road blew up dust along the side of the car. He slowed down, navigating the bumps, hoping he wasn't jostling his passengers too much.

"This. Is. Amazing," Anya said. "So much space. Do you know how much land there is to roam around in New York City? None. Not at all."

"That's not true. There are plenty of places to get out and walk. And there's Central Park," Katrina said.

Leo snorted. "That's not what I would call land, Kat. How many acres do your parents have here, Grant?"

"About four hundred acres. You can do plenty of roaming around while you're here."

"Freakin' awesome," Anya said.

The dirt road turned onto the paved one about a quarter mile from the house.

"Wow," Katrina said as she spied the house up ahead.

"That's the main house where my parents live."

She tore her gaze away from the house to look at him. "There's more than one?"

His lips curved. "Yeah. There's more than one."

He pulled around the circular drive and parked along the side of the house. Grant got out, as did everyone else.

The front door opened and he saw his mom first. He'd been busy a lot lately so he hadn't seen her since the spring. He walked over to envelop her in a hug.

"How's my baby boy?"

He always smiled hearing her say that. She said it to his brothers, too, which always amused them since they all towered over her small, five-foot-four frame. "Good, Mom." He kissed her, then put an arm around her. "Come meet everyone."

She gave him a squeeze. "I can't tell you how surprised—and happy I am that you brought company."

Katrina and the kids were standing by the side of the SUV he'd rented. He motioned for them to join him, so they walked over.

"Okay, everyone. This is my mother, Lydia Cassidy. Mom, this is Katrina Korsova, her brother, Leo, and her sister, Anya."

Katrina felt suddenly nervous, but stepped forward and shook Lydia's hand. "It's very nice to meet you, Mrs. Cassidy. Thank you so much for having us."

"Please call me Lydia. Nice to meet you, too, Katrina."

Anya and Leo shook her hand, too.

"This ranch is awesome, Mrs. Cassidy," Anya said. "I can't wait to get out and explore. Grant made us buy several types of boots—the non-fashion kinds without heels."

Lydia laughed. "First, call me Lydia. Yes, you definitely might need boots. It's always dusty around here, and Grant might have a mind to take you hiking. Grant, bring the kids' luggage in while I show them around. I'm putting you and Katrina in over at the other house."

"Sure, Mom."

Katrina hesitated. The other house? She wasn't going to second-guess his mother on housing. "The kids and I can help him with luggage."

Lydia waved her hand. "He's used to being on chore duty when he gets here. Luggage will be the least of what he does. Don't worry."

Interesting. Katrina wondered what kind of chores were in store for Grant. He didn't seem to mind with the luggage though, and Katrina's attention turned to the house as they walked in.

It was a two story, and she'd already noticed the stonework out-side and the amazing landscaping. The front porch was a huge wraparound with multiple seating areas. She'd spied a garden out back as they were driving in, and she felt a little spark of envy, since she had always wanted a garden to grow things, which she couldn't do in her apartment.

Inside, there were dark wood floors and an extremely spacious living area that led into a massive open dining room with the big-gest table she'd ever seen. That room led to a beautiful kitchen that made Katrina's eyes widen.

"Your house is incredible."

"Thank you. We've remodeled over the years, opened things up some. As you can imagine, four boys ran roughshod over this place growing up. And our daughter did her part as well."

"You painted over my artwork on the wall is what you're say-ing, Mom."

Katrina turned to see a stunningly beautiful young woman walk in from out back. This had to be Grant's sister.

"Katrina," Lydia said. "This is my daughter, Mia. Mia, this is Katrina, Anya, and Leo."

Mia shook her hand. "I know who you are. I'm a big fan."

Katrina grinned. "Thank you."

"Mia is home from college for the summer. She'll be finishing up her last year at the University of Texas starting in the fall."

Katrina looked at her. "How great for you. What's your field of study?"

"Business and communications with a minor in mathematics."

"Wow. That's intense."

"Yes, but I like staying busy. And speaking of busy, you seem to be everywhere these days. I saw your cover of *Vogue*. It was gor-geous. I also love your commercials for the new shampoo. Not surprised they chose you for that campaign. Your hair is even more glorious in person."

Katrina laughed. "It helps when you have a team to style your hair for the commercials and photo shoots, but thank you."

A man who looked very much like an older version of Grant walked in through the back door.

"I heard our company had arrived."

"I hope you washed up," Lydia said.

"I did." He turned toward Katrina and held out his hand. "I'm Easton Cassidy. You must be Katrina."

"I am." She glanced at her siblings. Leo looked awestruck, like he was meeting the president. How sweet.

"This is my brother, Leo, and my sister, Anya."

"Hi, kids." Easton shook both their hands.

"I've seen your film," Leo said. "You were an awesome quarterback."

Easton grinned. "Thanks. Those days are over now, though. But I still keep my fingers on the pulse of the game, with my boys and with some of the teams I help out with."

"Mr. Cassidy helps coach one of the local high school teams nearby," Leo explained to her. "He's also part owner of the team in Houston."

Katrina was impressed. "I did not know that."

"No reason for you to," Easton said. "I take it you don't follow football all that much."

"I know some. Leo is the expert on sports. Anya loves sports as well."

"We've got a lot of experts around here. Some think they know more than others. All these youngsters coming up these days, trying to best the old man." He shot a look across the kitchen island at his daughter.

Mia shrugged. "I like statistics, Dad. I'm certainly not going to claim I know what it's like to play the game. I'll leave that to you and my idiot brothers."

"Aww, saying nice things about me, like always," Grant said as he came up behind Mia and put his arms around her.

"You're a jerk," Mia said, but smiled and bumped her head against Grant's chest.

Grant kissed the top of her head.

Katrina could see the resemblance between the two, especially in the shape of the mouth. But Mia was more petite, like her mother, with lighter brown hair and smaller features like Lydia. She also had her mother's blue eyes, whereas Grant looked a lot like his dad.

"What can I get you all to drink?" Lydia asked. "I'm sure you're thirsty from the drive. We have iced tea, beer, cold water, lemonade . . ."

"I would love some iced tea," Katrina said.

"Beer sounds good to me."

"Not yet. I want you to come look at the tractor with me," Easton said to Grant. "I think we might need to replace the carburetor."

Grant's lips curved. "In other words, Flynn isn't here yet, otherwise he'd have had it torn down and rebuilt by now."

Grant's dad let out a short laugh. "You got that right."

"Flynn had an afternoon game. He'll fly in later. Tucker will be in soon, and Barrett tomorrow morning." Lydia turned to her. "It's Easton's birthday tomorrow, and our thirtieth wedding anniversary, so the boys all decided to visit and help celebrate."

Katrina smiled. "Congratulations. What a milestone."

"It is a pretty big one. Easton and I are heading to the Caribbean for a vacation in a few weeks, but it's wonderful to have the whole family here for the occasion."

"I hope we're not intruding."

Lydia laid her hand on top of Katrina's. "You are no intrusion. We're so delighted to have the three of you here."

"Okay, Dad," Grant said. "Let's go take a look at the tractor. Leo, want to come out with us?"

"Sure."

Katrina saw the excitement on Leo's face. Being alone with Grant and Easton must be so thrilling for him. He nearly tripped over his own feet catching up with them as they headed out the back door.

"Now it's just us ladies," Lydia said. "Tell me, Anya. What grade are you in?"

"I'll be a senior."

"Wonderful. Have you visited colleges?"

She nodded. "A few, though I haven't made my mind up yet where I want to go."

"You should go to the University of Texas," Mia said, grabbing an apple from the island. "There are a lot of great programs there. Though I should ask what you're considering majoring in."

Anya took a seat next to Mia. "Actually, and I haven't discussed this with Kat yet, I really enjoy cooking."

Katrina's brows rose. "You want to go to cooking school?"

"I was thinking about it. I was also thinking about getting a bachelor's degree in hospitality first, then going to cooking school, so I'd have the management and business knowledge to go along with the culinary skills."

Mia finished slicing a few apples and had set the pieces on a plate in front of all of them. "Not a bad idea, actually. A lot of chefs don't have the business acumen to run their restaurants. I assume you're thinking long term, like opening a restaurant of your own someday."

Anya nodded. "Yes. I don't want to work in some kitchen for someone else. I have a lot of ideas."

Of course she did. "This doesn't surprise me at all. I know how much you love to cook. And you're certainly talented enough to do anything you set your mind to do. It's a wonderful idea."

Funny how she and Anya had never sat down and talked about this until now.

But it was good she knew where her sister's head was at—and her heart. Now they could make plans.

"Why don't you come upstairs with me to my room, Anya?" Mia asked. "I could clue you into some information websites I think you'd really like. They preview various colleges, what they offer, and you can link in to the specialties you're interested in. It might help you narrow down your choices."

Anya nodded. "Sure. I'd like that. Thanks."

Mia and Anya disappeared, leaving Katrina alone with Lydia.

"I would love to see the garden," she said.

"Really?" Lydia's face brightened.

"Yes. Living in New York, where space is at a premium, I can't have one. I have a terrace outside my apartment and I've tried to grow a few things in containers, with some success. But it's not the same. I saw yours when we drove up and I have to admit it was one of the first things I wanted to look at."

Lydia's lips curved into a genuine smile. "You are a woman after my own heart." She stood and Katrina did, too. "One of the things I swore when I was working the full-time grind as a prosecutor in the cold climate of Green Bay was that as soon as we bought land in Texas, I was going to have the best damn vegetable garden in the state."

Katrina laughed, and Lydia slipped her arm in Katrina's and led her out the back door.

It was amazing out there, with a full kitchen and a built-in grill, a gorgeous flagstone patio that led to a huge pool. There was plenty of area to entertain, with several spots set up for seating.

The space was fenced off, and Lydia led her through the gate toward the gardens.

"And do you have the best garden in the state?" Katrina asked.

"I'm not sure I give a damn about anyone else's garden, but mine sure does make me happy."

The garden was on the south side of the house, and quite extensive. There were a lot more beds planted than Katrina had noticed at first. She followed Lydia through.

"There's lettuce, tomatoes, cucumbers, corn way in the back there," she said as she pointed out the tall stalks growing in the field behind the beds. "Out here, there are beans and asparagus and carrots. I keep a separate bed for all the herbs."

"Anya is growing an herb garden in her bedroom window," Katrina said. "She gets plenty of light in there. So we at least have fresh herbs, but we walk down to the farmer's market on Sundays for most of our vegetables."

"A farmer's market is a great way to buy fresh produce."

Katrina leaned over to inspect one of the tomato plants. "But nothing beats the smell of a garden. It's something I've wanted my whole life."

"The drawback to city living, unfortunately. You have the advantages of everything within walking distance, though."

She straightened, then nodded at Lydia. "That much is true. I guess you have to decide what's more important."

"I've tried to talk Grant into putting a garden in his yard. He has plenty of space back there."

Katrina thought about it a moment, visualizing where it would go. "Southwest of the pool. On the side of the house. Yes, I agree, there's plenty of space for several beds. Of course, during the season he's not there. He'd have to have someone tend it for him."

"That's true. But he loves working the land here. He's been in the garden with me, harvesting vegetables."

Katrina slid a surprised look at Lydia. "Really. I can't see him doing that."

Lydia patted her arm. "Trust me. We'll have him pick some corn with us over the next few days. He's a lot more outdoorsy than you know."

Outdoorsy? Shirt off and sweaty? Yes, she would definitely like to see that. She'd look forward to watching Grant in the garden.

In fact, she was already getting a preview as she heard the noise of an engine starting up, and she could tell from the sound it wasn't a car. She saw a large green tractor with a giant scoop in front of it coming out of the barn. A shirtless Grant was driving. He turned left and disappeared around the corner of the barn.

Easton and Leo followed behind on foot, the two of them engaged in conversation. Her brother didn't even look her way. Or acknowledge her.

Obviously, Leo was comfortable with Easton. She was happy about that.

"Oh, good, they got the tractor started," Lydia said. "Come on, let's follow them and see what they're intending to dig up."

Katrina was glad she'd worn her tennis shoes, because Lydia had one heck of a fast stride, and considering Katrina was taller with longer legs, it surprised her how hard she had to hustle to keep up with Grant's mom.

But she did, and soon they'd made it to the other side of the barn, where Grant had engaged the bucket on the front and was scooping up a large pile of dirt, then relocating it to another area away from the barn.

She and Lydia stood and watched for a while. Katrina was impressed with how well Grant knew the operation of the tractor, how he could shove the bucket into the pile of dirt, scoop it up, and then maneuver the tractor between the two barns so effortlessly.

Wow. Who knew watching a man operate a tractor could be such a turn-on?

"I've been after Easton to move that pile of dirt between the barns for two weeks now. He'd dug it up to lay some drainage, and then the big tractor conked out. I'm so glad Grant was able to get it working again. Now they can get the job finished. Come on, let's go back to the house. It's hot out here."

Katrina could have stood out there for hours and watched Grant, but she followed Lydia back to the house and poured herself another glass of tea.

"Okay, about the sleeping arrangements. You and Grant will stay at one of the other houses," Lydia said.

"Oh. Okay."

"Flynn, Barrett, Tucker, and Mia aren't coupled up. I think I'm putting Barrett and Tucker at the guesthouse, and I was wondering if it would be all right if Leo and Anya stayed here at the main house with us."

"Um, you don't have to keep them here. I'm sure they can stay wherever I do."

Lydia offered up a knowing smile. "Then how will you and Grant get to be alone?"

The woman was entirely too knowing. "That's not necessary, you know."

"Please. I was young and dating once, too. I know what it's like to try and grab some time alone. And with your brother and sister along, I know you haven't had a lot of moments to yourselves. There's another house a few miles from here. You and Grant can stay there. There are five bedrooms in this house, so plenty of space for the kids."

This was the most bizarre conversation she'd ever had.

"Okay. Thank you."

"Not a problem."

She wanted to tell Lydia that there wasn't anything serious going on with her and Grant, but she supposed that would be up to Grant to discuss with his mom. It wasn't her place to define her relationship with him to his mother.

"How about I drive you over to the house? You can get your things unpacked and settle in and we can come back here and start dinner. Tucker should be here soon, and if Flynn hasn't arrived by the time we eat, then he can grab leftovers when he does."

"I don't want to put you out, Lydia. If you give me some directions, I'm sure I can find the house myself."

"Don't be ridiculous. I'm so happy to have another female here. Mia and I both are. You noticed she absconded with your sister as soon as she could, didn't you?"

"I did notice that."

"Trust me. There are a lot of men on this ranch. You just haven't seen them all yet. Easton's brother, Elijah, lives here as well. He's not here at the moment, but he'll be back tomorrow. Anyway, since his divorce six years ago, Elijah spends a lot of time hanging around us. Not that I mind. I love my brother-in-law very much. But the testosterone overload when those two get together is enough to make my head explode. You'd think they were teenagers again the way those two get on. I was happy having Mia home again for the summer, but she comes and goes a lot, as all kids her age do."

Katrina nodded. "Yes. I was just thinking the other day how it won't be long until Anya will be leaving for college. She's not my daughter or anything, but I think I was having some empty-nest pangs. I've been responsible for her since our mother died ten years ago."

Lydia grabbed a set of keys from a drawer. "Wow. That's a lot of responsibility for a young teenager to handle. Should we drive over to the house now? I'll text Mia to let her know where we are."

As Lydia and Katrina made their way outside and climbed in a bright red truck, Lydia asked more questions about Kat's parents and what had happened.

Katrina found it easy to tell her about her mother and father and raising the kids on her own as they made the drive over to the other house. It was odd to be so open and comfortable with Lydia, since it wasn't a story Kat typically told anyone.

Except Grant. And now his mother.

"That must have been so hard for you, being basically Anya's age when you had to become an adult."

"I managed."

"You did. And you managed well."

"Thank you." She never wanted kudos for doing what had been, for Katrina, the obvious choice. She couldn't imagine her life without Leo and Anya in it.

They approached the house. She'd expected something small, like a guest cottage, but it looked just as amazing as the main house . . . and almost as huge.

"Does someone live here?" she asked as Lydia stopped in front.

"Not at the moment. When we bought the property there was a home here, but it was run-down and in dire need of renovation. So we fixed it up, knowing we'd have family and friends who'd want to stay over."

She grabbed their bags and followed Lydia inside.

"There's a master bedroom at the end of the hall."

Lydia led her past a spacious living room and dining area, and a wide-open kitchen with a lot of room, much like the main house, only on a slightly smaller scale.

The master bedroom was good sized as well. Katrina put their luggage in there and turned to Lydia. "It's beautiful."

Lydia smiled. "Easton and I enjoyed the renovation, and I had fun decorating."

"You must get a lot of guests."

"Easton has a big family. I have two sisters. And of course all his football friends. There seems to always be someone visiting. Which we love, of course. Plus I'm waiting for the day these kids decide to settle down, get married, and start giving me grandchildren. We have a few houses on the property."

Lydia gave her a pointed look.

Uh-oh. Time for Katrina to make Lydia understand it wasn't going to be her and Grant. "Won't that be fun for you?"

"Yes. I can't wait." Lydia looked around. "Anyway, did you want to unwind and take a nap?"

"Oh. Not at all. I'd like to help you get dinner started. I'll go on back to the house with you."

"Great."

They drove back, and this time, since Katrina wasn't in deep conversation explaining her past, she had the opportunity to gaze out the window. She spotted deer in the thick woods, and saw a creek running parallel to the road.

"It's beautiful here," Katrina said.

"It is. I fell in love with the place as soon as Easton and I saw it, and I knew we had to buy it. The terrain changes in so many places. There are high hills and low valleys, and sparse vegetation along with lush greenery. It's really amazing."

"I can see why you love it so much. I live in an apartment in Manhattan that has zero greenery other than the plants."

"Oh, but Central Park is lovely. I've been there several times."

Katrina nodded. "It is, but it's not exactly my backyard, and I think they'd frown on me trying to grow a vegetable garden there."

Lydia laughed. "That's true. But you could surely buy another place out in the country somewhere if you wanted to."

She could. But the idea of being out somewhere remote with just her and the kids kind of unnerved her.

They pulled up to the house and she noticed an additional car parked out front.

"Oh, Tucker must be here," Lydia said.

"We went to one of his games the other night. He's very good."

Lydia put the car in park and turned to her. "Did you get to meet him?"

She shook her head. "No, he had to leave town for an away game."

"We'll take care of that now. Come on."

When Lydia opened the door, the noise level had increased. Katrina spotted her sister in the kitchen with Mia. Grant was in there, too, along with his dad and Leo. And another guy who had to be Tucker, because she noticed the glasses.

They seemed to all be arguing about something.

"They're arguing the curveball again," Lydia said. "A frequent argument around here. Mainly because Tucker's is so good. It mystifies them."

"You can't argue physics," Mia said. "It's a natural curve."

"Bullshit. It's an optical illusion," Grant said.

"And you're just jealous because you can't throw a baseball like that," Tucker said, offering up a smug smile to his brother.

Grant leaned against the island and folded his arms. "No, but I can throw a sweet spiral that'll land a wide receiver in the end zone. Which you can't do. There's a reason you chose baseball over football."

"Yeah," Tucker said. "Because I'm damn good at it."

Easton rolled his eyes. "How about we end this argument, and Tucker, give your mother a hello hug."

Tucker turned and grinned. "Hey, Mom."

Wow. Katrina was right. Up close, Tucker was incredibly good-looking. Very tall, a little leaner than Grant, but still built just . . . fine. And those glasses did nothing to detract from how very handsome he was. In fact, Katrina swore the glasses made him look even hotter.

When he pulled away from Lydia, his gaze zeroed in on her. "So I've met Anya and Leo. You must be Katrina."

"I am. Nice to meet you, Tucker."

"You, too." Tucker cocked his head to the side. "So my brother was lucky enough to do a photo shoot with you. I've seen your work. It's very impressive."

"Thanks. I've seen your work with a baseball. Also very impressive."

Tucker grinned, then looked over at Grant. "See? Your girlfriend thinks I'm impressive."

Grant shrugged. "Only on the field. She thinks I'm impressive off the field as well."

Dear God. Katrina hoped the floor opened up and swallowed her.

Easton only laughed. "Damn glad to have you boys home again."

Tucker lifted his gaze to his brother. "So . . . Kat and her family were your four tickets, huh?"

"Yeah," Grant said, coming over to put his arm around her shoulders.

She was surprised he'd show this kind of familiarity in front of his family. Putting his arm around her. Talking about the two of them as if they had some kind of . . . she didn't know. She wasn't sure what to think about it.

"Good call," Tucker said, looking at his brother, then turning his attention to Katrina. "I hope you liked the game."

"I liked it a lot. You're quite the athlete. My brother follows your statistics, as does my sister."

"That's what the world needs. More statisticians," Mia said to Leo and Anya with a wink.

Anya grinned.

"Okay, enough of all this," Lydia said. "I need you all out of my way so I can start fixing dinner."

"We'll help," Katrina said. "What can we do?"

"Easton will cook the steaks tonight out on the grill, but there are still a few side dishes I'd like to make. I've already made potato salad. I thought a big green vegetable salad and fruit salad would go well. I don't really want to heat up the kitchen cooking anything since it's so hot outside."

"Fortunately, Katrina and I wield knives very well," Anya said.

Mia pulled one out of the knife block. "As do I."

"Great. Now if you guys will get out of here, we'll start slicing."

"You okay in here?" Grant asked.

She smiled. "Doing just fine. Go hang out with your dad and your brother. How's Leo doing?"

"He's in heaven. Don't worry about him."

"Okay."

The guys disappeared outside again, leaving the women in the kitchen. They washed their hands and got started slicing.

"Are all of the fruits and vegetables from your garden, Lydia?" Anya asked.

"Most of them, yes. I grow the strawberries and melons."

"I'm going to have to move out of New York City," Anya said. "I have to live somewhere where I can grow things besides an herb garden in my bedroom window."

The words tugged at Katrina's heart. But the one thing she'd tried to always foster in the kids was a sense of independence, of knowing their own self-worth so when the time came for them to be out on their own, they'd have the confidence in themselves to fly.

"Any thoughts as to where that might be?" she asked Anya.

"Not yet. But Mia showed me some great websites and I have a few thoughts."

"I can't wait to talk about them with you." Now that she knew what her sister's career path was, she'd do everything in her power to see her dreams fulfilled.

"I need more tomatoes," Lydia said, frowning as she surveyed the bowl.

Katrina swiped her hand on the towel. "I can go get those for you, Lydia."

"Would you? I'd appreciate it."

"I'll be right back."

She headed out the door and walked back toward the gardens, trying to recall where she'd seen the tomatoes. She finally remembered, and when she found them, bent over to survey the tomatoes, wanting to make sure she picked only the ripest ones.

When a set of arms went around her waist, she nearly shrieked.

"You're going to fall face-first into the tomato vines." Grant flipped her around, and before she could say anything, his mouth came down on hers in a kiss hotter than the steamy weather outside.

They hadn't had a second alone since they'd left his house, and she had to admit, she'd missed feeling his arms around her, and his lips on hers. She leaned into him and tangled her fingers into his hair, enjoying the heat of his body and the taste of his tongue licking against hers. The feel of his hand sliding down her back to cup her butt only intensified her need for him.

Until someone cleared their throat. "Aren't you a little old to be making out behind the tomato patch, Grant?"

Grant broke the kiss and shot a glare at Tucker. "Aren't *you* a little old to be spying on your big brother, Tucker?"

Tucker just shrugged. "I'm on my way to get the steaks. Not my fault that *on my way* happens to be past Mom's garden. You two should get a room." He winked at Katrina and moved on.

Grant laid his forehead against Katrina's. "Sorry. The drawback of a big family—even on a ranch this size—is very little privacy."

"Your mom is putting us up—and by us, I mean just you and me—at one of the other houses."

He grinned. "Alone?"

"Apparently."

"Remind me to give her a big hug and a kiss for that."

"I need to pick some tomatoes and bring them into the house before she thinks I got lost."

"Okay." He brushed his lips against hers. "Later."

She picked several ripe and juicy ones and brought them inside. She was certain her hair was mussed up and her lips were kiss swollen, but Lydia never said a word. They finished up the salads, then went into the immense dining room to set the table.

The table was rectangular, dark and distressed, and looked handmade. "Who made this table?" she asked as they were setting the utensils.

"Easton and the boys." Lydia ran her hand lovingly over the surface. "It's reclaimed maple, and one of my treasured possessions. It's held up well over the years, and can seat at least twenty people. He even built extra leaves so we can expand it for larger parties."

Katrina nodded. "It's massive. And so impressive."

"Easton worked night and day on it for six months. The boys all pitched in and helped. Every gouge and nick has part of them on it. I love it so much."

Her heart clenched at Lydia's words. "I can see why. It's beautiful."

"Now, it's time for all of us ladies to have cocktails. Except for Anya, of course, who's going to have the virgin variety of whatever we have."

"Curses," Anya said, then smiled.

Katrina laughed, and they followed Lydia into the kitchen where she mixed up a very tempting concoction containing watermelon, agave nectar, lime juice, orange juice, and tequila. After shaking up the mix, she filled each glass with ice and decorated it with a wedge of watermelon.

"Melon margaritas for everyone," she said, though she'd fixed a special pitcher for Anya without the tequila, much to Anya's irritation.

"Someday I'll have tequila. Lots of tequila," Anya said as they made their way out to the front porch and grabbed seats.

"And someday I'll explain the tequila hangover to you," Mia said. "Everything in moderation is not just something adults say to be mean to you. Trust me on this."

Lydia laughed.

Katrina sipped the drink. It was cool and refreshing with just enough of a tequila kick. "This is so good, Lydia."

"Thank you. I like to experiment with icy cold drinks in the summer. And I do like watermelon."

"You also like margaritas, Mom," Mia said.

Lydia swirled the liquid around in her glass, then took a sip. "This is true. More than half the drinks I make have 'margarita' in their name."

Katrina laughed. What a lifestyle the Cassidys led. It seemed relaxed, yet busy at the same time. It didn't appear as if Lydia was sitting around bored. She had a garden and they'd remodeled two homes. She'd raised four boys and a girl. She must have been going nonstop for years.

"Do you miss your job as an attorney, Lydia?" Katrina asked.

"No. I sit on the board of the Cassidy Foundation. We run several charities, and I'm deeply involved with those. So as far as the legal side, I still have my fingers in that enough that I don't yearn for my days as a lawyer. But the courtroom? No, I don't miss that at all. I did my part for a lot of years and I thoroughly enjoyed the work I did. I made what I consider all the right choices for myself, for Easton, and for the kids. I have zero regrets."

"Tell Katrina how you and Dad met, Mom," Mia said, then looked over at Katrina. "It's such a great story."

"Easton was a key witness in a case I was prosecuting for battery."

"Really," Katrina said. "What was the case about?"

"He was involved in a skirmish in a nightclub. Though he wasn't a participant, one of his friends had been accused of assaulting another patron there. Since Easton had been present, he was one of the witnesses and I needed to talk to him. Of course, since the defendant was his friend, he did his best to make himself unavailable.

"I was an assistant DA during that time, and I was assigned to depose him. He didn't show up during the scheduled time, which irritated the hell out of me. He claimed scheduling conflicts, when I knew damn well he was trying to protect his friend."

"Did he ever show up?" Katrina asked.

"Finally. And he wasn't happy about it, either. But we got through it, and I gave him credit for being honest, though he was as . . . creatively evasive as he could be. And he claimed the other guy started it and his friend was just defending himself."

"Did he have to testify in court?" Anya asked.

Lydia shook her head. "The guy who was assaulted ended up dropping the charges and refused to testify. And without our key witness, we didn't have a case."

"So you lost," Anya said.

"More or less, yes. And then Easton asked me out."

Katrina laughed. "He did?"

"Yes. And I was pissed about losing the case and the media circus surrounding him and the other player."

"So you said no?"

"Of course I said no. I was young and hungry, trying to climb the ladder in the DA's office. I wanted nothing to do with him and his fame. But he was so persistent. He pursued the hell out of me. Of course I was also wildly attracted to him. There was my dilemma."

"And then Mom gave in and went out with him," Mia said with a wide smile. "They became an item, which caused another type of media circus."

Lydia sighed. "That it did. Which did not make the DA's office happy."

"Not much they could do about it, right? They couldn't tell you who you could date—or fall in love with."

Lydia nodded at Anya. "That's true. We became inseparable. Both of us so career minded, and yet so in love. And when he proposed to me, it kind of sealed the deal. I was going to be the prosecutor married to the football star."

Their story made Katrina's heart swell. "That is incredibly sweet. And so romantic."

"It was. He swept me off my feet. Damn man. He was kind of overwhelming."

Katrina knew that feeling. She'd felt overwhelmed ever since Barbados.

Like father, like son, she supposed.

While everyone talked, she sat and sipped her drink, looking out over the porch and onto the land. What an amazing feeling that must be for Lydia and Easton to have all this land, to know they could walk or drive for miles and still not see the end of what was theirs. She had been impressed enough with Grant's house in St. Louis. The property had been huge, especially the expanded woodland area with the surprise pond located beyond the woods.

This, however, was spectacular. She couldn't imagine having something like this, an oasis to shut yourself off from the world, but also spacious enough to welcome as many guests as you wanted.

She'd always been content in New York. It had suited her purposes, business-wise. It had everything she needed or wanted. But now it was starting to feel closed in to her.

Which was ridiculous, of course. She'd be fine once she got back home.

Easton opened the front door. "Steaks are ready, honey."

Lydia stood. "Okay. Let's go have some dinner."

Just as they were about to head inside, a dark SUV came flying up the driveway, dust flying in its wake. It slammed to a halt out front.

A tall, very muscular dark-haired man came out.

"Figures you'd show up just as dinner was being served," Lydia said.

He pulled off his dark sunglasses and came up the stairs, wrapping Lydia in a hug. "You know me, Mom. And it's good to be home."

He turned away from his mother only long enough to hug his sister.

"Brat," he said.

"Smartass," she replied. "Good to have you home again."

"Flynn," Lydia said. "This is Katrina Korsova, Grant's girlfriend. And this is Katrina's sister, Anya."

Girlfriend. She didn't know how she felt about that, but she didn't have time to think about it because Flynn took her hand and shook it.

"So, my brother's the first of us to bring a woman home to meet Mom and Dad, huh? Nice to meet you, Katrina. You too, Anya."

"Flynn," Katrina said.

"Hey, Flynn," Anya said, grinning the whole time.

"Well, come on," Lydia said. "Let's go eat before those steaks get cold."

"Nice of you to have dinner on the table just as I got here. I'm starving," Flynn said, putting his arm around his sister and walking inside behind their mother.

"Wow," Anya said, inching close to Katrina, stopping her as everyone else headed into the dining room. "Is every Cassidy brother that good-looking?"

"They're all too old for you, Anya," Katrina said.

"I know that. But that doesn't mean I can't ogle the goods. And maybe drool over them a little. Flynn is all lean muscle and dark hair and those eyes. Such an intense green. Gah. I need to take a picture of him to send to Leah. I need to take pictures of all of them. I wonder what Barrett looks like? Maybe I can get a group pic?"

Katrina shook her head and grabbed her sister's hand. "I think you need to stick to boys your own age."

Anya made a face. "Bleh. I don't want a boyfriend. I'm just enjoying the eye candy."

Sometimes, Katrina wondered about her sister. Seventeen and she hadn't had a boyfriend yet. She'd gone out on a few dates, but mostly in groups with a bunch of friends, which Katrina had thought was just fine.

Maybe it was time to encourage her sister to spread her wings a little.

She paused behind everyone else as they all entered the dining room. What was she thinking? A few weeks ago she'd have been deliriously happy to have her little sister stay boyfriend-free. Now she wanted to encourage her to date?

Katrina was twenty-seven and had just had sex for the first time. She was doing just fine. So was Anya.

"You know what, Anya? You're right. You don't need a boyfriend. Not anytime soon."

She needed to reevaluate her priorities, and fast.

Clearly, Grant was not a good influence on her.

And speaking of Grant, as they entered the room he came around the table and put his arm around her waist.

"I see you met Flynn."

"I did. He showed up outside just as we were getting up to come in for dinner."

"How timely of him. His stomach has a clock. He knows when a meal is being served."

Flynn came down the hall. "Oh, and you don't? You eat more than Tucker and me combined."

"I don't think so."

"Before this devolves into another one of your infamous hot dog eating contests," Easton said, taking his spot at the far end of the table. "Let's sit down to eat."

"I'd like to hear about the hot dog eating contest," Leo said.

Leo had taken a seat across from Easton, who motioned with his head down the table. "Ask Grant. He was usually the instigator."

"Tucker stupidly claimed he could eat more than I could. Then Flynn chimed in, and Barrett said he could eat twice as much as the three of us combined. So I challenged all of them."

"This was when I was outside working in the garden one day," Lydia said as she passed the salad around the table. "We were having company over that night, so I had hamburgers and hot dogs in the fridge. The boys snuck into the kitchen and took all fifteen packages of hot dogs out of the refrigerator, threw them on the stove and cooked them up, and proceeded to try and outeat each other."

Katrina looked at Grant. "How old were you?"

Grant lifted his gaze to the ceiling, obviously thinking. Then he looked at her. "Flynn was like twelve, I think. Which would have made me eleven and Tucker and Barrett eight."

"Foolish boys," Lydia said. "By the time I came into the house, they'd eaten every hot dog and their faces were green. I made them all throw up outside."

Leo snorted out a laugh. Even Katrina couldn't resist laughing.

Flynn pointed his steak knife at his brothers. "Yeah, but I won."

"I don't think so," Grant said.

"We all know I won," Tucker said with a smug grin. "I threw up four times."

"Can we please not discuss this during dinner?" Lydia said. "I don't think we want Katrina and her family fleeing the table because of our choice of dinner topics."

Katrina couldn't help but smile. "Oh, trust me. I've heard worse during dinner."

"This is true," Leo said. "We talk about really disgusting topics while we eat. Bugs. Vomit. Blood. Brain matter. We aren't squeamish."

Katrina leveled a glare on her brother. "Thank you so much for that, Leo. I'm sure you've endeared us to the Cassidy family quite nicely now."

"Actually, you have," Tucker said. "You're our kind of people."

Lydia cut into her steak. "Don't worry about it, Katrina. *After* dinner I'll tell you about the time Easton decided to discuss every detail about his gallbladder surgery during one very graphic dinner conversation."

"With photos," Grant added with a proud glance over at his father. His dad grinned.

This family was wildly amusing. And so obviously close-knit.

Katrina leaned over to whisper at Grant. "I can tell you have some kind of obsession about hot dogs. This worries me."

He winked at her. She shook her head.

"How long can you stay, Flynn?" Easton asked.

"Just two nights. I leave Tuesday morning. I need to get back to San Francisco, because we have a meeting, then we fly out to Denver for the game next weekend."

Easton nodded. "Your defense is looking solid this year. How are the rookies?"

"They're doing good. Our line is strong, our safeties better than ever. I think the D is going to kick some ass this year." Flynn looked over at Katrina, then the kids. "Sorry for saying ass."

Katrina laughed. "Nothing they haven't heard before."

"You play with Mick Riley. He's really good," Leo said.

Flynn gave a quick nod. "He's the best quarterback there is."

"Hello," Grant said. "I'm sitting right here."

Flynn shot Grant a smug smile. "I know you are."

"Asshole," Grant muttered, then looked over at Flynn. "San Francisco's on our schedule this season, you know."

"I know. You prepared to be flattened by your brother?"

"I'm prepared for my offensive line to kick your ass. You won't get anywhere near me."

Flynn calmly cut into his steak and slid a piece into his mouth. "We'll see, won't we, Brother?"

"Yeah, we will."

Katrina watched the interplay between the two of them. "Does this happen a lot? Brothers having to play each other?"

"On occasion. None of us play in the same division. Barrett plays for Tampa, too. So yeah, we have to play each other."

"And how does that work?" Leo asked. "I mean, you all are brothers. But on the field, you're competitors, right?"

"We put our best play out on the field," Grant said. "Family is for off the field."

"As it should be," Easton said.

"But what about you, Lydia, and you, Easton?" Katrina asked. "When your boys play each other, who do you root for?"

"I expect them to play the best they can," Easton said. "Their best game, and leave it all on the field. If Flynn as a defensive back had an opening, but pulled up and didn't lay Grant down because he's his brother, I'd be disappointed. And if Grant saw a wide open receiver who was beating Flynn and didn't take the shot and put the ball in that receiver's hands for a touchdown, I'd be disappointed in him. Their best game. That's all I've ever asked of any of my sons."

"I root for all of them. I feel bad when they lose, and I'm happy when they win. When they play each other, it's awful for me," Lydia said. "My stomach is in knots the entire game, because I know one of them will lose."

"Awww," Flynn said. "We're big boys, Mom. Honestly, we talk crap to each other, but really. We can take it. Win or lose, we can handle it."

"That's right, Mom," Grant said. "After the game is over, we're still brothers."

"I don't care which of them wins and which of them loses," Tucker said. "And I never have to play any of them. Lucky for them."

Grant laughed. "You mean lucky for you, sissy boy. You opted out of the tough game and decided on baseball."

Tucker leveled one hell of a confident look at Grant. "Oh, is that right? You want to try and hit one of my pitches and see how tough you really are?"

"Anytime."

Tucker squinted his eyes at Grant. "How about right after dinner?"

"I'll take you on right after Grant," Flynn said. "We'll see who gets their asses kicked."

Lydia sighed and leaned over to Katrina. "It's like this all the time when they're together. It's always the Cassidy Olympics. Lots of bragging. And a lot of sports being played out in the yard. That's why there's a clearing out back behind the garden. They played a lot of sports back there when they were kids."

Lydia gave each one of them a look. "I thought they'd grow out of it when they became adults. I was wrong."

In turn, each of the boys gave her a wide smile. "But you can cheer us on, Mom. Free games, right in your backyard."

She shook her head.

Katrina smiled and scooped up some fruit salad on her fork.

After dinner, everyone helped with the cleanup, so it was done in record time. By then it was dark, so Easton decided the baseball game would have to wait until tomorrow. Instead, they fixed s'mores on the outdoor fire pit, and pulled up chairs to watch the stars, which were amazing with no city lights to distract from the view.

Easton had lit the torches to keep away the mosquitos. It was quiet except for the sounds of nature. Katrina could have sworn she could hear a running stream.

"Is that water running somewhere?"

"Yeah. There's a creek not too far behind us," Easton said. "We've had a lot of rain this year, so it's pretty swollen with water. If you open the windows at night, you can hear it."

"Which reminds me, Tucker, you and Barrett are in the guest-house," Lydia said. "I'm putting Leo in your room here."

"Fine with me."

"Are you sure that's okay?" Katrina asked Tucker. "We really don't want to put you out."

"Honey, I've slept in some of the worst places imaginable when I played in the minor leagues. Wherever Mom wants to put me has a nice bed with a great bathroom and awesome sheets. Trust me, I'm good."

She smiled at him. "Thank you."

"No problem."

She went inside to refresh her lemonade. Leo followed her.

"Easton's taking me fishing in the morning. Like at dawn or something," he said.

"You did tell him you've never fished before, right?" Katrina asked.

"Yeah. He said it's time I learned."

Leo sported a wide grin. She could tell he was so excited to spend time with Easton. She grasped his arm. "Have a good time."

"I will." He started to walk away, but then stopped. "It's pretty great here, Kat, isn't it?"

She smiled at him. "Yes, Leo. It sure is."

Anya appeared from upstairs.

"I'm hanging out in the room next to Mia's," Anya said with a wide grin. "We're going to watch movies tonight and she's going to give me some insights on college."

"Sounds great. If you need anything, text me."

Anya nodded. "I'm not going to need you. We're good. Trust me."

Katrina sighed. Neither Leo nor Anya really needed her for much.

That strange realization kept pummeling her over and over.

Her siblings were growing up, branching out, and needing her less and less.

She refilled her glass and went back outside, pausing on the porch stoop to see Grant laughing with his brothers.

She hadn't seen him that unguarded before, so at ease with himself. It was truly a sight to behold. Flynn shoved him, then he shoved back, but it wasn't with malice. There was an ease to him here, a difference to him. He was so affectionate with his mother—and with his father, too. She could tell how much he loved his parents.

She felt a pain of loss so hard and so deep for her mother right then. She missed her so much. It had been so long, but she could still vividly see her mother's face, smiling and laughing as she'd sit with all of them, read a book, play board games, or just watch television. It could be the simplest of things, a small gesture, like when she'd tuck Katrina's hair behind her ears. She could still feel her mother's touch, and she tucked her hair behind her ear, as if she could sense her mother's presence at that moment.

Those gestures had meant so much to Katrina. She knew how much her mother had loved her.

She wished she could remember the sound of her mother's voice, but it had been so long, her voice had faded with time. She could still picture her face. She had a few old photos around the apartment and every now and then she'd pull them out and look at them. Photos of her mother with the three kids all together.

The best of times.

She shuddered out a sigh, closed her eyes for the briefest of moments, trying to hold on to that sweet memory, then let it fade up into the night sky.

"I miss you, Mama," she whispered into the darkness, choking back the tears that threatened before pushing off the top step and heading back to the crowd.

TWENTY-SIX

GRANT HAD NOTICED A CHANGE IN KATRINA'S MOOD
after she'd gone inside to refresh her drink. He'd watched her as
she stood on the back porch, her arm wrapped around the railing,
staring off at something in the distance.

For a minute there she'd looked so damn sad, he'd wanted to
get up and go to her, put his arms around her and comfort her. But
then she'd closed her eyes for only a few seconds, sighed, then
come back down the stairs to sit next to him.

He wondered what was wrong, but this wasn't the right time to
ask her. He'd taken her hand in his and squeezed it, and she'd
smiled at him. Still, that sadness in her eyes lingered.

When the night started to wind down, he stood. "I think we're
going to head out."

"Okay," his mom said. "We'll see you in the morning for breakfast. You two sleep well."

"Thanks, Mom. Good night, all."

"Thank you all for a lovely evening. And for dinner," Katrina said.

They said their good nights and headed out to the car. Grant drove the few miles to the other house, parked in front, then came around to the passenger side as Katrina was getting out. He slipped his hand in hers and squeezed.

"This place is okay?" he asked.

"This house is amazing. It was so nice of your mom to offer it to us."

"I think my mom really likes you. I think she likes you and me together."

She didn't say anything, just offered up a faint smile. He let it go, and walked them up the steps and to the front door. He opened it and switched on the light.

"We brought the luggage in earlier today, so that's in the bedroom," she said.

"Great." He closed the door, then pulled her against him. "How about we talk?"

"Okay. What would you like to talk about?"

"You."

Her lips tilted. "I'm not a very interesting topic."

"I disagree." He brought them over to the sofa in the living room, then sat, putting her on his lap. "You came outside after going in and refilling your drink. You stood on the back porch and you looked so sad."

"I'm surprised you noticed that."

"I notice a lot of things about you, Kat." He brushed his hand down her hair, loving the way it felt like wet silk against his fingers. "Tell me what made you sad."

"I was thinking about my mother. About how much I missed her."

He thought about that for a minute. "Being with my family— around my mother—makes you miss your mom."

She looked down at him. "For a guy, you're very adept at reading a woman's emotions."

"I have a pretty good mom. And I have a sister. I've had some experience in this area. Plus, I'd like to think I've been around you enough that I might be starting to grab signals about how you feel."

She sighed. "Yes. You have an amazing mother. She's reminded me that I also had an amazing mother. It was just a momentary thing. I'm past it."

He sat her down next to him. "I'm sorry you were sad. I couldn't imagine not having my mother."

"She's obviously had a very strong influence on you."

"Yeah, she has."

"You know, for some reason, I thought you would have been heavily influenced by your father."

"To some extent I was. As far as sports, he was my role model. My mother taught me about a lot of other things, mainly about women. She used to think I wasn't listening, but I was."

She traced her fingers across his brow, then over his cheekbone and jaw. "Your mother has done an amazing job. You're quite the man, Grant Cassidy."

"I don't know about that. More like a work in progress. I haven't always been the best as far as women, but as far as you? You do something to me, Katrina Korsova."

"Is that right? And what do I do to you?"

He studied her for a few seconds, and she wondered if there was something on his mind. But then he took her hand and guided it down his chest, over his stomach and settled it over his quickly hardening cock. "That's what you do to me. You make me hard. I'm like a walking erection around you."

She quirked a smile. "That's not necessarily a bad thing, you know." She slipped down off the couch and nestled on her knees between his thighs. "Let's see what we can do about that."

Grant laid his palms flat on the sofa as Katrina unzipped his pants and pulled out his cock. Her mouth was on him in record time, and he was arching upward, sliding his cock between her sweet lips.

"Oh, yeah," he said, leaning forward to grasp a handful of her hair. "Do you know how much I want to fuck your mouth?"

She gave it up to him, opening for him so he could slide against her tongue, giving him access to pump between her lips until he was ready to explode. But instead of coming in her mouth, he wanted to be buried deep inside her. He pulled her up onto the sofa and dragged her pants and underwear off, making her stand while he put his mouth on her sex.

She let out a soft moan while he explored her pussy with his lips and tongue until she was the one arching against his mouth.

And then, when she was shaking and he knew she was ready to come, he laid her on the sofa, and left only long enough to grab a condom. He put the condom on, spread her legs wide, and draped them over his arms. He slid inside her, leaning in to kiss her while he ground against her.

She whimpered against his lips and he thrust deeper, feeling her squeeze tight around his cock.

Neither of them were going to last long, and that suited him just fine. He wanted her, needed her, and had done nothing but think about this moment the entire day. So when she shattered, he pressed his body against hers, needing to feel her body quiver. She wrapped her legs around him and he dug in deep, thrusting over and over as he released. Now he was the one shuddering against her as he poured out everything he had.

He pressed his body against hers, feeling both their hearts beat fast against each other, then slow to normal rhythms again.

"I'm not sure I can move," she finally said.

He fixed that by scooping her up and carrying her into the bedroom.

"Let's try out this awesome shower," she suggested.

They took a quick shower, dried off, then unpacked and crawled into bed.

Katrina laid her head on his shoulder and flung her leg over his hip.

"Feel better?" he asked.

"I feel perfect now that we're in bed together."

He couldn't help but smile at that statement. He was content to listen to the sound of her breathing. Within minutes, she was asleep.

Katrina was right. Damned perfect. He closed his eyes.

TWENTY-SEVEN

THE BASEBALL GAME IN THE MORNING WAS PRETTY epic. True to what he stated, Tucker cleaned up the field with his brothers.

Then they all complained that of course Tucker would toss that nasty curveball at his brothers.

"What? You wanted me to throw easy pitches at you?"

"Well . . . yeah," Flynn said, letting out multiple curses as he swung on three pitches and missed.

They all got tired of missing pitches, and finally, Barrett arrived, who, Katrina realized with a surprise, looked nothing like his twin brother, Tucker.

"Oh, they're fraternal twins, not identical," Lydia said. "I guess Grant didn't mention that."

"No, he didn't."

Barrett was tall and dark and oh so handsome, like Tucker. But he didn't wear glasses, and he was a lot more muscular. And where Tucker's eyes were green, Barrett's were blue.

But Barrett had the same Cassidy sense of humor, standing on the sidelines during the baseball game and calling them all pussies.

"I'm happy to toss a few balls your way, Barrett." Tucker stared down his twin brother.

"No. I'm good. Besides, I already know I can hit you, and I don't wanna embarrass you in front of the ladies."

That caused Mia to laugh so hard she started coughing.

"Enough of this," Grant said after striking out—again. "How about some football, where we wipe the floor with our brother?"

"Now we're talking," Barrett said.

"You can all cool down and get drinks, then you can pick corn for me first," Lydia said. "After that you can play football. Besides, I'm sure Leo and your father would like to get in on a football game."

"Aww, man. You're gonna make us play with Dad?" Grant asked. "He'll get to play quarterback, which means I'm gonna have to run."

"Wimp," Barrett said. "I'll run you down and intercept you."

"Care to put some money on that?" Grant asked.

"I've got a hundred that says I take one away from you."

"You're on."

"And so it begins," Lydia said to her, heading toward the cornfields.

Katrina had to admit she was more excited about picking corn. They dove into the fields.

"Check the end of the corn husk with your hands as you go along," Lydia told Katrina and Anya after she handed them baskets. "If it's rounded or blunt, it's ready to be picked. If it feels pointy, it's not ready yet."

She demonstrated by going down the row with them, and feeling a few of the ears, then having them run their hands over the ears after she had. "These are ready. This one's not."

It didn't take long for Katrina to get the feel for an ear that was ripe. After that, she and Anya were on their own, and Anya disappeared down a different row. Grant and his brothers had been assigned different rows, and wow, were they fast. They had obviously done this before because they moved at a much more rapid pace than she did.

Before long, she had filled her basket and walked to the end of the row, where they dumped the corn into a bin. She went back to refill.

All in all, it took about an hour.

"That's good enough for now," Lydia said.

"What do you do with all the corn?" Katrina asked as they headed toward the house.

"Some we'll put on the grill for dinner tonight. Some I'll blanch and freeze for the rest of the summer."

"That sounds fun," Anya said. "I hope we're around to help with that."

Lydia put her arm around Anya. "I could keep you for the entire summer, you know."

"I'd enjoy that as well. Too bad school's starting up in a couple of weeks."

Anya gave her a wishful look. Katrina laughed. "No. Sorry. You don't get to forgo your senior year to stay here on the ranch."

"See how she ruins all my fun, Lydia?"

Lydia laughed. "I ruined a lot of the kids' fun over the years."

Katrina caught sight of Easton and Leo returning in the truck, so she stopped and waited for them.

When her brother climbed out of the truck, he looked sunburned, dirty, and he smelled like fish. He was also grinning like crazy.

"Catch any fish?" she asked.

"I caught two," Leo said. "Easton said I didn't do badly at all."

"He's a natural fisherman," Easton said. "Born to it. With a little more practice, I could take him out on the boat at sea and I'd bet he'd be catching bigger fish in no time."

She was certain Leo's face might explode if he smiled any broader. "I'm glad you had a good time. I hear there's going to be a football game out here soon."

Easton nodded. "Then we're back just in time."

Lydia decided it might be better for everyone to have lunch first, and let Easton and Leo cool off a bit inside the house, so they made sandwiches and had leftover fruit salad from the night before. Easton told them about fishing and told everyone how well Leo did baiting his first hook.

"Yeah, the kid was born to live in the country," Easton said. "You'll need to drag him out of the city more often, Katrina. Plus, I hear he wants to play football."

"So he tells me."

"I guess we'll find out during the game this afternoon if he's any good at it, since he'll be playing with the best there is."

"And Tucker, who sucks," Barrett said before taking a bite of his sandwich.

"Screw you. I'm going to knock you flat on your ass," Tucker said.

"You wish, pansy."

"Someday, Katrina, maybe you'll end up with a houseful of boys who love each other as much as ours do," Easton said. Then winked at her.

She laughed. "Oh, I have siblings who love to give me a hard time. This is not unfamiliar to me."

"This is true," Anya said. "Though we don't beat each other up."

"You don't know what you're missing, Anya," Barrett said, winking at her.

"Please don't give her any ideas, Barrett," Katrina said.

Anya laughed, then shot Katrina a look of pure devilish delight.

It was a good thing she knew they'd never get physical with each other, or her sister would be in deep trouble.

After lunch everyone scattered to rest up before what everyone had now dubbed the first annual Cassidy football tournament to the death.

Or until everyone got tired, or until Lydia decided enough was enough. Whichever came first.

"They call it the first annual," Lydia said to her as they all marched out to a clearing behind one of the barns. "But honestly, they've been doing this for years. Someone will get their ego in a knot over something, and then it's a free-for-all."

"And you're not worried one of them will get hurt?"

"Not really. They're all athletes, all in shape, and I think they know their limits as far as how much they can hurt themselves—and each other. They have professional careers to watch out for and none of them will put any of their brothers' careers in jeopardy. It's all in good fun."

Katrina wasn't so sure about that. With all the guys dressed in shorts and sleeveless shirts, the muscles on display were impressive. And they were all incredibly tall. They all looked fierce and prepared to kill their opponents. Even Easton was still in amazing shape for a man she guessed had to be in his mid-fifties. She supposed working a ranch kept a man in good shape.

Which was no doubt why Lydia had that gleam in her eye.

And in the middle of that mix of giants and testosterone was her brother, who looked so small in comparison.

As if Lydia could read her mind, she said, "They'll protect Leo, so don't you worry. They'd never put him in harm's way. They'll mostly pound on each other."

Which meant Grant could take a pounding.

Not that she thought Grant couldn't hold his own, because standing out there in the field, sweat soaked and looking just as determined as his brothers, she was convinced he'd be victorious. But she couldn't help the tiny feeling of trepidation that had crept in.

She didn't want him to get hurt. And there was a small voice inside of her—call it competitive spirit—that really wanted to shout to him to kick his brothers' asses.

A voice she decided would be prudent to keep silent. But when Grant came over to where they were sitting to grab a bottled water from the cooler, she went over to him, grasped his arm. "You'll watch out for Leo?"

He smiled at her. "Of course. He's not going to get hurt."

"Okay. And Grant? Kick their asses."

He grinned. "I intend to." He gave her a quick kiss, which caused his brothers to whistle at him. He rolled his eyes, then headed back out on the makeshift field.

Katrina pulled up one of the chairs they'd brought out to the field. She and Lydia, Mia, and Anya had taken seats under a group of trees in the shade and sipped glasses of lemonade from the jug Lydia had prepared.

It looked like Easton, Barrett, and Leo were going to be on one team, and Grant, Flynn, and Tucker on the other.

They flipped a coin, and Easton's team would have the ball first. After a quick huddle, Easton dropped back and threw, but Leo missed the catch.

Leo was disappointed, too. She could tell from the way his chin dropped to his chest.

"You'll get the next one, kid," Easton said, slapping him on the back. "Even the best receivers drop passes."

"Dad's right," Grant said. "Brush it off and go after the next one."

"Hey," Tucker said. "Quit talking him up. He's the enemy right now. Drop another one, Leo."

That made Leo smile, and then it was back to the game.

After a series of downs, Easton's side turned the ball over. Grant had the ball next, and as soon as he dropped back he threw a long pass to Tucker. Flynn and Barrett crashed into each other in an awful collision, and Tucker caught the pass for what Katrina assumed was a touchdown.

"Ha!" Tucker said, slamming the ball to the ground. "In your faces, all of you."

"That's only because you had me as protection," Flynn said. "Without me, Barrett would have flattened you."

"Whatever." Tucker calmly walked back to the huddle. "Face it. I'm better than all of you. At any sport."

Grant shook his head, then looked over at Barrett. "Even though he's on my team, you have my permission to turn him into a pancake the next time he has the ball."

Barrett nodded. "Consider it done."

Tucker just laughed, but on the next play, Barrett did just that, slamming Tucker to the ground.

Tucker just stared up at the sky.

"You okay?" Grant asked, grinning down at him.

"Fuck off," Tucker said with a slight wheeze in his voice.

Grant laughed, then helped Tucker up. "You never did know how to keep your mouth shut, dumbass."

When it was Easton's turn at quarterback again, he threw it right at Leo. Flynn and Barrett did battle again. Katrina could swear the two of them crashing into each other sounded like two freight trains colliding. Tucker went after Leo, but even Katrina had to admit, Leo was fast. This time he caught the ball and scored.

Katrina was out of her seat, screaming. It might be makeshift play and mean nothing, but these were all pro players. And the ego boost for her brother was going to be tremendous. She could see the joy on Leo's face, and all the Cassidys celebrated with him.

"No one gets an easy score in this family, Leo," Easton said. "You did good."

There were several skirmishes, and the score seemed fairly even. Katrina kept her eye on both Leo and Grant. Her brother was filthy and seemingly having a great time. After every play, whether they scored or not, he came out of it grinning. He apparently was being accepted by the Cassidys, and she knew that, to Leo, it was all that mattered.

On one play, Barrett knocked Flynn to the ground, stepped on him, and flew into Grant, knocked him flat and took the ball, scoring for his team. He raised his hands over his head, then slammed the ball to the ground.

Barrett looked fierce. "That's how it's done, boys."

Katrina held her breath, even reaching over to grasp Lydia's hand.

"Grant's fine," Lydia said. "Trust me."

Grant leaned over and glared at his brother. "I think you broke my rib."

Barrett went over and held out his hand to Grant. "Don't be such a puss."

Grant shoved a shoulder into his brother, then laughed.

Only then did Katrina exhale.

"I was going to suggest we join in the game because it looked like so much fun," Anya said. "But now I think I'll pass."

"Yeah, you'd have to be insane to want to take part in that bloodbath," Mia said. "I'm comfortable making fun of them on the sidelines."

To prove her point, Mia shouted, "Is that the best you all have? I'm getting bored over here."

Flynn glared at his little sister. "You're welcome to join in, princess."

She laughed. "Not on your life. But try and make it a little more interesting, will ya?"

The game went on for another half hour and ended in what Easton called a tie, much to the grumbling and complaining of his sons. They were dirty and sweaty and Easton said his knee hurt, so he called it quits.

"Good game, boys. Now everyone shake hands," he said.

They all did, surprising Katrina, because it had gotten rough out there. Though they'd gone easy on Leo, but not too easy. He was banged up, and still grinning from ear to ear as he followed the guys to the backyard, where everyone rinsed off under the outdoor shower, then changed into swim trunks and cooled their hot bodies by diving into the pool.

All the women changed as well. They might not have played football, but sitting in that hot sun had been grueling. Katrina had no idea how the guys had played for an hour in that intense heat. She supposed they were used to the extreme temperature, and they had taken frequent water breaks.

Now, though, they all played in the pool like kids. Grant swam his way over to her.

"Did you enjoy the game?" he asked, hanging on to her raft.

"It was brutal. Do you and your brothers always play like that?"

"Like that? No. That game was mild by comparison, and only because Mom and Dad were around. There wasn't even any major bloodletting. You should have seen us when we were kids."

"This is true," Mia said. "When I was old enough to get involved in watching them play, someone was always needing stitches after a fight broke out. All those trips to the emergency room were tedious."

Katrina laughed. "The drawback of having injury-prone older brothers, I suppose."

"Indeed. Though the nurses all thought I was cute and I got lollipops."

"Suck up," Flynn said, tossing Mia off her raft. She retaliated by hopping on his shoulders. Then they decided a game of chicken was in order. Katrina ended up on Grant's shoulders, Anya on Leo's, and there was a free-for-all. By the end of it, Katrina had gotten dunked several times.

She couldn't recall ever having more fun. That was the one thing she'd discovered quickly about the Cassidys. They knew how to have fun, no matter what they were doing.

Lydia announced it was time for everyone to get out. They had to wash down the back patio and clean up to get ready for tonight's party. She and Grant headed back to their house to shower so they could be back to help with the party preparations.

Katrina followed Grant into the bathroom.

"You have a few cuts and scrapes on your back," she said as he pulled off his shirt.

"Do I? I didn't even feel those."

She'd noticed the scars on his body when they got naked the first time. But now, after seeing him play close-up, she ran her fingertips over each one of them. There was one on his right shoulder blade, one on his left arm—a pretty long one.

"What's this from?"

"I fell off a set of rocks when I was nine. Broke my arm and cut myself pretty good. Had to get fifteen stitches."

He was smiling.

"Ouch."

He shrugged. "It was a clean break and healed good. My friends thought I was a badass."

She shook her head. "I wonder how many times your mother had to visit the emergency room with you and your brothers."

"Too many times for me to remember. One of us was always

leaping off something, falling off something, or running into something. One time during Halloween, some girl whacked Barrett on the back of the head on the way home from trick-or-treating for making some smartass comment to her. He ended up with four stitches just for that. Pretty embarrassing for him to get the shit beat out of him by a girl."

Katrina's lips lifted. "I can only imagine the hellions you all were."

He cocked a brow. *"Were?"*

She laughed. "Come on. Let's get in the shower."

They took quick showers. Katrina insisted on cleaning up Grant's scrapes, even though he told her they were minor in comparison to what he usually got playing football games every week.

"Yes, but you don't play games in the dirt every week, do you?"

"You don't need to baby me," he said, watching her in the mirror as she cleaned his wounds. "I'm tougher than you think."

"I know that. Humor me, anyway."

He did. Then she dried her hair, put on makeup, and changed into a sundress and sandals.

"Do I look okay?" she asked as Grant put on a pair of shorts and a sleeveless top.

He came over to her and put his hands around her waist. "You're beautiful. I don't know if I tell you that enough, but every time I look into your eyes I'm mesmerized by you. I always want to stop whatever I'm doing so I can kiss you and lose myself in you."

The way he spoke to her made her heart squeeze. What kind of man talked like that? None that she'd ever known. "Thank you. And you know what? The feeling is mutual." She smoothed her hands up his arms, wishing they had a spare hour or so to take off all these clothes and explore each other.

"If you keep looking at me like that, we're going to be late. Then Mom is going to call asking me what we're doing. And I'd have to lie to her and tell her you're taking a nap or something." He pulled her closer, letting her feel his erection.

She took a deep breath, desire wrapping around her like the heat of the day. "We can't have you lying to your mother, so we should stop this now."

He let his hands slide down her back to cup her butt. "Yeah. One of us should have enough willpower to walk away."

She arched into him. "Okay. You go first."

His gaze narrowed. "Katrina."

"Grant." Her nails dug into his arms.

"I can make you come in less than five minutes."

"I want you so much, I'm pretty sure I could come in less than two minutes."

"You're on."

He scooped her up and stalked the few steps to the bed, then laid her down on the edge. He had her panties off in record time. When he spread her legs and put his mouth on her, she was already throbbing, lifting to get closer to his lips and tongue and the magic he did with them. Watching him today, but not being able to have access to him, to touch him at will, had been an exercise in torture.

That had been her foreplay.

Now was her reward, and she was so ready for this release that when it happened, she cried out with the pure, unadulterated joy of feeling his tongue lap over her sex. She quivered as her climax raced through her, and barely had time to come down from the high before Grant had his cock out, a condom on, and was thrusting inside of her.

She gasped at the delicious sensation of still feeling the aftereffects of her orgasm, his cock driving inside her over and over again, building that sensation to a fevered pitch. And when she felt herself getting close again, she wrapped her legs around him and urged him to go with her.

It didn't take much urging, because when she came, he was right there with her, arching his back as he let go. It was the most beautiful thing to see his muscles tighten as he came, to see his body shudder along with hers as they rode out their orgasms together.

He bent and took her mouth in a sweet, gentling kiss before nuzzling at her neck.

"I forgot to time us," he said.

She let out a soft laugh. "Trust me. The clock was the last thing I was focused on."

They did a quick cleanup. She brushed her hair again, then they were on their way back to the main house. Grant held her hand in the car the entire way, and she couldn't resist the more than satisfied smile on her face.

"You keep smiling like that, my entire family is going to know what we did back at the house."

"Do you care?" she asked.

His lips curved in a wicked grin. "Not at all."

TWENTY-EIGHT

IT WAS GOING TO BE ONE HELL OF A GREAT PARTY tonight. Grant hadn't seen his uncles and aunts in a while, and his parents had a lot of friends. Not everyone would make it, since the party was on a weeknight, but Easton Cassidy was a popular guy, and if there was a celebration, Grant would guarantee that a lot of people would be here.

Uncle Elijah had made it back just in time for the get-together. Grant saw him as they came through the front door.

"Hey, kid," his uncle said. "I heard you were here."

His uncle pulled him into a hug.

"Uncle Elijah. You look good."

"Eh. I look older all the time. And this pretty woman must be Katrina. I'm Elijah Cassidy. The good-looking Cassidy."

Katrina smiled. "Very nice to meet you."

"I already met your brother and sister. Everyone's in the kitchen, bugging Lydia."

Grant knew no one bugged his mother. The bigger the crowd, the happier she was.

Lydia was in the kitchen directing traffic.

"I need those wineglasses put on the bar in the dining room. And those cases of wine set out."

"Where've you been?" Grant asked his uncle as they carried the wine out and set it up behind the bar.

"Had a line on some horses we were interested in picking up, so I took a trip into Oklahoma for an auction."

"And?"

"Picked up about four of them."

"I'd like to see them."

"Sure. Soon as we're finished here, we'll head on out to the horse barn and take a look."

"Are Uncle Eddie and Uncle Elgin coming?"

"Eddie will be here," his dad said. "Elgin and Patsy are in Italy on vacation, so they won't be able to make it."

"I'm supremely jealous of their vacation, too," his mom said, eyeing his dad.

"Europe's not really my thing, honey, but if you wanna go, just make the plans and I'll tag along."

His mom pointed her finger at his dad. "I'm holding you to that, Easton."

Once the glasses and wine setup was finished, they were all shuffled into the living room.

"It's time for everyone to relax." His mom turned to head back into the kitchen.

"No, Mom," Mia said. "It's time for *you* to relax. No fixing food or spending your evening in the kitchen."

Mom laughed. "Please. I have a ton of food to prepare for tonight."

"Actually, you don't," Mia said. "All of us got together and arranged for tonight's dinner to be catered. The caterers will be arriving shortly."

Grant couldn't help but smile when his mom teared up and laid her hand over her heart. "Really?"

"Really. So we're going to open some wine and you're going to let someone else work tonight. Tonight's the night you get to have time with Dad. Happy anniversary."

She hugged them all individually, and when she got to him, whispered, "Thank you for this."

He gave her a little squeeze, and said, "You deserve it. Now have some fun and enjoy your guests."

He liked seeing his mom so happy, especially with a glass of wine in her hand, leaning into his dad.

He'd been lucky—damn lucky—to have grown up with a family he could always count on. As they all raised their glasses and toasted not only Dad's birthday, but his parents' anniversary, he glanced over at Katrina. She looked genuinely happy for his parents, but he wondered if she was thinking about her own parents.

A mother who was gone too soon, and a father who'd abandoned her and her siblings. That had to eat away at her. He went over to her and put his arm around her.

"I hope you're having fun."

Her lips tilted in a smile. "I'm having a great time. You have a wonderful family, Grant. You're very lucky."

"I know I am. And I'm glad you, Leo, and Anya decided to come down here with me. Thanks for that."

She gave him an enigmatic smile, but then guests started to arrive, so he didn't have a chance to talk to her, because he had to introduce her to his other uncle, Eddie, and his Aunt Cecile, and soon the door was open and the house filled with guests.

His dad's old coach from Green Bay, now retired, made the trip. Grant hadn't seen Fred Arendale in years, so he spent some time getting caught up with him. Fred talked to Grant about his team this year and how proud he was of Grant's career. Then they were surrounded by Grant's brothers, all of them having a great amount of respect for Fred.

He'd lost sight of Katrina because he was swallowed up by all the guests. Fortunately, he knew she could hold her own.

He'd just have to catch up with her later.

KATRINA WAS IN AWE OF THE FAMILY AND FRIENDS who'd showed up for Easton and Lydia's party. She knew Grant was busy greeting people, and she was fine on her own.

Not that she spent a lot of time on her own. Neither did Leo or Anya. The one thing she'd learned quickly about the Cassidys was that they didn't let their guests stand alone. One of Grant's brothers would introduce her to someone, and she noticed Mia had stuck close to Anya all evening, making sure she didn't feel like a wallflower.

Her brother had met a new friend in Easton, and when he'd taken a moment to go get a soda, he'd stopped by and told her he'd met Easton's former coach and some of his old teammates from Green Bay as well.

Her brother was going to have stars in his eyes for a while, she could tell. She didn't have to worry about the kids feeling left out.

Or herself. Right now she was sitting with Lydia and talking to a few of the women who were a part of the charity foundation she and Easton had founded. Some of these women were wives of Easton's former teammates. She found them to be highly intelligent, most of them career women who had either retired or were still actively working. They were all formidable, and she sat with rapt attention listening to them talk about items on the agenda for their next meeting.

"We have a few scholarships to go through," Lydia said. "I have the paperwork that we'll need to review, but I believe there should be about ten we'll give out this year."

Lydia turned to her. "The foundation gives full-ride scholarships to underprivileged children in high risk areas. These are kids who might not qualify financially otherwise, but we believe stand a great chance at making a good life for themselves and their families. They just need someone to believe in them and give them the opportunity."

"What a wonderful idea," Katrina said, remembering what it was like to be seventeen, poor, and alone. If she hadn't gotten that big break that had sent her career soaring, who knows what would have happened to her—and to Leo and Anya?

"Is this something every football player does?" she asked.

"Not everyone, but players who want to give back," Varella, one of the women, said. "Everyone who wants to make a difference. Some of these men make a lot of money during the course of their careers. It's a chance to pay it forward."

Katrina liked the idea, and not just for athletes. She'd spent so much of her career hoarding her money, concerned about Leo's and Anya's future, that she hadn't taken the time—or the money—to give back as much as she should have.

It was time she changed that.

She made a mental note to speak to her lawyer about that when she got back to New York.

In the meantime, she was learning a lot listening to these women.

The caterers came to Lydia to announce dinner was ready.

Lydia smiled at her friends. "Wow, how nice is that? I didn't have to do any cooking tonight."

"You should have a night off more often." Mary, one of Lydia's friends, laid her hand on her arm.

Lydia laughed. "Trust me. I have Easton take me into the city for dinner at least once a week. It's not like I'm trapped in the kitchen."

Everyone assembled and filled their plates, buffet style. She finally caught up with Grant, who got in line behind her.

"I'm sorry I kind of left you to yourself tonight," he said.

"Are you kidding? I've been having a wonderful conversation with your mother and a few of her friends. I've been learning about the Cassidy Foundation."

"Oh yeah?"

They found a seat together near the fireplace. "Yes. It's quite the charity, and the causes they give to are incredible."

"Yeah. My dad taught me all about it when I was in college. We all got to take part in some of the decision making as soon as we became adults. It made us hyperaware of how lucky we all were, and how important it is to give back. All of us have formed our own foundations, while continuing to participate in the main Cassidy Foundation."

She had no idea. "As I was listening to your mother talk about scholarships and benefits, I thought about all the money I've made. I've done nothing charitable. I mean, I make charitable donations, of course. But nothing like your foundation."

"You have a family to support."

She shook her head. "I can still give back. I need to do something about that."

He nodded. "Even the smallest thing can make a big difference. Building a playground in your neighborhood, or setting up an annual scholarship. One thing. You'd be surprised."

She lifted her gaze to his. "I had no idea you thought about things like this."

"See how we're learning things about each other? Stick with me, Kat. Maybe we'll build a foundation together."

He winked at her, but she wondered about that. She felt a little thrill at his words. The things they could do together could be tremendous.

But they weren't together. They'd never be together.

And that thought kind of . . .

Sucked.

She was getting way too involved. But what was she supposed to do about that? She knew it, just now as she thought it, that her heart was getting tied up in Grant. In his family.

She decided the best way to cope with that was simply not to think about it. At least not tonight.

After dinner, she poured another glass of wine. Oblivion was an awesome solution.

She checked on the kids. Anya had met a few of Mia's friends, who were in town for the party and staying to visit. Some exposure to college kids was good for her.

"They all go to the University of Texas," Anya said. "Did you know I could get an amazing business degree at the university? And Mia is thinking of getting her master's degree there, which means she'd be there when I would be. Plus Suz and Della are sophomores, so they'd be there when I attended."

"That's so interesting." Katrina let it all flow through her, deciding that tonight she wasn't going to freak out about anything, the least of which was Anya's college choice. By next week, Anya might decide on something else entirely.

Like going to college in Poland or something. She knew how her sister's mind worked.

Leo was currently talking to Flynn, who was gesturing about . . . something.

Football related, was her guess, and she didn't want to interrupt, since it looked like Leo was paying rapt attention and was in very good hands.

She realized as she made the circle back to the bar that she'd emptied her wineglass.

So she refilled it, and just in time, because Easton's brother—which one was he?

Elijah. That was the one. He clinked his glass to get everyone's attention.

"I wanted to take a moment to wish my brother a very happy birthday. He's not the oldest, so we can't give him a hard time about that. But I can say that he's a great brother, a damn fine husband, according to Lydia, and since I've been around him all these years, I can tell you he is one hell of a good father. He's lived a rich, happy life and has had monumental success over the years.

"Here's to a lot more years, Easton. Happy birthday."

Everyone cheered and clinked glasses. Easton raised his glass and drank.

Then Grant stood.

"I wanted to take another minute to say a few words, since for some reason I was elected to speak."

"Because you have the biggest mouth," Tucker said.

There were some laughs to that, and Grant glared at his brother.

"Anyway, I want to tell you all how we kids admire and respect our parents. We weren't exactly the easiest of children."

That got him a lot of laughter, and a couple of coughs from his parents.

"There were several fights among us and maybe a little more than the average amount of bloodshed, but that's what you get when you have four boys. Fortunately, they had Mia, and she might not want to admit it, but she threw herself in there and scrapped with us. It was a lot of fun for us, and a lot of headaches for Mom and Dad, who handled us with toughness, and a hell of a lot of love.

"Our lives have been blessed because of the parents we had. We all agree we're the luckiest kids ever, thanks to our parents, and that's because we were raised in a house filled with love.

"Everyone, I invite you to toast to love. Happy anniversary to Easton and Lydia Cassidy."

Katrina blinked back tears. Their gazes met as they raised their glasses.

While everyone was busy giving congratulations to Grant's parents, she made her way over to Grant.

"Beautiful toast," she said.

He shrugged. "I'm not much of a public speaker. I just said what was in my heart about my parents."

"You did good."

He swept his knuckles across her cheek, swiping away a tear that had escaped. "Thanks."

Someone turned on music, a slow song, and a makeshift dance floor cleared in the middle of the living room. Grant's dad swept his mom up and the two of them swayed together. Grant put his arm around Katrina as the two of them watched his parents, who clearly only had eyes for each other.

"It must be wonderful to see your parents so happy with each other after all these years," she said.

"Yeah. Kind of sickening how much they love each other."

She nudged into him. "It's sweet."

When Easton bent Lydia over and gave her a passionate kiss at the end of the dance, Grant shook his head. "Those two should get a room."

Katrina laughed. "Can you imagine that with your spouse? That kind of passion after thirty years of marriage? To know the person you married still wanted you that much would be amazing."

He turned to her, his hands sweeping down her arms to grasp her hands. "I can't imagine any man you marry wouldn't lust after you until his dying day."

She stared at him. "Do you always have the perfect thing to say?"

"Uh, no. Why?"

"I don't know. It seems you always say the right words to a woman."

His lips curved. "Trust me, it hasn't always been that way. Maybe I just have the right words to say to you."

She didn't know what to say in answer to that, and his parents came over and pulled them onto the dance floor for a fast song. Soon, the floor was crowded with people all hopping up and down. Her sister and Mia joined in. Even Flynn and Barrett had dragged Leo onto the floor, though Katrina couldn't help but laugh at her brother's attempts at dancing.

At least he was having fun.

The music slowed and all that was left was couples. Grant pulled her into his arms, their gazes met, and she connected to him, to the music, their bodies touching. There were other couples on the floor, but Katrina could only see and feel Grant.

Their heads were touching, and he whispered in her ear.

"Speaking of people who should get a room."

"Yes. We definitely should. And soon."

She loved the feel of his body against hers. She felt his heartbeat, the heat of him, and wanted nothing more than to be alone with him.

She tilted her head back and searched his face, saw more than just lust there.

Tonight, though, she was in oblivion and reveled in the warmth and desire mirrored in his eyes. All her feelings wrapped around her like a cocoon. She felt safe.

She felt loved. She felt *love*.

She waited for the panic, the worry. But it never came. Not now, not when this amazing man held her so close.

She was going with it tonight.

She'd worry about the mix of her feelings tomorrow.

Or if she was lucky, maybe the wine would cloud her memory and tomorrow she wouldn't remember these emotions at all.

TWENTY-NINE

THE PARTY WOUND DOWN AROUND MIDNIGHT, AND Grant helped escort people to their cars and made sure the older folks found their way off the property.

Once the place was cleared out, he made his way back to the ranch to find Katrina in deep conversation with his sister. His parents had already gone up to bed, and his brothers were off in a corner of the living room talking.

"See you all for breakfast," he said.

"Yeah, early, because I have to catch a flight," Barrett said.

Grant nodded, then headed over to Katrina, who looked up at him and smiled.

She looked tired.

"Ready to go?" he asked.

"Yes." She grasped Mia's hand. "Thank you. I'll talk to you tomorrow."

"Sure. Good night, you two."

Grant didn't know what Katrina and his sister had been talking about. He didn't need to know. He liked that she'd bonded with Mia, though, and with his mom.

It was important to him in ways he hadn't had a minute to sit down and think about yet. He wasn't going to do it tonight, either, not when she was giving him a look that told him she was as ready to leave as he was.

They got in the car and drove to the house. He opened the door and she walked in, but he left the light off.

"I can't see," she said.

"We don't need to see." He shut the door and drew her close. "We just need to feel."

He captured her lips in the kiss he'd been dying to take all night. She met his kiss with fervor, sliding her hands along his shoulders, then along his neck and upward, her nails in his scalp.

His passion rose with her touch. He backed her against the door, pressing into her, letting her feel how fast she could ignite him. Her answer was a whimper, her body arching against his.

He'd spent all night watching her. They hadn't had much time together, but every time he'd searched the room, he caught sight of the way she tilted her head when she was listening to someone talk. And all he could think about was kissing that spot on her neck. Or he'd hear her laugh and he'd search out the sound so he could hear it again.

It was like she was a part of him now, embedded in his senses, and he couldn't get enough of her.

He turned her around and unzipped her dress, letting it slide down over her hips, admiring every curve as his hands followed. He took off her bra. Her panties were next, and then she was naked. He knew her body well now, and let his hands roam over her breasts, cupping them, letting his fingers tease until her nipples were tight points, her breasts straining against his hands as he fit his body against hers, rubbing his cock against her butt as she moaned against him.

He flipped her around again and shed his clothes, grabbing the condom he'd stuck in the pocket of his shorts. He put it on, sliding his hands between her legs to caress her sex, rub the tight knot of her clit until she lifted.

"Make me come," she whispered, leaning into him. "Make me come, Grant."

There was nothing that gave him greater pleasure than feeling Katrina coming apart against his hand. He slid his fingers inside her, using the heel of his hand to brush her clit. Her body gripped his fingers as she released, quaking against him as she dug her nails into his skin.

It was hot as hell, not being able to see her. All he could do was feel, touch, and breathe in the scent of sex.

He flipped her around and pushed her against the door, kicked her legs apart and entered her from behind, once again filling his hands with her breasts as he drove deep.

Her pussy latched onto his cock, a tight sheath of quaking sex that made him close his eyes. For a few seconds, he only wanted to feel her, listen to her gasps, and slide his thumbs over her nipples.

He laid his chin against her shoulder. "You and I fit perfectly together, Katrina. No one will ever do this to you like I can."

He had no idea why he'd said that to her. Maybe because he knew she'd had no one else. Maybe because for some reason, tonight he felt possessive of her.

She was his. She always had been, and always would be. The thought of another man having her made his blood boil.

He drove into her, sliding his hand down to rub her clit. He wanted to make her come again. And again. Until she wanted no one else but him.

Ever.

She laid her head against his shoulder and cried out, tightening around him with another climax. He pumped hard and fast into her and released, groaning as he came in hard, rhythmic spasms that made his legs shake. He palmed the door for support as he rode it out, giving everything he had until he had nothing left.

He fought for breath, for sanity, for some clarity to the thoughts that had grabbed hold of him while he'd been making love to Katrina.

He wasn't a possessive man. He didn't have those kind of caveman ideas about women.

Until Katrina.

What the hell was wrong with him, anyway?

They disengaged and he turned her around, cupped her jaw and kissed her. He meant to make it light and easy, but it ended up strong, passionate, igniting his fire all over again.

By the time they made it upstairs and he brushed his teeth and got ready for bed, Katrina was in bed, naked.

He pulled her toward him, intending to turn out the lights and go right to sleep.

But she turned to him, and there was something in her eyes, something he couldn't define.

He rolled over and kissed her, that passion he'd felt downstairs still not extinguished. She climbed on top of him and it was Katrina who reached into his nightstand for a condom, rolled it onto his erection and rode them both to another blistering orgasm.

Finally, they collapsed together and she fell asleep.

But he lay there for a while after, staring at the ceiling while he stroked her back.

Maybe it was because this time at the ranch, where he had her all to himself, was coming to an end. Maybe he knew Katrina and the kids would be heading back to New York soon, and his season was gearing up to start. He'd be busy.

Then what was going to happen between them? And how did he really feel? He hadn't taken the time to sort out his feelings for her. Or maybe he hadn't allowed himself to admit them.

Maybe it was time to do a little soul-searching. On both their sides.

THIRTY

KATRINA AND GRANT HAD TO GET UP EARLY THE NEXT morning. He wanted to say good-bye to his brothers, and Lydia had told her she was making a super early morning breakfast.

Katrina was used to early calls, so it wasn't a big deal for her, though her head was a bit fuzzy from all the wine she'd consumed the night before. She felt better after taking a shower, though, and she headed straight for the coffeepot when they arrived at the main house.

"I had a wonderful time at the party last night," she said to Lydia in the dining room after she'd taken a couple sips of coffee.

"It was a fun party, wasn't it?" Lydia said, cradling a cup of coffee in her own hands. "More people came than I expected. And I got to enjoy it more than I thought, since the kids surprised me with the catering."

"You should be able to enjoy your parties. Who wants to be stuck in the kitchen all night?"

"I never mind that part. I like to cook for my guests. But I freely admit to having no complaints about being freed from the kitchen last night."

Everyone showed up for breakfast, including—and quite surprisingly—her brother and sister, who looked awake and happy to be there.

"How come you're not this alert when I have to wake you up early in the morning?" she asked Leo.

Leo shrugged. "I guess because you're not Easton Cassidy."

She laughed at his honest answer. "So I should drag Easton back to New York with us and he can be your personal alarm clock once school starts?"

Easton came over and put his arm around her shoulders. "You won't have a problem with him in the future, Katrina. He's promised me he's getting up early every morning and hitting the gym before school so he can put some muscle on. I've also promised him that I'm going to talk to his high school football coach."

Katrina looked at Leo. "Is that right?"

"Yup. I promised. I've got college to think about, and only a few years to impress potential colleges."

"He's welcome to come out here in the summers. I run a few summer programs for high school kids. We'll get him college ready in no time. Once I have a chat with the high school football coach and get him on the team, we'll have him college bound in no time."

"That's awfully nice of you, Easton. But shouldn't he make the team only if he's qualified?"

"Pfft. He's more than qualified. He survived a football game with all the Cassidy boys. Name one kid on your high school team who could do that, Leo."

Leo smartly stayed mute.

Easton cracked a smile. "See? Coach and I will have a chat."

"Best not to argue with Dad when he has an idea in his head,"

Flynn said, popping his head into the dining room. "And Mom says breakfast is ready."

Breakfast was a feast of eggs, bacon, biscuits, hash browns, and fruit. After two cups of coffee, Katrina realized she was starving. She had a few minutes to talk to Anya while they ate. Or, rather, listen to Mia and Anya talk.

"So you'll come out for a campus visit during your fall break?" Mia asked. "I think you'll love the programs at UT."

"I plan to," Anya said. "I'm really excited about it. I've already looked at their curriculum and I think this is something I want to do. Plus, there's a culinary school in Dallas I'd like to take a look at as well."

Katrina ate her meal silently. Easton was taking care of Leo, and Mia seemingly had Anya's college trajectory in hand.

Not that she was complaining.

It appeared the Cassidys had it covered.

This was what it was like to have a family—a support system—other people to help out. She'd been on her own for so long, had done everything herself for her entire adult life, that she didn't know what to make of other people doing things for and with the kids.

It made her happy, but it was a little unnerving. She didn't want the kids to fall in love with this family, to get used to having other people in their lives who might not always be there. They were connected to the Cassidys by a very thin line, and only through her relationship with Grant.

What was going to happen when she and Grant weren't connected anymore? It was going to sever Leo's tie with Easton, and Anya's tie with Mia.

It sounded so awful to think it, but it was a reality she was going to have to address sooner rather than later.

These people were amazing. Kind and warm and wonderful, accepting her and Leo and Anya as if they belonged to them.

The problem was, they didn't. She was realistic enough to know that. Last night she'd been in sweet oblivion. This morning she was a lot more clearheaded. And no amount of wine, lovemaking, and sweet words were going to make her forget this reality.

But the kids? The kids were going to be hurt when she and Grant walked away from each other, and suddenly he—and his family—weren't in their lives anymore.

She had a lot to think about. And a lot to talk to Grant about.

But not now, because after breakfast they helped Lydia clean up, then Barrett, Tucker, and Flynn had to leave.

"We have all your schedules. Tucker, we'll be at your game on the fifteenth," Lydia said. "And the series you're playing against Houston and Dallas."

"Can't wait to see you again," he said, giving his mom a kiss on the cheek.

"I'll be in touch," Barrett said. "And you know I'll pop down to stay when I play Dallas."

"Here, too," Flynn said.

"I'll be seeing all of you soon enough," Grant said, then hugged his brothers.

One by one they all hugged Katrina as well.

"We like you," Tucker said to her. "We don't know what you see in Grant, since we think he's ugly, but we like you anyway."

She laughed, then said her good-byes.

She headed over to the house to pack, so Grant would have some time alone with his parents.

She was going to miss them all, and felt a tug in her heart.

She'd fallen in love with his family. It wasn't just going to hurt the kids when the ties were cut to his family. It was going to hurt her as well.

As she started putting things back in her suitcase, she paused, the realization smacking her, hard.

She hadn't just fallen in love with Grant's family. She'd fallen in love with Grant. That's why all of this had been so difficult. Why the prospect of the kids getting close to his family was so difficult.

She loved him. He was hot, sexy, gorgeous, but her feelings for him went so far beyond simple chemistry.

He was also kind and funny and smart and honorable. He loved his family and he was so good to hers.

And she had no idea what to do with all these feelings.

Did he even feel the same? He might, or he might not. To him, this might just be a fun interlude. Or he might love her.

Either way, it was a disaster. She wasn't ready for a relationship. She might never be ready for one. She had spent her whole life remembering her father, how many times he'd told her mother he loved her. How many times he'd told Katrina he loved her and how he'd always be there for her.

And look what happened there. She knew better than to trust in love. That was why she'd spent all these years saving her money and protecting her siblings.

Her independence meant everything to her. She had a road map she'd carefully constructed for her entire life, and nowhere in there had it included a man. A crazy, sexy man who would disrupt everything.

How had she allowed this to happen?

She didn't know what to do. She needed time to think, and her heart was getting in the way.

GRANT FOUND SOME TIME ALONE WITH HIS DAD WHILE his mother was in the kitchen. They sat down outside by the pool.

"It's been a fun couple of days, Dad. I'm glad we came."

"I'm glad you came, too. It was good to see you." His dad studied him. "You know what? You're different."

Grant arched a brow. "Different? How?"

"You've always had this crazy energy. Always up and doing things. You seem a lot more . . . settled now."

"Yeah? I hadn't noticed."

"I'm not surprised. I'm sure that difference has a lot to do with Katrina."

"You think so?"

His dad gave him that all-knowing "Dad" smile, the one Grant had seen a thousand times over the years. "I know so. Of course, the same thing happened to me when I fell in love with your mother. I'd been cock of the block, chasing women like there wasn't a pair of panties I couldn't get into. It was like a big, fun challenge to me, and one I enjoyed winning."

It sounded an awful lot like how Grant had lived his life for the past several years. One woman after another. He'd had fun. A hell of a lot of fun.

"Then I met your mom and bam. Game over."

And then Grant met Katrina. And nothing had been the same since.

"I fell in love with your mother. I never wanted to look at another woman after her."

The "love" word. Grant hadn't allowed himself to think it, let alone admit it, but there it was. His dad said the word so easily. He wondered if it had been so easy for him all those years ago. "So it was like that, huh?"

"She was it for me. My skirt-chasing days were over once I met your mother. The thought of ever being with another woman lost its appeal after her."

That's exactly where Grant was now. He took a few seconds to let the realization wash over him. "I don't think I knew it until spending time with Katrina here, but that's exactly where I am. I don't want anyone else but her. I don't want her to be with anyone else but me. Is that love?"

His dad gave him an all-knowing smile. "It was for me. Are you saying you don't know?"

"I don't know. I guess it is."

His father gave him a stern look. "I think you'd better do more than guess. Before you mess with that girl's heart—and those kids, too. They're crazy about you in case you hadn't noticed."

Yeah, he'd noticed all right. "I know how I feel about Katrina, Dad. And about Leo and Anya. I've never felt this way about a woman before. And I know she's part of a package. The kids have been in her life—in my life—since the beginning. I love her. I love all of them."

He'd said the words out loud and it had felt good. So there was step one.

"Have you told her that?"

"No."

"Do you know how she feels about you?"

"No."

Dad gave him that look again, the one that told him he was being a dumbass. "I guess it's time the two of you sit down and talk about your relationship."

Grant scrubbed his hand over his chin. "That's the thing. She hasn't exactly had an easy go of it over the years. Her dad skipped out on them and her mom died when she was young, leaving her the burden of raising Leo and Anya on her own. I think she might be reluctant to give up her independence."

"I think love and independence are two different things, Grant. You just have to show her that loving you doesn't mean she has to give anything up. And look at what she gains."

"What's that?"

His dad spread his arms wide. "Us."

Grant laughed. "So true. That's a big win in my opinion."

His dad stood and brought Grant in for a hug. "Talk to the woman you love. You'll figure things out."

"I will, Dad. Thanks."

He walked away, thinking about the conversation he'd just had.

Never in his life did he ever think he'd get love advice from his dad.

Of all people. Mom, maybe, but Dad? He shook his head.

But his father had been right. He and Katrina needed to talk.

But not here, and not right now. He had to get up to Dallas and start getting prepped for the game on Thursday night. It was time to put all his focus on that.

After his game, he and Katrina would have that talk.

THIRTY-ONE

KATRINA HAD EVERYTHING PACKED BY THE TIME GRANT returned to the house.

She also had her mind made up. She knew what she had to do.

Now she had to hope Grant understood.

He came in the room and started toward her, a very sweet smile on his face.

Oh, no. She knew what would happen. He'd put his hands on her, his mouth on her, and all her resolve would dissipate. She purposely put a suitcase in front of him to block him from touching her.

He stared down at the suitcase and looked over at her, then frowned. "What's wrong?"

"The kids and I are leaving."

"I know. We're all leaving for Dallas. I figure you all could sightsee and maybe do some shopping for a couple of days. Then the game on Thursday night. After that, we'll head back up to my place . . ."

She cut him off. "No. We're going back to New York."

She saw the confusion on his face. "What? New York? You mean today? That's kind of what I wanted to talk to you about. I thought maybe you and the kids would stay at my place. Like . . . permanently."

"What?"

"St. Louis is a major airport. You shouldn't have any problems catching flights wherever you want to go. There are great schools there, both public and private."

She held up her hand. "Wait. Just stop there. What are you talking about?"

"You. Me. Leo and Anya. There's plenty of room at the house. And I've already talked to a contractor about all the renovations. We can make this work, Kat. We can be a family."

Her head was spinning. This wasn't at all going like she planned. "Are you saying you want us to move in with you?"

"Okay. Yeah. I'm kind of handling this backward. It's not like I've done this before." He was smiling at her. He looked genuinely happy, as if he hadn't just turned her world completely upside down. "I love you, Kat."

The words should have elated her. After all, she loved him, too. But love changed things. It made everything messy and complicated. As if their lives weren't messy and complicated already.

And why would she uproot the kids and move in with him? She'd established a life for them in New York. A life that worked well. She was successful there. She had a launching point for European travel.

So typical for a man to think she'd give up everything and follow him. Wasn't that what her mother had done? She'd left Russia and followed her father to a new life in America. And then he'd made her life miserable, abandoned her . . .

Abandoned them.

Abandoned Katrina when she'd needed him most.

Because that was what men who loved you did to you. They made promises, and then they left.

She shook her head, the past mixed with the now.

No. She would *not* do this.

It was like she'd been living in a dream these past couple of months. A hazy fog where everything had been hot and sexy and uncomplicated. And in the middle of all the hot and sexy and uncomplicated had been Grant, who'd swept in with all his sweet words and his incredible body and made her feel like a princess in a fairyland.

But that wasn't real life. She had other people besides herself to think about, which was nothing like a fantasy.

She'd worked so hard all these years, had sacrificed so much, so the kids could have their futures. So she could have her future. So she'd never have to rely on anyone. It had taken order and discipline and a precisely structured plan. All the order and discipline she'd carefully crafted would never work with him, living with him at his house.

Her heart sank.

She shook her head. "No."

His smile evaporated. "No to which part?"

She lifted her gaze to his. "No to all of it. We can't make this work."

He circumvented her luggage barrier, took her hands and sat on the bed, taking her with him. "Tell me what you think won't work and we'll talk through it."

She didn't want to talk through it. She didn't want him to try and convince her. All she wanted right now was to go back to the way her life was. When it was simple and uncomplicated and didn't have Grant in it. When her heart didn't hurt and her mind wasn't confused. When the kids wouldn't be hurt—again—because they couldn't have what they wanted.

Only this time it wouldn't be Dad who hurt them by leaving, or Mom by dying. It would be her who was going to hurt them, because they'd fallen in love with Grant—and with his family— just as she had.

This was just as much Grant's fault as it was hers. How could she not have seen this coming?

Dammit.

She stood and paced back and forth. Grant got up, too.

"Kat. Talk to me."

She stopped, turned to face him.

"I have to get the kids. We have to go home."

"No, you don't. You have to tell me what's bothering you so I can fix it."

Anger and frustration boiled inside of her. She pointed a finger at him. "That's the problem. You think you can fix everything when you can't. You exploded into my life and made all these changes to it. You expected me to blindly follow along as if you knew best. Well, you don't know best. You don't know me or my family or what's best for us. And while I appreciate you taking my brother and sister under your wing, and while I really love your family, you're all a little overwhelming for me. And you never once asked if this was what I wanted."

He frowned. "If what was what you wanted?"

She opened her arms wide. "This. All of this."

He looked around the bedroom, then frowned. "You're not making any sense. Are you saying you don't want to be part of my life?"

She knew she wasn't making sense. None of it made sense to her, either. All she knew was she didn't want to be here anymore, because it hurt too much. She didn't know what she wanted, only that she had never been so scared of the way she felt, of the possibility of change in her life.

The possibility that he could hurt her someday.

"I need to go home."

"No, you need to stay here and talk to me."

She shook her head. "The kids and I have been doing fine. I'm perfectly capable of supporting them and myself. I don't need you to take care of me. To take care of us."

"I know that."

She gave him a pointed look. "Do you? Do you really? I don't know if you care about me, or feel as if you need to shelter us, to protect us."

He reached for her. "Kat, it's not like that. It's never been like that."

She took a step back. "I don't know if it is or it isn't. I need some distance, some time to think about all of us. About all of this. You can't upend our lives like this, Grant. You just . . . can't."

He stared at her, and she knew then he was out of things to say. So was she.

"I'd really appreciate it if someone could drive us to the airport. I've already booked flights for us to New York."

"Don't do this. Stay and talk to me."

"I need to get back home. Please don't ask me to stay."

He stared at her. She stared back.

"Katrina."

"No. I mean it, Grant. No."

He threw up his hands. "Fine. I'll drive you. But this isn't over. We're not over."

Yes, they were. They had to be, because she couldn't allow someone to take over her life like this. It had already gone on too long.

She said her good-byes to Lydia and Easton, as painful as that was, knowing she wouldn't see them again. She made up a flimsy excuse about having booked a last-minute job and needing to catch a quick flight back to New York.

The kids didn't say anything, but she knew they felt the tension in the car all the way to the airport, especially when Grant dropped them off.

They both gave him tight hugs. And she saw the tears in his eyes when he looked at her. But he didn't hug her, and it took everything in her not to throw her arms around him.

But she held back. Because she was doing the right thing and she knew it.

When they got back to the apartment in New York City, it felt cold and empty. The kids were quiet, and it didn't take long for them to realize she lied.

"You don't have a job, do you?" Anya asked the next day when she saw Katrina sitting on the sofa, leafing through a magazine.

"No."

"Then why are we back here when we could have gone to Dallas with Grant?"

She rubbed at her temple where a headache had formed yesterday and had yet to go away.

"Grant and I have some issues to work out. It's really not your business, Anya."

"You screwed things up with him, didn't you?"

She gave her sister a stern look. "I'm not discussing this with you."

Anya marched off in a huff and hid in her room.

It was even worse with Leo, who was inconsolable. Despite his promises to Easton, once he realized her relationship with Grant was over, he could put two and two together. He slept until noon, dragged himself out of bed and shoved his earbuds into his ears. He was silent and sullen, barely speaking to her.

She'd done a fine job of alienating her siblings. She'd hurt them—badly.

But she knew what was best for the kids, long term, even if they didn't think so.

Didn't she?

Thursday night they ate dinner, then crowded around the television. Grant's game was on, so Anya and Leo cuddled together on the sofa to watch, making sure to keep as much distance from Katrina as they could. They had barely spoken to her for the past couple of days. Not that she could blame them. She was the one breaking their hearts.

It only made Katrina feel more miserable to see Grant play. He looked so good in his uniform, throwing the ball with his rocket arm to his receiver, Cole Riley.

"He looks really good," she said to Leo and Anya, who only shot glares in her direction as replies.

At halftime, Leo and Anya refreshed their drinks while Katrina checked her e-mail.

"Why did you do it?" Leo asked.

It took her a minute to realize he was speaking to her. "Do what?"

"Break up with Grant. Did he do something bad to you?"

"No. He didn't."

"Then why? And don't treat me like a kid."

She sighed. "I just felt it was better for us to be here."

"Instead of . . . St. Louis?" Anya asked.

"Yes. I think he was suggesting too many changes to our lives. And that's not always a good thing. You don't just move into someone's life and change everything."

"But didn't you—didn't we—all do the same thing to him?" Anya asked. "He was a hot, single guy who could have any woman he wanted, right? But he chose you. But with you came us, and suddenly we presented an entire family to him. Plus, we made all those suggestions to renovate his house and plans for the future. And you know what? He never even blinked. He just accepted us. All of us. And all the change that came to his life that we brought. So if he could do that, and love us all, why couldn't you?"

It took a full minute for Anya's words to soak in.

"I . . . don't know, Anya."

Anya shook her head and went back to watching the game.

It was only after the game—that the Traders won, after Anya and Leo had gone back to their rooms and she was alone again, that she really had time to think about what Anya had said to her.

They had completely upended *his* life, not the other way around. Anya was right. He was a hot single athlete who could have had his choice of any available woman. Instead, he'd chosen her and her siblings. And then they'd gone and made suggestions to renovating his house, and he'd loved their ideas and had made plans to move forward.

At every step in the process, he'd welcomed her and her family into his life. He'd always included Anya and Leo, because he knew that if he wanted her, she came with a brother and sister. And when he told her he loved her and wanted to move her into his home, he'd invited Leo and Anya as well. That would have meant huge changes in his lifestyle. He'd never even blinked.

Because that's what you do when you love someone—you allow change in your life.

She stood and went over to the window, looking out over the city she'd always called home. Now it just seemed foreign to her, because Grant wasn't here to share it with her.

Grant wasn't a man who ran from responsibility. He was a man who would have welcomed it with open arms.

Tears pricked her eyes and she swiped them away, so angry with herself she wanted to scream.

"Stupid, Katrina. You are so stupid."

She'd gone along on this wild, crazy journey with him because she'd known, probably as early as Barbados, that he was the one for her.

The only one.

She'd have never done any of these things with any other man.

Just Grant. Because he was it for her. The one, the only, the man she loved.

The only man she would ever love.

She laid her head against the windowpane.

"So, so stupid."

And now she'd lost him.

DESPITE THE GREAT GAME AGAINST DALLAS, GRANT wasn't in the mood to celebrate. His parents had come to the game, and damn he was happy to see them. Fortunately, the media was happier to see Easton Cassidy than they were to talk to him, so he let his dad field questions from reporters while he grabbed his mom and snuck away from the inevitable postgame interviews.

They waited in the car for his dad to finish with the reporters.

"I'm sorry Katrina couldn't be here tonight," his mom said.

"Yeah, that's too bad." It was as much of an answer as he was willing to give.

"Are you going to tell me what happened between the two of you the day you left the ranch, or should I just call Katrina and ask her?"

His head shot up. "I don't think it's a good idea to call Katrina, Mom. We're not . . . seeing each other anymore."

His mom crossed her arms. "Okay, what did you do?"

"Why do women always assume the guy screwed something up?"

His mom shot him a look.

"Okay, fine. You want to know what happened? I asked her and the kids to move in with me, and she decided to flee back to New York."

"Because?"

He threw his hands in the air. "Because . . . hell if I know why.

She said I took charge of her life and made all these decisions and I never gave her the chance to decide if that's what she wanted or some bullshit like that."

"I see."

He looked over at his mom. "Which is not at all what happened, by the way."

When his mother didn't say anything, he thought about it. About how he'd just showed up at Katrina's apartment in New York, and basically took over all the decision making from there.

"Okay, maybe I did. Just a little."

"You do realize how important her independence is to her, don't you?"

"Yes. And maybe I bulldozed my way into her life more than I should have. And maybe I could have been a little gentler in my suggestions." He turned in the seat to face his mother. "I love her, Mom. I don't want to lose her."

His mother leaned forward and patted his hand. "Then go see what it's going to take to get her back. My guess is she's miserable without you and doesn't know what to do, either. The two of you need to communicate your needs to each other and figure out how to make it work."

He sighed and leaned back in the seat. "Why couldn't this be easy like you and Dad were?"

His mother laughed. "You think he and I getting together was easy? Your father was a bullheaded alpha male who thought women would fall at his feet. And I was an independent feminist who in no way wanted anything to do with an arrogant athlete. He decided one day that we should just get married. I told him I intended to stay single, and no way in hell would I ever marry a man like him anyway. He didn't have a romantic bone in his entire body, and I was convinced that, even though I loved him like crazy, we could never see eye to eye on anything."

Grant arched a brow. "So not the story Dad tells."

"Of course it isn't. He always has to come out the hero."

"So how did you end up saying yes?"

"He finally swallowed his pride and was honest with me and told me he wouldn't make it if I wasn't in his life, and that he was only half a man without me. And then your strong, testosterone-filled father got down on one knee and, with honest-to-God tears in his eyes, proposed marriage to me."

Grant couldn't imagine. "Wow."

"Yeah. And so your independent feminist mother bawled like a baby and said yes. It was sloppy and romantic and if you ever tell anyone I told you this story I'll totally deny it."

Grant laughed. "Your secret is safe with me, Mom. But thanks for sharing it."

"Sometimes you just have to let the woman you love know how you really feel. And own up to the mistakes you've made."

Now he understood where he'd gone wrong. And how he had to fix it.

THIRTY-TWO

KATRINA HAD TRIED MULTIPLE TIMES TO CALL AND text Grant, but he wasn't answering. She knew he wasn't playing a game today. She'd checked his schedule, and he was due to play New England in the opening game of the season on Sunday, which she knew was a big deal.

So maybe he was in meetings or practice or traveling or something. Either way, she was going to keep trying until he answered his phone. Though he was probably avoiding her.

She couldn't blame him.

Leo and Anya were spending the next couple of days at camp, the last before school geared up. She figured they mainly just wanted to get away from her. Not that she could blame them.

She had to admit, the quiet unnerved her, forcing her to think about all the stupid mistakes she'd made.

She had walked away from the best thing that had ever happened to her, and all because she was afraid of change, of losing her independence.

Afraid of the past.

Now the only thing she was afraid of was that Grant would never agree to give her a second chance.

Her doorbell rang. She frowned, knowing she hadn't ordered a delivery.

She pressed the button. "Yes?"

"Katrina."

Her heart slammed against her chest. "Grant?"

"Yeah. Can I come up?"

"Yes, of course." She pressed the button, unable to believe he was here.

She took a step back and looked down at herself. She wore a pair of workout capris and a tank top, and her hair was in a high ponytail.

It would have to do, because he was going to be here in a . . .

He knocked on the door and she opened it. She wanted to cry seeing him standing there in his cargo pants and white T-shirt. He looked tanned and gorgeous and it took every ounce of willpower in her to stop herself from hugging him.

"Come in."

He stepped inside and she closed the door.

"Thanks for seeing me. I wasn't sure if you'd be home."

"Yes. I'm home. Just . . . hanging out."

Well, this was awkward.

"Where are the kids?" he asked as he looked around the apartment.

"They're at camp for a couple of days. I think they're mad at me."

"Oh."

"Grant . . ."

"Before you say anything, I have something I need to say to you."

"Okay."

"First, I'm sorry. You were right."

She was confused. "I was?"

"Yeah. I did take charge of your life. I barged in here and made you go sightseeing and eat hot dogs and go to ball games and take all those trips without once asking if that's what you wanted. I was kind of . . . I don't know what the word is . . . bowled over by you, and I guess I didn't want to give you the option of telling me to take a hike, so I wanted to insinuate myself into your life and not give you the chance to say no until you fell head over heels in love with me. Or something like that. Even I can't explain it, Kat. All I know is from the moment I met you, I wanted to see you all the time."

Her lips curved. "That's not necessarily a bad thing."

"Maybe not. But it is if in any way I trampled all over your independence. I know how important that is to you, and for that, I'm sorry. Because if anyone has earned the right to be independent, it's you. So if you and the kids don't want to move to St. Louis, then you don't have to."

"Thank you."

"So I'll move to New York."

Her gaze shot to his. "What?"

He took a few steps toward her and picked up her hand. "I love you, Katrina. I need to know if the feeling is mutual."

She shuddered in an inhale. She had been so worried that she'd lost him. Hearing those words made relief fall over her like a heavy rainstorm. "Yes. The feeling is mutual. I love you, too."

His entire expression changed, from guarded to happy. "You don't know how happy that makes me."

"I'll have to live in St. Louis during football season, but I can sell the house and buy a condo there. Then during off-season, I can live in New York with you and the kids."

She realized the sacrifices he was willing to make to be with her.

"Why would you do that?"

"Move?"

She nodded. "You would give up your amazing house in St. Louis to come live in New York with me?"

"That's what you do when you love someone, Kat. Home is a place you live with your family. And you, Anya, and Leo are my family. So it can be any place where you and the kids feel safe and happy. And I will always support you emotionally, because you're important to me."

"You wouldn't be happy in New York."

"I'll be happy being with you. Wherever that is."

Tears pricked her eyes and she tried to swipe them, but they just kept coming.

For so long she had it wrong. So very wrong.

Home wasn't a place, it was a state of mind, a place in the heart.

Grant was in her heart. He had been from that zing she felt in Barbados during their first photo shoot when their eyes met and their bodies touched. It didn't matter where she lived, because as long as they were together, she'd be happy.

She laid her palm on his chest over his heart. "This is home to me. No matter where we live, geography doesn't matter, this is always going to be home. And the kids want to be with us, so as long as we're together, they'll be happy.

"I love the house in St. Louis. I can sell this place and keep a smaller apartment here for when I need to work here, and I can continue to fly all over to do my job. Neither of us has to give up anything, Grant. But we can have everything we both want—each other."

He gathered her close. "All I want is you. All I need to be happy is you."

"That's all I want. You."

He kissed her, and all her fears and uncertainties dissolved.

She had everything she'd ever wanted right here, sheltered in the arms of the man she loved. A man who would never abandon her, who would never ask her to give up anything.

Because he would always be everything she needed.

He kissed her, and warmth turned to passion. His lips were everywhere. On hers, on her neck, her shoulder, and she pulled off her shirt so she could feel the burn of his kisses everywhere. She tunneled her fingers under his shirt to feel the heat of his skin under her hands.

He drew his shirt off, and they kissed and walked their way into the bedroom, clothes flying as they did. She fell onto the bed with Grant following on top of her. His mouth came down on hers as he gathered her close, his hand cradling the side of her neck.

"I was meant to be with you," she said.

"Yes."

And those were the only words they said as passion took over. She pulled a condom out of her bedside drawer and he put it on, then slid inside her.

Perfect. How could she ever think she could live without this man, when he made her feel so much? When he moved inside of her and shook her very world on its axis every single time.

He clasped his fingers with hers and took every stroke, every thrust with his gaze locked in hers. And when she shattered, they were looking at each other in the most intimate way. It was heady and it made her cry.

After, he held her and kissed her, neither of them moving for a very long time.

She loved him. She trusted him and she'd never let him go.

Finally, he rolled to the side to dispose of the condom, but came right back to gather her in his arms. It was an idyllic, perfect day. She swept her hand over his chest, then looked up at him and smiled.

"One thing we need to get straight, though," she said. "It's pretty serious."

He looked down at her. "What's that?"

"I don't think I'm ever going to learn to love hot dogs."

He laughed. "I can probably live with that."

She affected a huge sigh of relief. "So glad to hear it."

They got dressed and Katrina fixed them glasses of iced tea, then they settled in the living room.

"So, when can we tell Leo and Anya?"

She looked over at him, so happy that he'd think of her brother and sister. It was one of the reasons she loved him so much. "I'll call them tomorrow. Tonight, you're all mine."

He leaned over and pulled her onto his lap. "No, Kat. I'm all yours forever."

Yes, he was.

Dear Reader,

Thanks so much for reading *Quarterback Draw*. I hope you enjoyed Grant and Katrina's love story.

Coming up in August of 2015 is *All Wound Up*, the next book in the Play-by-Play series, which features Tucker Cassidy, one of Grant's brothers. Tucker's got his hands full with Aubry Ross, daughter of Clyde Ross, the St. Louis Rivers baseball team owner. You met Aubry briefly in *Changing the Game*. She's been in medical school, and she's busy enough with her residency and doesn't have time to play games with a hotshot pitcher. The sparks fly between these two, though, and I hope you enjoy the excerpt from *All Wound Up* included here.

Also coming up next in my Hope contemporary romance series is *Love After All*, releasing in April 2015. *Love After All* is Chelsea and Bash's story. Chelsea's looking for the perfect man, and to land him, she's compiled a top-ten list of the things she's looking for in a man. Bash doesn't fit the criteria, but the chemistry between them is explosive. Can a man who doesn't match her list be the perfect man for her after all? I hope you enjoy a peek into Chelsea and Bash's story with the *Love After All* excerpt included here.

Happy reading,
Jaci

KEEP READING FOR A PREVIEW OF THE NEXT
PLAY-BY-PLAY NOVEL FROM JACI BURTON

ALL WOUND UP

AVAILABLE AUGUST 2015 FROM BERKLEY BOOKS

IT WAS COOL, DARK, AND MOST IMPORTANTLY, PRIVATE in Clyde Ross's wine cellar, which was why Tucker Cassidy had brought Laura, his girlfriend, down here.

She'd had a lot to drink today, and when she drank, she got loud. She was also pissed at him at the moment.

Laura pissed off, drunk, and loud? Not a good combination at the house of the owner of the St. Louis Rivers. Clyde Ross was his boss, and the last thing he needed was his girlfriend making a scene. He had enough of a bad-boy image without Laura making things worse by screaming at him in the middle of Clyde's very nice backyard garden.

"I'm not going to tell you again, Tucker. We're moving in together."

Yeah that so wasn't happening. "We can talk about this when I take you home tonight, Laura."

He'd brought her to the wine cellar in the hopes of cooling her down. Plus, they were alone here and no one could hear them. Okay, mainly Laura, who had a tendency to get on a roll once she had a topic in mind she wanted to discuss.

"We've been dating two whole months, Tucker. Don't you think it's time we make it official?"

It had been the most awful *two whole months* of his entire life. Okay, maybe not at the beginning. Laura was a knockout. Tall, with long dark hair and curves that just didn't quit and the best ass he'd ever seen. She was a cocktail waitress and they'd met one night when he'd been having drinks in the bar where she worked. They hit it off right away and had gone out, had a night of hot sex, and had started dating. She'd been fun, adventurous, great in the sack, and they had a lot in common.

Plus, she liked baseball, and he played for the Rivers. Not that it was a deal breaker if a woman he dated wasn't a baseball fan, but it didn't hurt. She'd come to his games and she actually knew the game, as opposed to other women he'd dated who claimed to know the game but in fact didn't know balls from strikes or a curve from a fastball. In his mind, that was a goddamned crime.

But as the weeks progressed, he'd noticed she didn't hold her liquor well, and when she drank, she was not a fun drunk. She was loud, obnoxious, and she insulted his friends. She'd also grown more demanding of his time. Whenever they weren't together, she wanted to know where he was and how soon he was coming over. He didn't need a mother—he had a pretty great one already.

And now the past few times they'd been together she'd thrown down hints about the two of them moving in together. He was so not ready for that.

So now he had to redirect her and calm her down before things got out of hand.

"How about we check out Clyde's awesome wine collection?"

She pushed at his chest. "I don't give a shit about Clyde or his wine. I want you to make a commitment to me."

He sighed and raked his fingers through his hair. He didn't want to do this here, but she hadn't left him much of a choice. "That's not gonna happen. We've only been dating two months and I'm not ready to live together."

She poked at his chest. "You know what? You're a sonofabitch. I thought we were heading somewhere. You led me to believe—"

He was going to have to stop her there. "I never made promises to you, Laura."

And now the tears. He'd seen a lot of those lately, too. Especially when she'd been drinking.

"I thought we were in love."

"I never said that, either."

She broke down then and sobbed.

Well, shit. He walked over to her and pulled her into his arms. "I'm sorry."

He didn't know how a woman could be so drunk, yet so accurate, but her knee hit his crotch at just the right angle, and he went down like a fighter getting a perfect punch.

Lights out. Only instead of a hit to his jaw, she'd KO'd him right in the balls.

"You're an asshole. We're done, Tucker. I'm out of here. I'll call a taxi to take me home."

He heard the click of her heels on the stone floor as she walked away.

He couldn't even breathe, let alone care that she'd just fucking left him on the ground.

Jesus Christ, that had hurt. His balls throbbed like someone had—

Well, someone *had* shoved a knee into them.

He lay there for what seemed like hours, but he knew it was only minutes before he managed to stagger to his knees. He found the wall, still struggling to catch his breath.

In a minute. He'd be able to stand in just a minute.

"Oh, my God. Are you okay?"

He heard a female voice.

Great. Just what he needed. A witness to his humiliation.

Then cool, soft hands swept across his forehead.

"Are you hurt? Did you fall?"

He shook his head. "I'm fine."

"You are not fine. You're practically hyperventilating. Tell me what happened."

His eyes were still closed and he was concentrating all his effort on trying to determine if his balls were still attached to his body. He did not want some female being nice to him.

Actually, he wanted nothing to do with any female. Possibly ever again.

He finally managed to stand—with the woman's help, unfortunately.

"Tell me where you're hurt," she said.

He shook his head. "I'm not hurt. Just go away."

"I am not going to go away. I'm a doctor and I can help you."

Awesome. This night was getting worse by the second. "I don't need a doctor."

"How about you let me be the judge of that?"

He finally managed to open his eyes and look over at his unwanted savior.

She was, of course, gorgeous. Which made her immediately untrustworthy, since he'd just vowed to never again fall for a beautiful woman.

She was average height, with short blond hair and the most intense blue eyes he'd ever seen. She also had the most perfect mouth—

Not that he was ever going to think about a woman in a sexual way again. Thoughts like that only led to trouble, and crushed testicles.

He leaned against the cool wall and closed his eyes. She slipped her fingers around his wrist.

"What are you doing?" he asked.

"Shhh."

Fine with him. Maybe if he didn't say anything, or look at her, she'd disappear.

But she didn't. She kept holding on to him.

"Your pulse rate is a little high."

He opened his eyes and looked down at her. "Not surprising since I just got kicked in the balls."

She pursed her lips as she met his gaze. "Literally or figuratively?"

"Literally."

"Ouch. I can't speak from experience, of course, but that must have been painful. What did you do to deserve that?"

Figures she'd think he was deserving of a knee to the groin. "Nothing. I had a drunk girlfriend who had it in her head we were supposed to move in together. When I tried to let her down easily, that was her response."

"Ouch again. Sorry."

He shrugged. "Not your fault."

She rubbed her hands together. "I should examine you."

He let out a laugh. "Honey, no offense, but the last thing I want is any woman near my balls tonight. Or possibly ever again."

Her lips curved. "You say that now. You'll change your mind once they feel better. And you need to let me take a look and feel them to make sure your girlfriend—"

"Ex-girlfriend."

"Okay. To make sure your ex-girlfriend didn't seriously injure you."

"Uh, no. I'm okay."

She put her hands on her hips. She had nice hips, showcased in a white, lacy sundress, which showcased one very cute figure. Not that he was into noticing that kind of thing at the moment. Or ever again.

"Who's the doctor here? Me or you?"

"You. Or so you say. This could be some conspiracy. You could be a friend of Laura's setting me up for round two of let's-destroy-Tucker-Cassidy's-manhood night."

Now it was her turn to laugh. "I can assure you I have no idea who your girlfriend—"

"Ex-girlfriend."

"Right. I can assure you I am not in league with your nefarious ex-girlfriend."

"I like that." He finally had something to smile about.

"Like what?"

"Nefarious. It fits her. But you're still not getting in my pants."

"Playing hard to get, Tucker?"

"I'll show you mine if you show me yours."

"I see you're starting to feel better. That's a very good sign. But no, I'm not showing you mine. I am going to look at yours, though. And in your weakened condition, I'm pretty sure I can get into your pants."

His balls still throbbed. What if Laura had broken them? What if he was unable to have kids? Not that he wanted any— right now. But someday . . .

"Okay. Fine. You're really a doctor?"

"I really am. So drop 'em and let's take a look at the goods."

He reached for the zipper of his pants. "If I had a dollar for every time a woman said that to me . . ."

She snickered, came over, and he caught a light citrusy scent. He breathed it in, the best thing he'd smelled all night. It smelled like renewal, like starting over.

Which was ridiculous because he didn't even know the doctor's name. But if she fixed him, she'd be his savior.

She cradled his ball sac in her hand, then examined his dick. There was something about having a woman so close to his goods that should be exciting as hell. But he wasn't getting hard. He hurt too damn bad.

"A little red and swollen, but she didn't break your penis."

"Well, hallelujah."

She tilted her head to the side and gave him a wry smile. "Right? She hit you pretty hard, though. Your testicles are swollen and red."

She took a step back. "You can pull your pants up now. You're going to be sore for a couple of days. But I think you're going to be fine."

"Thanks."

"You're welcome."

He zipped up. "I hope your husband or boyfriend doesn't mind you inspecting my stuff down here in the wine cellar."

"No husband. No boyfriend. I'm a resident at Washington University here in St. Louis and way too busy for that."

"I see. So who are you here with?"

"Oh, my father is Clyde Ross." She held out her hand. "I'm Aubry."

Shit. Shit, shit, shit. The boss's daughter. This night couldn't get any worse.

"Oh. I didn't know that. I mean, I knew he had a daughter in medical school or something. I don't know why I didn't make the connection."

"No reason for you to. Nice to meet you, Tucker. I've seen you pitch. You're pretty damn good."

"So are you, Doc. Thanks for the once-over."

"You're welcome. I actually came down here to grab a bottle of wine for my dad." She wandered off as if she knew exactly where she was going, plucking a bottle from the rack before turning to face him. "Got it. Shall we go upstairs, or do you need more time to reflect on your evening?"

"No, I think I've spent enough time down here."

He followed her toward the stairs, hoping like hell Aubry was discreet enough not to tell her father what had happened to him.

But there was something he needed to know, so he stopped and turned to face her. "One question."

"Sure."

"Did you make me drop trou because it was medically necessary, or because you wanted to get a good look at my dick?"

One side of her mouth curved up in a sexy-as-hell smile. "Tucker. I'm surprised you'd ask that question. I am a doctor, after all."

She turned and headed up the stairs.

Which wasn't an answer at all.

The night was starting to look up.

But his balls still hurt like hell, and after the debacle with Laura, and the fact that the doc was Clyde's daughter, he should definitely avoid Aubry Ross.

Or . . . maybe not.

KEEP READING FOR A PREVIEW OF THE NEXT
HOPE NOVEL FROM JACI BURTON

LOVE AFTER ALL

AVAILABLE APRIL 2015 FROM JOVE BOOKS

CHELSEA GARDNER SAT AT THE NO HOPE AT ALL BAR, waiting for her friends.

While she waited, she got out her notebook and doodled.

Okay, maybe she wasn't doodling. She was on a mission.

The ten-point list made perfect sense to her. She'd fine-tuned it, but really, she'd had this list in her head for a while now, and decided it was time to memorialize it, get it down on paper. Maybe even laminate it.

Chelsea was thirty-two years old, and the one thing she knew and knew well was men. She had years of dating history, and she could weed out a decent man from a loser in the first fifteen minutes of a date.

She should write a book about it. She'd probably make millions.

Okay, in reality, maybe not. But she had a lot of experience in dating. She could offer up some valuable advice. At least advice on how to date the wrong man.

Hence the list.

Her list would ensure she found the right man—finally. She was tired of going out on useless dates. From now on, she was going to ask the correct questions, so she wouldn't waste any more time on the wrong man. If a prospective date didn't possess each and every one of the listed qualities, then he wasn't the perfect man for her.

Her list wasn't going to focus on personality traits. She already knew in her head the type of guy she wanted—warm, caring, compassionate, with a sense of humor. If he didn't possess those basics, he'd be out of the running before they even got started. And those she could suss out right away without a list. Nor did she have a preference for looks. No, this list was compatibility based. That's where she'd run into roadblocks in the past and where she was going to focus her efforts in the future.

She scanned her list, nodding as she ticked off the attributes in her head.

1. Never married.
2. Has to be a suit-and-tie kind of guy, because it means he cares about his appearance.
3. Has to work a 9-to-5 job, so he'll be available for her.
4. No crazy ex-girlfriends.
5. Likes fine dining and good wine.
6. Hates sports. Everything about sports.
7. Must want at least two kids.
8. Must love animals—preferably big dogs, not those yippy little dogs.
9. Doesn't spend all his time at the bar with his friends.
10. Idea of a perfect weekend getaway is somewhere warm and tropical. With room service.

She studied the list, tapping the pencil on the bar top.